UNNERVING

UNNERVING
A NOVEL OF SUSPENSE

KAREN J. GALLAHUE

AuthorHouse™
1663 Liberty Drive
Bloomington, IN 47403
www.authorhouse.com
Phone: 1-800-839-8640

Published by AuthorHouse   04/30/2013

ISBN: 978-1-4817-4726-4 (sc)
ISBN: 978-1-4817-4723-3 (e)

Library of Congress Control Number: 2013907630

This book is a work of fiction. All of the characters, names, places, incidents, organizations, and dialogue in this novel are either the products of the author's imagination, or are used fictitiously. Any resemblance to actual persons, living or dead, business establishments, events, or locales is entirely coincidental.

Any people depicted in stock imagery provided by Thinkstock are models, and such images are being used for illustrative purposes only.
Certain stock imagery © Thinkstock.

This book is printed on acid-free paper.

I dedicate this book to my husband, Greg. Thanks again for all the encouragement.

CHAPTER 1

"**Y**ou're kidding me! You're telling me that Ralph Kendrick, the bogeyman of my worst nightmares, has escaped from jail?" Eyes wide and unbelieving, Fiona Morgan asked the detective standing at her front door, as she reached for the door frame to steady her wobbly legs.

Detective John Tremayne from the Naperville Police Department had already shown her his badge when she answered her door. "I would never kid about something this serious," the brown haired man said patiently. "And actually I'm afraid the situation is worse."

"How could it be worse? He threatened to kill me and my two friends when we testified at his trial twenty years ago."

"We know that, and they're being contacted as we speak. The thing is, Kendrick's cellmates have come forward to say that Kendrick knows that you have identical triplet sisters, and he doesn't know which one of you testified. They say that, even recently, he's vowed to kill all three of you Morgan women, in addition to Tory Girard and Sandy Johnson."

"Oh, no! Not my sisters, too."

"They're being notified as well."

"But I'm the one who testified."

"We didn't know which one of you was the witness either."

"But how could he kill us if he's on the run?"

"Unfortunately, he may have wealthy connections."

"Please come in. I need to sit down." Fiona gestured him into the living room of her town house. Her stomach clenched. Tiny, icy beads of perspiration formed along her hairline and on the sides of her nose. The same reactions she'd had as a child when she had nightmares about Kendrick. She groped for a chair.

"Ms. Morgan, are you all right?"

"Water. I need a glass of water," she croaked. Her voice felt as dry as old paste, and she slumped in the chair before her legs deserted her.

The tall detective with the kind eyes found the kitchen and came back with the water. Fiona gulped it down.

"Please, tell me what you know of this," the slim, woman asked, as she twisted the strands of her blond shoulder length hair.

"Police Chief Jansen received a phone call from Warden Elmore of the Minnesota State Prison. Three days ago, a prison bus was involved in a bad accident outside Minneapolis. A few inmates escaped, including Ralph Kendrick."

"Why wasn't I notified earlier?"

1

"According to the warden, things were hectic," he replied. "The driver and the armed guard died in the accident. Several convicts were injured, and six escaped. The pictures of the escaped convicts were in the Twin City papers."

"How can my sisters and I protect ourselves?" she whispered. "I've heard that, in the real world, no police department can provide continuous protection, especially for an indefinite time."

"We'll do everything that we can for you." Tremayne shifted uncomfortably. "We just can't guarantee twenty-four/seven."

"I need to hire a bodyguard, don't I?"

"Probably a good idea. The chief will provide back-up for him, and the entire PD will be aware of the situation. I'm assigned to you until you can make arrangements."

"Do you have names of bodyguards?"

"I don't, but the chief will."

"I need to make a phone call. Please have a seat. It should only take a couple minutes." She punched the buttons on her cell with nervous fingers. "Hi, Mom, I have a question for you. Remember that blind date I turned down when you tried to fix me up with your new neighbor's son? Didn't you say he was a former policeman?"

"If you changed your mind about the date, I can't arrange it," her mother said. "He wasn't interested either."

"No, I didn't change my mind about dating him. I might want to hire him as a bodyguard."

"What?" Her mother's voice shrilled. "Why?"

"Ralph Kendrick escaped from prison, and he's made recent threats against me."

"Oh, no!" her mother moaned. "Oh, Fiona, I can barely swallow. My heart's stuck in my throat. My new neighbor's son's name is Ted Collier. He was a Naperville detective before he went to work on a special project for the FBI the last four years. His new job doesn't start for a while."

"Hold on, Mom," Fiona covered the phone and turned to Detective Tremayne. "Do you know a cop named Ted Collier, who used to be a Naperville detective?"

"Ted Collier, yeah, I worked with him. He was a captain at the Naperville PD. But I thought he was working for the FBI on the east coast."

"According to my mother, he's back in this area. Would he be a good bodyguard?"

"The best. If he's willing and has the time to take the job."

Fiona uncovered the phone. "Mom, would you ask your friend to have her son call me ASAP if he's interested in talking to me about this job?"

"Of course," her mother said.

"And, Mom, I hate to upset you, but Ralph Kendrick doesn't know which triplet testified against him, which means . . ."

"Don't tell me all three of you are at risk?" her mother interrupted. "Oh, no!"

"Afraid so. They're being notified as well."

"At least Kailee's husband has some Army background. Thank God she has him! And Regan and her family will be out of the country tomorrow," said her mother. "But what about you?"

Fiona sighed. "A police detective has been assigned to me for now, but they don't have the manpower to protect me continuously."

"Then I'd better contact Lucy about her son right away. I'll be praying for the safety of all of you."

"What's your schedule for today?" Tremayne asked when Fiona closed her cell phone.

"I have to be at the TV station for my news broadcast from three to six. Then I have dinner at my mother's house at six thirty. Is there anything I should be doing?"

"No, but I'll do a security check on your windows and doors," he said. "I'll start that now. Your alarm system looked pretty good."

"It should be; it cost enough."

Fiona jumped when her phone rang. A deep, steady masculine voice said, "Ted Collier here. I'd like to speak to Fiona Morgan."

"This is Fiona."

"I understand you're in a situation which requires protection."

"Yes." Her pent up air whooshed out.

"I'll need to meet with you before I make a decision," he said. "How about eleven at Quigley's Pub?"

Fiona checked her watch. She had just enough time to change out of her shorts and tank top. "That's fine," she said. "How will I recognize you?"

"I'll recognize you; I've seen your picture. Your mother said you had a policeman with you. Have him drive you to Quigley's."

Fiona relayed the information to DetectiveTremayne. He checked the doors and windows while she changed. A slim blond woman, she pulled on black slacks and adjusted the turquoise floral top that matched her eyes.

This morning she'd felt a pang when she realized today was the second anniversary of her husband's death.

Now this! I hope I didn't rush into things agreeing to meet the Collier man. Will this be embarrassing, or what? Apparently both Ted and I didn't want to meet each other. And he still has to check me out before he takes the job. Well, I might decide against hiring him!"

The thought was immediately chased away as she remembered the danger she was in.

CHAPTER 2

Detective Tremayne double-parked, escorted Fiona inside the door of Quigley's, and left to find a parking spot. As Fiona entered the pub whose entire interior had been designed, built, and shipped from Ireland, she wondered if she had been too impulsive about meeting this Ted Collier. After a few seconds, her eyes adjusted to the dark teakwood interior, and she saw a lean, well-muscled man with a wide shoulder span walking toward her. A commanding-looking man in his prime, with smoky gray eyes.

"Ted Collier," he said, reaching out to shake her hand. Curving his hand under her elbow, he escorted her up a few steps to the right to a smaller room. It didn't have the ambiance of the main bar area with its etched and painted glass and its ornate booths called snugs, but it offered privacy.

As Fiona sat across from Ted, she could tell by his intent look that he was assessing her just as carefully as she was assessing him.

"I'm drinking coffee," he told her. "Would you like a drink or something to eat?"

"No food," Fiona replied. "I don't think I could choke any down. But I am a coffee addict."

Ted signaled to a waiter as Fiona said, "I almost didn't come. I was afraid your mother and mine pressured you into this."

"It's been a long time since I allowed myself to be pressured by my mother," he replied laconically.

"Of course not," she said, reddening. "I can see that now. I guess I'm the one with problems dealing with motherly pressure."

Ted angled his head toward the door. "Where's your police escort?"

"Detective Tremayne's assigned to me, and he's parking the car. I asked him if I could speak to you privately, and he'll sit at the bar until we call him over."

"Fine. You didn't want to come, but you did. Why?"

"Because I'm afraid, and I don't know which way to turn," she replied, a little unsettled by his piercing gaze. "My worst nightmare has come true. I've had many sleepless nights worrying about Ralph Kendrick coming after me. And now he probably actually may be doing just that." She twisted her hands together on the table top. "I'm also furious that he's disrupting my life. And I'm worried about my sisters because he doesn't know which one of us testified against him. I feel as if I've lost control of my life."

"Then you need to get back in control."

"How can I do that?" she asked sharply. "I'm a target for a killer." She bit her bottom lip so hard, she could taste blood.

4

"Be proactive. You need to have a plan and prepare yourself for any eventuality. Get a bodyguard whom you can trust. Let him or her cover your back at all times. Adapt your schedule to reduce vulnerability.

"How would I do that?"

"For example, if you take a two mile run along the same path every day, you need to change that. Go on a different path each day. Or use your treadmill. If you go out, carry pepper spray. Practice self defense moves. You're not a helpless ten year-old anymore. You're a mature adult who is aware of danger and intends to protect herself."

They stopped talking when the waitress placed Fiona's coffee on the table. Fiona reached for the cup and took a deep breath. "You're right. I've been so busy feeling like a victim that I've forgotten there are some things I can control. I don't know your background, other than that you were a former police officer."

"I was a detective with the Naperville Police Department for ten years, as well as a member of the SWAT team. I spent the past four years in on the east coast with the FBI. In two weeks, I start my new position as Chief of Police in Plainfield. I'm living with my mom while I search for a place of my own."

Fiona swallowed hard. "Mr. Collier, or is it Captain Collier?"

"Call me Ted."

"I feel very humble that you've even agreed to see me. Your qualifications are more than excellent." She inhaled and took the plunge. "What can I do to convince you to take on my case?" Twisting a few strands of hair, she continued. "I have an unusual schedule. I sometimes interview people in odd places, and I have to appear at crowded functions. I can't just crawl into a hole."

"Have you thought of the Witness Protection Program?"

"Only for a second. Regan and Kailee would have to go, too. And I can't leave my mother alone. And for how long? It just doesn't seem feasible."

"I'll only agree to protect you if I have your full cooperation."

"Of course," she said, sipping her coffee.

"Don't be too quick to reply. I mentioned the example of a morning run along the same path. I would probably forbid it if I feel it's too dangerous. Would you accept that without an argument and use a treadmill instead?"

"Yes, if I can see a logical reason for the request, I'll accept anything you say."

"Wrong answer. It won't be a request. It'll be an order. If I tell you to drop to the ground and you want to know why first it might be a second too late for me to protect you."

"I see your point, but I haven't taken orders from anyone for a long time. What if I forget?"

"Forgetting isn't acceptable."

"You're not some kind of control freak, are you?"

"Only when I'm risking my life to protect someone." His intelligent gray eyes held hers. She broke the gaze.

"What other issues require my full cooperation?" she asked.

"If I take the job, we'll be sticking together like Velcro. Which means I'll sleep at your place."

"Now wait a minute." She reached for her coffee again. "I haven't done sleepovers with any man since my husband died. And how can you protect me if you're asleep?"

"Item one: I'll be sleeping at your place, not in your bed. Item two: Most detectives can wake at the drop of a paper clip. It's an acquired skill. And if I get too tired, the Naperville PD can help out."

"If I agree to all your terms and let you call the shots, will you take the case?"

"Yes, I will. Before I came here, I called Police Chief Jansen with a few questions. He'll deputize me so I can access the PD's facilities and data bases, as well as get backup." He smiled briefly. "I'd like to head over to the PD when we leave here. We need to have them take your picture to distribute to all officers. We also need a recent picture of Kendrick so we know what he looks like now, although he may be hiring out the kills if he can access any money."

"You think he might do that?" Her hand wavered, and she sat her coffee cup down with a clunk.

"We have to look at all possibilities."

"So I might not even be able to identify my enemy." She twisted her hands in her lap.

"Possibly."

"He came from a wealthy family."

"Hopefully, they'll know enough to turn him in."

"About your fee. I'm not very businesslike. How much do you charge?"

"Five hundred a week. Your mother said she'd take care of it."

"My mother? Absolutely not!" Fiona's eyes flashed. "Submit the bill to me. There's no deal unless I pay. And I have a feeling rates for bodyguards are twice that."

"Five hundred suits me. But I can only protect you until I start my new job in two weeks."

"I understand."

"If your schedule will permit it, we need to travel to Minnesota tomorrow to speak with the prison warden and selected inmates to find out as much about Kendrick as we can. I need to develop some kind of personality profile on him. The more I know about him, the better I can predict what he might do.

"Since you're a reporter, you may think of questions to ask that I might miss. And I can protect you at the same time. We also need to talk to the Minneapolis detective in charge of the murder case twenty years ago, if possible. If you can't get away, I'm sure Tremayne could take over protecting you here for a day."

"Let me call someone." She hit speed dial on her phone and said, "Maureen, could you take over my show tomorrow? I have all the human interest stuff ready and I can have the rest organized for you before I leave the studio tonight."

When she rang off, she turned to Ted. "I'm good to go."

"Excellent. From now on, I'll drive you in my car. Do you have a one car garage?"

Fiona nodded.

"We can ask Tremayne to get someone to park your car at the PD so I can park in your garage. We need to keep you safe from any car-tampering. A friend of mine is getting a patent on a device to prevent car sabotage, and I have it installed on my car. It raises holy hell if someone even lifts a windshield wiper to put a flyer on the car."

"I'm glad to have any protection you can offer."

Ted gestured to Tremayne to join them. The two men shook hands, and Tremayne said, "Glad to see you back in town."

"Thanks. Please sit down. Fiona has hired me for the job." Ted turned to Fiona. "Will it bother you to describe to us the murder you witnessed?" he asked.

"Yes, but I'll do it." She took a deep breath.

CHAPTER 3

A s she began her story, Fiona's stomach did its usual clench and flip. "I was ten years old. My family lived outside Minneapolis at the time, and I attended a Girl Scout picnic at a park called Minnehaha Falls. Tory Girard, and Sandy Johnson, and I decided to explore the area around the picnic site. We hiked about fifteen minutes. Suddenly, we heard a terrible scream, and then another."

She hesitated and tugged a strand of hair behind her left ear. She also picked up her coffee cup, but forgot to sip from it. "We were saucer-eyed, and we looked at each other before we all raced in the direction of the scream. We came to a small clearing and saw a man sitting on a woman with a big rock in his hand. He crashed it down as hard as he could on the lady's head. She stopped screaming. Blood gushed from her head. We all froze." Fiona stopped for a minute and finally took a gulp of her coffee.

"The man suddenly turned and saw us. His eyes bugged out. We ran screaming back to the picnic site. Our Girl Scout leader's husband was a policeman, and he was at the picnic.

"When we took Officer Grant to the site, the man was gone, but the woman was still there on the ground, and she wasn't moving. Officer Grant ordered us to stay back while he checked her and called 911. He told us not to look, but we saw all the blood."

She shuddered. "He cautioned us not to talk to each other about the incident until a police officer questioned us. Fortunately, when Officer Grant followed us to the clearing, he immediately started looking for the rock we described, which he found in the brook. It still had bits of hair and blood on it and a partial print."

Fiona's voice strengthened as she plunged on. "Later Tory, Sandy, and I each worked separately with a sketch artist. I know now that Kendrick had raped the woman, Rose Wilson, before he killed her, and the police suspected him of another rape and murder, and they were being super careful with all evidence. When they arrested Kendrick, we each had to go separately to the police lineup. Each one of us picked out Ralph Kendrick as the killer."

Fiona twisted her hair again.

"My mother told me later that Kendrick lied about everything. First, he denied being in the park at all. But another person remembered seeing a black Porsche with a University of Minnesota sticker in the parking lot near the clearing. It didn't take detectives long to narrow the search to Kendrick." She looked up. "How many University students drive a Porsche? Once they matched his tire treads, Kendrick admitted he was at the park, but claimed he never saw the woman. When the results came back from her rape kit with his semen, he admitted that he met her, had consensual sex with her, and left. He denied killing her.

"My mother didn't tell me, but I read the newspapers about the trial. Kendrick's response after the juryman read the verdict was to beat his hands on the table in front of him and roar, 'I'll make those three little bitches pay for ruining my life.'"

Fiona's mouth felt really dry. She took a sip of coffee before she continued, "Then Kendrick yelled at his lawyer, that he should have done a better job, and punched him in the face, breaking his nose. The judge called for order. It took three policemen to hold Kendrick. The judge said he couldn't have threats issued in his court, and he increased Kendrick's prison sentence by a year. He told Kendrick that if any harm happened to us girls, he would be the first suspect, even if he was in jail." She gave a sigh of relief and sank back into the booth.

"Thanks, Fiona," Ted said. "Every bit of information you can share will be of help to us. I think we can all head to the PD now, if possible. What's your schedule for the rest of today?"

"I have to stop home and change and get to the TV station by three o'clock to be ready for my newscast at five. At six thirty, my mother has planned a going away party for my sister, Regan, who is leaving for Spain with her family tomorrow.

"Okay, why don't we head for the PD now," Ted said.

When Fiona excused herself to go to the rest room first before they left, Tremayne said to Ted, "Tough break you have. You get paid to live with and guard that gorgeous woman. Your luck is phenomenal! Couldn't you have waited a few days to take over . . . so I could at least work up the courage to ask her for a date?"

"Can it, Tremayne," Ted replied. "See you back at the PD."

When Tremayne left, Ted leaned back, tenting his fingers on the table. A week ago he had turned his mother down when she had tried to arrange a blind date with Fiona. What a fool he had been! She was something very special. He'd seen her telecast at five yesterday, but she was even more beautiful in person than on TV. She had the wide eyed blond look of Christy Brinkley, although her eyes were more turquoise than blue. She also had the straightforward look and intelligence of Katie Couric. She was certainly a lot more than a chirpy commentator. Her look of vulnerability spoke to him. Her ladylike sexuality intrigued him. Her heart-stirring smile touched him in a way that he hadn't felt since before his wife died.

"Ready?" he asked Fiona as she approached the table.

"As well as I'll ever be," she replied, straightening her shoulders.

9

CHAPTER 4

As they left Quigleys, Ted again cupped Fiona's elbow and propelled her to a late-model black Mustang GT parked in front of the pub. She still wasn't sure if she liked being herded by him, but after all, that's what she was paying him for. He expertly jockeyed the car out of a tight parking place outside Quigley's and headed down Jefferson Street, a traffic-clogged downtown thoroughfare.

"I'm surprised at how easily you could talk about the incident with Kendrick," Ted commented.

"Actually, I never talk about it, but I knew it was necessary today. In reality, I quit Girl Scouts because of my fear of going into wooded areas, and I still have an aversion to dark haired burly young men that remind me of Kendrick. Thankfully, the nightmares only occur once or twice a year now."

"One asshole can cause a whole lot of damage."

"Yeah, worst of all, I hate for my sisters to be in danger because of me. It makes me wish I hadn't testified."

"If you hadn't testified, Kendrick probably would have killed more women," Ted said bluntly.

Fiona shrugged and concentrated on how ordinary and safe the shops and restaurants and people looked after so much grim discussion. Or were they? Could any of these people be sinister? Not that perky mom pushing that expensive stroller or the elderly gentleman crossing the street. *But what about that odd-looking man just entering the crosswalk? Could he be scoping out Naperville trying to locate her? What if someone jumped out from behind that parked car to their right?*

Fiona was glad Ted couldn't hear her ridiculous what-ifs. She deliberately pushed aside the wayward thoughts and said brightly, "Have you noticed any changes in downtown Naperville since you came back from the east coast?"

"Plenty. I see more locally owned shops and restaurants have been bought out by the big guys . . . Talbots, Eddie Bauer, Chicos, etc."

"But Naperville still has a hometown ambience. It has a downtown, with sidewalk sales and old fashioned parades. And some great traditions. When I was a kid I ate ice cream at the bandshell and listened to Sousa playing in the park. I think the population was around forty thousand then. Now the population is over one hundred forty thousand, but the band still plays on every Thursday night."

"You sound like a Chamber of Commerce lady."

"Good. That's my work coming out in me. I love this city and hope to get that across on my TV show."

Within minutes they approached the Naperville Police Department. Located on a large piece of land and sharing space with other city offices, the police department looked like an impressive fortress. They wound past Safety Town, a child-sized village where Big Wheel and tricycle riders learned the first rules of driving safety. A small man-made lake glistened just west of the complex.

"In 1990 when this new PD opened, it was the most state-of-the-art facility of its kind in the country, with its bar-less cells. Now they're commonplace," Ted said.

Fiona looked around the huge lobby. She was sixteen years old the last time she set foot in the police department. She had gone to a party with Billy Turner, a football player she liked, and she didn't know that kids would be drinking and smoking. She and Billy were dancing, and she was just ready to tell him that she wanted to leave when someone yelled, "Police!"

Everyone ran for the exits, including Billy, who never gave her a backward look. Before she could grab her cell phone in her purse across the room, someone said, "Stay right there, young lady." Fiona and a few other kids who were slow on the uptake were taken to the police department. And their parents were called. Her mom came. Even if her dad was alive, he never would have come. Fortunately she hadn't had anything to drink and they let her off with a warning. Billy was history, of course.

She followed Ted to the chief's office. He was greeted several times by police officers who apparently had worked with him before he took the FBI assignment.

Chief of Police George Jansen greeted Fiona and Ted and ushered them into his office where Detective Tremayne joined them. Chief Jansen shook Ted's hand and said, "Glad you're back to this area. We missed you." He turned to Fiona, "Sorry to have you here under these circumstances. You made a good choice in hiring Ted. I'm going to deputize him right now, so he'll have access to our facility and our data bases.

"John Tremayne will be the officer assigned to your case. He'll also cover your protection, Fiona, whenever Ted needs time off. And even though we can't give you continuous protection indefinitely, Ted can call us at any time for backup or whatever he needs. Your sister, Regan, will be given protection until she leaves the country tomorrow. Also, we'll want to take your picture so that all our officers can be watching out for you, as well as for Kendrick."

After Ted was deputized, he asked for a recent picture of Ralph Kendrick. Chief Jansen pulled an eight by ten picture out of a folder, and said, "All our officers will be on the lookout for this man."

Fiona took a long look at the man who still appeared in her nightmares, and a shiver passed through her whole body. "Except for his mean looking, pale blue eyes, Kendrick doesn't look anything like the person I remember. I'd never recognize him as this balding, middle-aged man."

"Don't forget. By now, Kendrick could have a false beard and a full head of hair," Ted reminded her. "About the only thing he can't change is his height which I see is five feet ten inches."

"According to Brady, the Minneapolis detective who called us, Kendrick worked out and is very strong," Jansen said. "Brady also said Kendrick came from a wealthy family. Let's hope he can't access any of their money without getting caught."

"Chief," Ted said, "Fiona and I would like to travel to Minneapolis tomorrow. Could you arrange a meeting between us and the prison warden, and perhaps some inmates who knew Kendrick? I want to do a personality profile on him, so we know what we're dealing with. We'd also like to meet with the Minneapolis detective who contacted you."

"Tell me your arrival time and I'll take care of it," Jansen said.

"Do you have any information about Tory Girard and Sandy Johnson?" Fiona asked.

"Only that they haven't yet made contact with Ms. Girard yet. The Minneapolis police department has her address and phone, but she's out of town visiting her mother in Florida. Evidently Ms. Girard turned her cell phone off, when she and her mother went off sightseeing somewhere. She's due back in Minneapolis tomorrow sometime according to co-workers. As for Ms. Johnson, they still haven't found her location."

"One more thing, Chief," Ted said, "I don't want to risk a tail following us to the airport. Can I drive my car here and take one of yours out a different exit?"

"We'll set it up for you. We'll also get your tickets bought under an assumed name."

Ted turned to Fiona, "The chief and I might be busy for awhile. While you're waiting, make up a detailed schedule of your activities for the next two weeks."

Fiona opened up her I-Pad, which she carried every place, and began typing. When she finished the schedule, she called her sister, Regan, who was moving to Barcelona the next day with her husband and two boys, aged three and five.

"The moving van finished at noon," Regan said. "And I just came to the Hyatt to get cleaned up. I have a policeman tailing me, thank God. Naperville's finest will protect me until we fly to Barcelona tomorrow. Brad has talked to people at the Embassy there, and they'll provide protection when we arrive. How're you doing?"

"I hired a bodyguard. He's the son of mom's new neighbor."

"I heard," Regan said. "The more I think about this situation, the madder I get. I think you and Kailee should just come to Barcelona with us until Kendrick is caught."

"If I were sure they'd capture Kendrick at the end of a week, I'd consider it. But I can't just put my whole life on hold."

"We all need to put Kendrick's threats in a compartment, be smart enough to take precautions, and concentrate on something else. Right now I need to concentrate on two boys who each need a time out. See you at Mom's." Regan rang off.

Next Fiona called Kailee and said, "I'm so sorry you're at risk because of me,"

"Now that's just stupid. This is certainly not your fault. And no one thinks it is." Kailee was her usual unflappable self. "Justin is taking the next two weeks off to be my shadow. I'm lucky he was in Special Ops when he was in the service. I only have a couple more classes in Abnormal Psychology to teach and one test to give. Then we'll leave for an undisclosed location. Justin also talked to the police chief here in DeKalb, and they'll provide protection until we go."

"That's good. I'm at the Naperville PD waiting for my bodyguard to finish conferring with the police."

"I saw your bodyguard the other day as he was leaving his mom's house. First time I've seen him since his mom moved in a few weeks ago. He's a hunk."

"I feel a little awkward with him. When his mom and ours tried to set up a blind date for us, we both refused."

"Silly you!" The two sisters rang off and Fiona picked up her I-Pad to do some research for her job while she waited for Ted.

CHAPTER 5

Unincorporated western Wisconsin

In the secluded woods of a large lodge in Wisconsin, Ralph Kendrick paced an opulent room with massive black leather furnishings. As he walked, he repeatedly fisted his right hand and smashed it into the palm of his left hand. Although the room was far bigger than the size of his former cell, he decided that it wasn't much better than being in jail.

Attached to a massive hunting and fishing lodge, the rooms were entirely underground. Although lavish, his quarters were actually no better than a damned windowless bunker. He didn't know who the lodge belonged to, but he'd been brought here on the order of Joe Toro, his dad's buddy and former partner, the man who visited him in prison after his father died.

He'd heard his dad talk about safe houses owned by the "club," a loosely knit few, formerly headed by his father and Toro, with no ties to the mobs. He was told to lay low for awhile. Already he'd been here a few days, and he was chomping at the bit. Although he enjoyed the unlimited booze, steak dinners, and expensive cigars, he was impatient to arrange for five kills before he left the country permanently.

He could thank his dead father for his attention to detail. He had convinced his old man that he was innocent. Good thing the old man was so gullible. Kendrick senior had set up a plan the last time he and Ralph had a private conversation before Ralph's trial. First of all, his father set up an offshore account for Ralph under the name of Anthony Clark and made him memorize the number. If Ralph could ever escape, he was to call a special telephone number for a pickup. His father or Toro would arrange for a person to pick him up, bring a disguise, and get him out of the area.

On the day of his escape, when Ralph left the old lady's place, he drove her car just long enough to steal another one. As he drove the second car, a black Taurus, he used the old lady's cell phone to call the special phone number and told the person where he was and what car he was driving. He was told to wait for his contact in a small, busy strip mall on the eastern skirt of Minneapolis.

His contact, Bud, was an old guy with no teeth who arrived in twenty minutes. Bud brought a white wig and facial hair, as well as padding and old man clothes for Ralph. He said a collapsible wheel chair was in the trunk. Ralph donned the wig and shirt as they drove to Wisconsin, sticking to side streets and secondary routes. When they reached the lodge, Bud turned Ralph over to a skinny, but tough-looking, guy named Pete, who would take care of him. Then Bud left.

The only good thing about this place was the computer in his room. Pete showed him how to use it. Ralph caught on fast and was soon surfing the web. He especially liked the porn sites.

A knock at the door interrupted Ralph's thoughts. He wondered what was up. It wasn't time for lunch yet. When he opened the door his eyes widened at the glimpse of a face from the past. Jimmy Ponzo. Nephew of Joe Toro. Ralph never liked Jimmy. And the feeling had been mutual.

"What are you doing here?" he asked.

"Figure it out, asshole," Jimmy said.

"You're my new handler?" Ralph frowned at the guy.

"Yeah. Our next stop will be the hotel that's attached to the HoChunk casino near the Dells. You'll need the old man duds and the wheelchair. The hotel's huge. First, I'll check us in for a few days. Then I'll wheel you in, and nobody'll pay attention to you.

"I've arranged for your first two kills, one in Naperville, and one in Minneapolis. The Sandy Johnson search took longer, but we finally found her, and that deal should be set tomorrow."

"How about the other two?"

"Chill out. This is not like an order for someone to deliver pizza. Sometimes it takes a few days before a hit can be set up. And no killer wants his ass on the line."

CHAPTER 6

Naperville, Illinois

As they left the police department, Ted cupped Fiona's elbow on the way to the car.

"I notice that you still flinch when I place my hand on your arm."

Fiona's face jerked to face Ted's. "What are you talking about?"

"When I protect someone, I cup the person's elbow to steer him or her. You don't like it."

"You're right," she confessed. "I have this independent, feisty streak. I don't like to be herded."

"Get used to it. It could save your life."

"I'll try," she murmured.

"Have you met anyone socially in the last week?" Ted asked as they drove to her town house. "I need to know the names so I can check them out."

"I met someone a few days ago when I went to Bar Louie's with some friends. His name is Rich Clement. He's a Loan Manager at First Continental Bank. I'm sure he's okay, though. He's too goal oriented to be a criminal type. We're meeting again for lunch at Malnati's this week."

"I'll check him out. When you print your schedule, include his personal info."

Fiona was normally an open, outgoing person. She had to be in her profession. She hated to be suspicious of the people in her life. At least the new people in her life. Well, that wasn't quite so bad. She realized that she was twisting the strands of blond hair over her left ear again. It was a habit she'd conquered years ago.

She jerked back to the present when Ted asked her a question.

"What?" she asked

"What was it like to grow up as a triplet?"

"Cool. Fun. I always had a playmate. Since I didn't have anything to compare it to, it seemed normal."

"Back when you were born, the birth of triplets must have been big news."

"Yeah. Not anymore. Edward hospital here in Naperville delivers more triplets than any other hospital in the United States."

"Any reason why?"

"Fertility options. Affluence. Women conceiving later in life."

"Did your mom dress you girls alike when you were young?"

"Never." Fiona pointed to the right. "Turn here into this subdivision. "Mom was determined that each one of us develop her own individuality. Trust me,

16

she didn't have to worry about that. From the time we could talk, each one of us was outspoken and opinionated. Over the years, we pulled a lot of pranks that involved switching places with one another."

"How long did that last?"

"Until the fourth grade. Up until then, Mom always kept our hair long, but she styled it differently . . . a ponytail, a topknot, or pigtails. However, the year we were in fourth grade, all three of us had an important math test, and we were in separate classrooms. Regan was the best mathematician. We changed our hairstyles, and she took the test three times. Got almost perfect scores. That was how we got busted. All three answer sheets were the same. From that day on, Mom insisted on one long hair, one short hair, and one permed. She held her ground no matter how much we complained."

"Did you learn a lesson about cheating?" Ted laughed.

"Apparently. We didn't pull that again. As a Trip, I never dared to get a big head because I knew the other two would put me in my place. That was true for Kailee and Regan, too. We kept each other grounded in the real world."

When they entered Fiona's subdivision, Ted saw a large retention pond on the right with three fountains. A few weeping willow trees graced the thick carpet of grass around the pond. On the other side of the street, gray brick, one-story townhouses with white trim clustered in groups of four.

Entering Fiona's townhouse, Ted saw hardwood floors gleaming under white furniture. An L-shaped sectional couch separated the living area from the kitchen. Two rattan chairs with white cushions flanked the built-in entertainment center with its flat screen TV. Turquoise pillows dotted the upholstered furniture. Light streamed in from a large picture window that overlooked the front yard. The room looked like a picture in a decorating magazine.

Ted eyed all the pristine white and groaned inwardly. "Are ordinary people allowed to sit in here?"

"Sure," she straightened a pillow. "And all the slip covers are washable. My nephews have spilled a few times."

"Did you choose the turquoise accents to match your eyes?"

"No, this is my Florida condo look. I change the accessories according to the season or my mood. In the summer, the pillow covers and throws are a cool navy. In the fall, they're gold, orange and brown. And so on."

"Let me guess. Red and gold at Christmas."

Fiona nodded.

"So you're a chameleon. And if you're in a bad mood, do you haul out black accessories?" he asked.

17

"No, then I'd use my buttery yellow accessories—to cheer me up," she smiled.

"Walk me through so I can view the floor plan, mainly for windows and exits."

Fiona pointed to the small kitchen and dining area, all open to the living room. After showing him a small powder room located off the kitchen, she led him down a short corridor to a small office on the left. Her bedroom, with its attached bath, sat to the right and was decorated in a nautical theme. "You'd better plan to sleep in my bed since you're longer than I am," Fiona offered.

"No, I'll take the couch if you throw a tarp over it or something, so I don't mess it up."

"Don't be silly. They're slip covers. Even chili spilled on a cushion washed right out. I don't worry about it."

"Yeah, right," he thought, and he moved back to the kitchen, where sliding glass doors led to a small patio and a postage-sized back yard. The patio overlooked a grassy divide with a row of townhouses about one hundred feet behind Fiona's town house. Several mature oaks and maples formed a long queue down the center of the grassy verge between the two rows of townhouses, giving a sense of permanence to the relatively new subdivision.

"I like to sit out here on the patio and work on my tan."

"This place is off-limits for now, especially if you sit here regularly. Too many opportunities for a sniper. Not in the trees yet, because they're still budding out. But the town houses."

Fiona frowned at him. "Isn't that far-fetched?"

Ted flashed her a dark look.

"I know, I know," she interrupted. "No objections from me."

They went inside. "This leads to the basement." Fiona opened a door off the kitchen.

As they moved down the steps, Ted looked with approval at a treadmill, an elliptical, a stationary bike, and a weight machine.

"Are these for show, or do you really use them?" he asked, then felt like an ass. Just looking at her perfect, well-toned figure, he could answer his own question.

"Uh-huh. And my sisters and I use the big exercise mat to practice our self defense moves. A friend of ours was attacked three years ago. After that, we took self defense classes, and we review the moves every month or so."

"Good idea." He noticed that the other side of the basement was devoted to a laundry area and a storage area, and he noted the location of four windows. "Tremayne said he checked all your doors and windows, and you have an up-to-date alarm system. That's good."

Back upstairs, Ted pulled out his laptop and said, "I'll start the searches on Rich Clement and Sandy Johnson, and the people on your schedule."

"I'll print it out for you right now. I already took off my morning run, and I blocked in time on my treadmill instead."

When she handed him the printed sheets, he said, "Good. But I see you're all over Naperville."

"Pretty much. Sometimes other suburbs. Sometimes Chicago."

"In the future, make all appointments for new interviews at least six hours ahead, so I can run a background check on the person. If he or she seems legitimate, I'll give you the go-ahead. From now on, schedule your appointments for a restaurant when you can, or your TV station. I'll need to accompany you for all interviews."

"That might be awkward. People might not open up."

"Tell them I'm a reporter new to the area, and you're bringing me up to speed."

"Great," Fiona muttered to herself. When she stood up, she knocked off some of her folders at the end of the couch.

As the papers scattered. Ted came to help her. "Hmmm," he said. "Here's an interesting document."

Fiona looked at the folder and blushed. "It's information I gathered on you before we met at Quigleys. It's the reporter in me. And I bet you have a file on me as well."

"You'd be right."

"Let's see, you have two brothers. One's an investment broker. One's a priest. You grew up in Glen Ellyn, and received your master's degree from Northern Illinois University. You made captain at the Naperville PD and also Policeman of the Year. Your wife died four or five years ago, about six months before you went to Quantico. Also, in relation to your character, according to my mother you go to church regularly and have good morals." Fiona grinned.

"You get good marks for accuracy." He tapped his forehead. "You grew up in Naperville except for two years when your father was transferred to Minneapolis. You received a master's in broadcast journalism at Northwestern. You married Jeb Travis, news commentator for Chicago's Channel 4, who was killed in a traffic accident two years ago. You worked as a news reporter for the same Channel 4 until you accepted a job at Naperville's NKTV. And my mother gave me the same character reference as yours." He changed the subject, "Any reason you left the Chicago station?"

"Quite a few, but I don't have time to go into them now. I need to shower and change so that I can get to the station well ahead of my show."

CHAPTER 7

Fiona turned the water on hard and hot, hoping it would beat the tension kinks out of her shoulders. She wanted to scream out loud like a banshee to release her frustration. But she didn't want Ted or her neighbors to come running. *She wanted Kendrick out of her life.*

She thought about Ted. He wasn't really a handsome man, but he had a virile, well-seasoned look that was actually more attractive. She liked the deep creases that bracketed his mouth, but she sometimes found his probing gray eyes unsettling. On the job, she was open and outgoing, but she liked to keep her personal life private. She wasn't sure she would be comfortable with Ted opening up any drawers of her personal life.

She quickly changed into an ice blue silk suit for her show at five. She grabbed a pair of designer jeans and a sleeveless top to wear at her mom's house when they went for dinner afterwards.

Ted tossed a handy afghan over the white couch, opened his computer, and re-examined Fiona's schedule, jotting notes here and there. He answered his e-mails and typed in her information about Rich Clement. His concentration was poor. He kept thinking about her. She intrigued him, and he hadn't been intrigued by a woman since his wife died.

In the past, he'd developed a bias against press and TV reporters. They had often made his life miserable with their pushy ways when he was trying to protect people. Fiona seemed different from other reporters. She seemed like a genuinely nice person who was scared to death. He was glad he decided to protect her.

As she came out of the bedroom to leave for the TV station, he was even happier with his decision. She looked like a million bucks in a blue suit that fit her in all the right places. And she had some very attractive right places.

"Can your boss be trusted to keep the details of your situation under wraps?" Ted asked as they drove to Fiona's station.

"Yeah, Mackay's okay. But the minute another station gets a whiff of the story, he'll want an in-depth account."

"Fair enough. If anyone of your co-workers asks, just say you're being stalked, and I'm watching out for you."

"Okay."

Fiona's TV station sat in a one story brick building, part of a strip mall near a large drugstore. The station faced Chicago Avenue, and an elementary school stood across the street. Inside the building, Ted saw black and white tweedy industrial carpeting. Black office furniture. Some white walls. A few black ones for contrast.

Fiona introduced Ted to the station's receptionist, Daphne Adams. Daphne, a perky young woman in her mid twenties, batted her eyes at Ted. Dressed in trendy clothing and accessorized with dangling chandelier ear rings, she reached out her hand to give him a welcoming handshake, showing her black-tipped fingernails. Her straight black hair was skewered into side ponytails, and her dark brown eyes had irises almost as black as her pupils.

"Is Daphne an NCIS fan?" Ted asked, after they were out of earshot. "She reminds me of the computer whiz on that show."

"You mean Abby? Yeah, Daphne tries hard to maintain the Abby look, and she's a dedicated flirt, but she manages several jobs around here and doesn't complain. And she makes excellent coffee."

Fiona led the way to her boss's office. When she knocked on the door, a gruff voice barked, "Five minutes, just five minutes."

Fiona introduced Ted to Gordon Mackay, a grizzly bear of a man with furry white eyebrows that matched his hair. Mackay looked at Fiona. "Spit it out," he said.

Fiona explained her situation and Ted's new role in her life. She also explained the reason for secrecy at this time.

Mackay nodded. "Point taken. If I can help in any way, let me know."

"Just approve Ted accompanying me everywhere for the time being," Fiona said.

"Done. When this dirtbag is caught, you'll have a story for us. Right?"

"Definitely."

Gordon looked at his watch. Fiona and Ted took the hint and rose to leave.

"Collier," Gordon said as they were going out the door. "Keep her safe."

"I intend to."

A strikingly handsome, blond man, probably in his early thirties, stood outside Mackay's office. Fiona said, "Ted, meet Ben Hamilton. He's my counterpart on the morning news show." Ben gave a perfunctory smile, shook hands with Ted, and knocked on Gordon's door.

Once in Fiona's office, she said, "Ben has ambitions to be a big time newscaster, but he lacks professionalism, and he's way too pushy. I try not to be judgmental, but I don't respect him. Of course, I aggravate him because I'm not impressed with him."

"I see." Ted looked around her office. Same black and white décor. A cluster of framed family pictures on top of a file cabinet. And a potted plant with red flowers. Fiona's desktop looked neatly organized, and included a computer and several black wire bins, each full of papers.

"Fiona, we need to find you another office temporarily. You'd be a sitting duck working at your desk in front of the picture window."

"You're kidding. I finally got desk space with a view."

"It would just be temporary."

"Just another example of how Kendrick has hijacked my life."

They were interrupted by a knock at the door, and Fiona's cameraman entered. Charlie Hunt's long neck encased an impressively protruding Adam's apple. His arms and legs looked as if they were only loosely attached to his torso. He advanced toward them with a loping gait. Fiona introduced the men. After she and Charlie conferred about a segment for the upcoming show, he left.

Fiona said, "Charlie's a gem. When he focuses his camera, he's loose enough to marshal his body parts into the most amazing positions to get the perfect shot or the best angle. He's got a dry wit, and we've developed a good relationship based on mutual respect."

Fiona gave Ted a quick tour of the rest of the facility so he could check out exits and windows. The oblong building was divided into thirds. In the front third, a row of offices, including Fiona's, faced Chicago Avenue. The middle third contained a row of storage rooms, and the rear third contained the newsroom where they filmed the shows.

When Fiona moved into the studio to broadcast, she settled herself at a draped table in front of a backdrop that showed a segment of Naperville's Riverwalk. Ted found a spot where he could watch the broadcast and the studio's exit doors.

When the first camera zoomed in on her opening words, he could see she was a real pro. Her voice had a special rich quality, and she radiated warmth. Her smile was wide and engaging in spite of the stress she was under. First she covered the general news in Naperville and the surrounding suburbs. She had a direct, but relaxed delivery. Her presentation was more like a local Today show rather than a usual news broadcast, with emphasis on recent and upcoming area events, and also short interviews. She showed footage of the annual plastic duck race down the DuPage river, and she mentioned the upcoming live event of border collies actually herding sheep at a Naperville location.

When she introduced today's guest, Molly Maguire, born in Naperville in 1918, Ted thought the next few minutes would be relatively boring. He was wrong. Ms. Maguire was plump, lively, and sharp. Fiona encouraged Mrs. Maguire to talk about her girlhood life in Naperville. Ms. Maguire told a story she'd heard from her father about the dispute between Naperville and Wheaton over the placement of the county seat which was once in Naperville. One night in 1868, a group of men from Wheaton stole the county records from Naperville in a daring midnight raid . . . and got away with it. Mrs. Maguire's father was awakened by the church bells ringing in the dark of night. He and others were too late to stop the theft, though, and from that time on, the county seat remained in Wheaton.

The show ended with a local sports update and a short weather commentary. "Nice broadcast," Ted said, as he steered her toward his car.

"Thanks." Fiona reminded herself to stop being irritated by his protective gesture. "By the way, I have to warn you about my family. They can be overwhelming. My sisters and I have a special connection, sort of an intuitive awareness of each other . . . probably from being jammed together in the womb. When we're together, we tend to monopolize a conversation. And, we often finish each others' sentences."

"Tell me about them."

"Regan's the oldest by twenty minutes. Then me. Then Kailee. Regan's married to Brad Daly, who's with the State Department. They and their two boys, Carson and Tyler, are moving to Barcelona tomorrow where he'll be working at the American Embassy for the next year. That's the reason for this get-together. Kailee and her husband, Justin Hughes, live in DeKalb, where he works for the city, and she teaches psychology at Northern Illinois University. Justin spent a few years in Iraq with the army, and he plans to take time off his work as a city engineer to protect her."

As they drove south on Naperville-Plainfield Road, a loud, sharp noise crackled through the air. Fiona ducked down toward the floor and covered her head with her hands. Breath hitching and shaking like a leaf, she quavered, "Are you all right, Ted?"

"I've never been injured by a backfire yet," he commented mildly.

"A backfire? I'm ducking from a backfire?" She pulled herself back up onto the seat, red-faced from the burn of embarrassment. "What a heroine I am!"

"Don't be embarrassed. You did the right thing. Duck and cover was a good response under the circumstances."

"Duck and cower was more like it."

"If that had been a gunshot, I would have burnt some rubber and gotten you the hell away from the shooter. For now you can relax. Nobody's following us. I've been watching."

"I hate being afraid. I'm so tense. Right now I feel like a balloon that's being pumped with so much air that I'm afraid I'll explode into little rubbery pieces."

"Breathe in through your nose. Hold it for four seconds. Blow it out through your mouth. If you do it a few times, it usually helps."

Fiona tried it three times, then leaned back and relaxed against the seat. "Thanks."

"Not a problem. By the way, Chief Jansen authorized an unmarked car for the front of your mom's house and also an officer to patrol the back yard. He didn't want to take any chances with all three of you being in one place tonight."

"That's good." No, that's not good, she thought bitterly. "It's like we're under siege."

CHAPTER 8

As they turned right into Blackberry Court, Ted's mother's house was the first one on the right. Fiona's mother's house sat in the middle of the three-house cul-de-sac, surrounded by mature oaks and fragrant lilac bushes. After her day of stress and fear, Fiona's mom's home, with the pale gray siding and white trim and its wraparound porch, represented a safe haven to her. As they left the car they heard the sound of horns tooting, and two more cars pulled into the driveway.

"Even though we come from different directions, we Trips generally arrive at the same time," Fiona said. "It must be some ingrained punctuality thing."

When Ted saw the Morgan triplets embracing each other, he realized that his jaw had fallen open. He quickly realigned it. It was like seeing a gorgeous model times three. The long-legged triplets were lovely, with their streaky, honey blond hair, classic features, and unusual turquoise eyes, but they also brought an energy and charisma into the atmosphere that was almost overwhelming. Fiona performed the introductions.

Dressed in black slacks and a black and white diagonally striped top, Regan wore her hair shorter than Fiona's, just to her shoulders, in a sculpted cut. Her two small boys raced to hug their aunts. Regan's husband, Brad Daly, was a tall, thin man who epitomized Ted's conception of a distinguished diplomat.

Kailee wore a trendy outfit, a gauzy, floaty skirt, with the current layers of long and short tops and funky jewelry. Her hair was permed into a curly halo. Her husband, Justin Hughes, looked like a football player. Ted noticed that the triplets all seemed to talk at once.

"This Kendrick thing is unbelievable!" Regan said.

"It couldn't come at a worse time," Kailee added.

"I think I should make a public statement that I was the original witness; then you two would be off the hook," Fiona said.

"Bad idea!" the other two chorused.

"I agree with your sisters," Ted said. "Right now we don't want Kendrick to know we're onto him."

By this time, the girls' mother, Barbara Morgan, came to the front door to welcome them. Ted saw his mother, Lucy Collier, right behind her.

Ted smiled at his mother and said, "Why am I not surprised to see you here?"

"Barbara invited me to the farewell dinner. She didn't want you to be the only outsider," Lucy said, with a twinkle in her eye. She introduced him to Barbara Morgan, Fiona's mother.

Mrs. Morgan resembled her triplets, with blond hair, softly feathered in a short hairdo and eyes the same unusual turquoise. Ted figured her to be in her fifties. His mother, Annette, who was sixty-one, had thick, short, salt and pepper hair, curly on top and short in back. Both women were trim and slender. Fiona had mentioned that her mother was an occupational therapist who worked at a nearby rehabilitation hospital. Ted's mother worked part time teaching remedial reading in her previous location, and had recently begun a full time position in the Naperville school system.

When Ted entered the Morgan house, he saw a cozy room of blue plaids, florals, and stripes. He guessed it was decorated in what they called country style. He noticed an assortment of pictures separately and together of the three Morgan girls. Most were candid shots. A few were posed portraits.

A large dining room table was set to accommodate the crowd. He could smell the aroma of roasted turkey. Barbara said, "I figured we could all use some comfort food. And since Regan and her family will be gone for Thanksgiving, I decided to make this an early feast."

"Here goes my diet," Kailee said, as she set the apple pies she had made on the large sideboard, already loaded with stuffing, cranberries, candied sweet potatoes, rolls, and mixed salad.

Barbara Morgan did not allow any discussion of Ralph Kendrick during the meal. Conversation focused on Regan and her family's move to Barcelona.

Regan said, "I've been practicing my . . ."

"Spanish," Kailee finished for her. "We can hardly wait to . . ."

"Visit you there," Fiona said. "I hear there's a spot called Las Rambas, where they sell everything from chickens to silver jewelry."

"Be sure to notice the assortment of balconies," Barbara said. "They're everywhere, in all different styles and shapes. I spent my trip there looking up constantly, because I was so fascinated with them."

During a lull in the conversation, Kailee said. "By the way, Justin and I have an announcement to make. We're looking at baby cribs."

"What?" Regan and Fiona squealed. "You're expecting?"

The next twenty minutes were devoted to baby talk and pregnancy issues. After dinner, while the women cleaned up the kitchen, and the men cleared away the chairs, Ted and Fiona's two brothers-in-law discussed the Kendrick situation. Both Brad and Justin asked Ted to update them.

"My embassy is aware of the situation and will give us additional security," said Brad, "I've hired a bodyguard who'll travel with us and stay as long as needed."

Justin said, "Kailee has to teach two classes and give a test this week. Then I'm taking her away from here where Kendrick won't find us. In the meantime, I've already taken time off to be with her around the clock."

"I recommend that you exercise caution at all times," Ted said. "We've heard that Kendrick threatened to kill all three Morgan girls since he didn't know which one testified. So far, the police have tried to contact Tory Girard, who evidently is on vacation. They haven't been able to hunt down Sandy Johnson. With a common name like that, the computer is going ballistic. The trouble is, we don't know if the killer will be Kendrick, a trained assassin, or a two-bit thug off the street. And sometimes the latter are the most dangerous because they're unpredictable. If Kendrick had any sense he'd leave the country and forget his vendetta. Maybe he has already."

The three men discussed the various strategies they could use to protect each of the triplets. Ted cautioned the other two men to be alert to any car that appeared to be tailing them. "A hitman will want to memorize your schedule and will look for a vulnerable time."

As the men moved to the family room, Regan joined them. "I got relieved of kitchen duty since I'm leaving tomorrow." She looked at Ted. "Could I talk to you in the den?"

He nodded, and they went into a comfortably furnished office containing enough books to be called a library.

"I get furious when I think about Fiona's having to deal with Kendrick again," Regan said, as she sat on a tan leather couch. "After he murdered that woman, Fiona had terrible nightmares, and she'd shout, 'I'm coming! I'll help you!'

"We'd wake her up, and she'd cry because she ran away and hadn't helped the woman. Kailee and I kept telling her that she was only ten years old, and Kendrick would have killed her, too. Mom made her see a counselor, and that must have helped because the nightmares weren't as frequent. But the incident changed her life forever.

"I want to speak plainly, since I'm going out of the country. I know you've been hired to take care of my sister. Just don't mess with her. She's not one for a one-night stand . . . or a one-week stand. Circumstances in her life have made her vulnerable."

"I'm her bodyguard, not her lover," Ted said laconically.

"Just so you keep it that way."

"You don't pull any punches."

"No, I don't." Regan stood and prowled the room as she spoke. "Fiona was the most exuberant and the most fearless of the three of us. Until she saw the murder. After that, it was as if her special spark dimmed. She saw evil in action, and became wary." She stopped abruptly. "Between seeing the murder and our father committing suicide shortly after the trial, Fiona had enough on her plate.

Then she married a jerk who could charm the skin off a snake, and who broke her heart with his infidelity."

"She seems like a well-grounded adult to me."

"Yeah, but you never knew her before. I'd sure like to see that devil-may-care twinkle back in her eyes. Take care of her." She turned to go back to the others, and Ted followed her.

As he entered the family room, Kailee asked him to step out on the front porch. She had a sweet natured, soft-spoken way about her. Ted wondered if she was going to give him more warnings.

"Take good care of Fiona," she said. "She'll pretend to be brave, but she can put on her newslady face and cover up her real feelings. She needs someone to watch out for her, especially if she's focused on some goal. She can be oblivious even to her own safety. I can tell she scared now, because I see she's twisting the strands of her hair again, and she worked so hard to break that habit. She never did it before she saw the murder."

"I'll do my best to take care of her," Ted said. "You take care, too."

"I'm lucky to have Justin. He'll watch out for me."

They joined the rest in the family room, except for Regan's boys who went to the basement playroom. Barbara Morgan settled in an overstuffed chair and turned to Ted. "What do you need to ask us that would help you and Brad and Justin to protect my girls?"

"They must have been a handful to raise," Ted said.

"Oh, they were, but I'd never trade them in. The three girls have many of the same preferences, such as fluffy slippers, Crest toothpaste, and oatmeal chocolate chip cookies. But they've each developed their own individuality. They also share many attributes, but they vary in degree.

"For example, there's fearlessness. They all love the roller coaster and downhill skiing. Regan is fearless in organizing huge parties and charitable events. Fiona is fearless in standing before a crowd and speaking. Kailee is fearless in avenging injustice. All three are outgoing and opinionated. All three are independent and stubborn."

"You used to call it bullheaded," Regan added.

"Or pig-headed," Kailee said.

"We call it determined," Fiona said.

"Being too independent and stubborn can get you dead," Ted reminded her.

"He's right," Mrs. Morgan agreed. "I just want to say to you girls that I wish I had never allowed Fiona to testify all those years ago. I feel as if my whole family is in jeopardy because of me."

Ted said, "Mrs. Morgan, with all due respect, your family is in jeopardy from Ralph Kendrick, not you. All three women now have protection. What about you?"

"I have an expensive security system that I installed last year. I also spoke to a family friend, Steve Wylie, who's a retired police officer. He's going to be here at night, just to be on the safe side. He'll be coming around ten tonight."

"Good," Ted said, and he heard several voices agreeing with him.

At that point Regan and her husband said they would have to leave for their hotel. The moving van had left their home earlier in the day, and they had an early morning flight. A flurry of hugs and tears ensued, with many promises to phone regularly and send lots of pictures via e-mail.

CHAPTER 9

When they were driving back to Fiona's town house, Ted said, "You were right. You do finish each other's sentences."

"Pretty much. What do you think of us Trips now that you've had a couple hours' exposure?"

"The words outgoing, outspoken, outrageous . . . and outstandingly beautiful come to mind," he answered. "But I think overwhelming is the best description I can think of."

"You thought we were overwhelming?"

"Absolutely."

"And here I thought you were a tough warrior type."

He threw back his head and laughed. "Guess I'm only mortal. I think I mentioned that the three of you are outstandingly beautiful?"

"That's funny," she said seriously. "We don't see each other that way. When you see your face looking back at you from not just one, but two people, you begin to think of it as ordinary. Do you think you could tell us apart if we were dressed alike and had the same hair style?"

"Absolutely."

"You seem very sure of yourself."

"I am. Regan has a tiny mole near her left eye, and she's the most direct and outspoken of you three. Kailee is the sweetest, and she talks softer than you and Regan. You are the most responsive. You get a kick out of little things. You're also a good actress. When you broadcast your show today, no one would have known what you've gone through earlier."

"I'm impressed. So I'm not the sweetest of us three?"

"You're sweet and *sassy* . . . that's an even better combination."

"Speaking of Regan's mole, our father always had trouble telling us apart. When we Trips were smaller, Kailee and I noticed that he patted her on the head and called her by name, but not us. One day Kailee and I took our markers and painted moles on our faces. Our father came home from work, looked at us, and couldn't figure out who was who. He gave us all a confused wave and went on into the house. Regan was furious. She always thought she was special."

When they arrived at her town house, Fiona started to pull on her knee-length Cubs shirt, then decided she'd better put a bra on first. She stepped into her red fluffy slippers and went toward the kitchen to brew a cup of hot tea. She hoped it would slow down the fearful thoughts that were like little plastic balls ping-ponging through her overtired mind.

She saw that Ted had changed into a white T-shirt and faded jean shorts. He sat on the couch working at his laptop. His long legs were stretched out and his

Karen J. Gallahue

white-stockinged feet rested on her glass-topped table. When he saw her, she laughed to see him pulling his feet down like a guilty school boy.

"Feel free to relax here. I put my feet on the table all the time," she said. She heard the Cubs announcers' voices in the background, and figured they must be playing on the west coast if they were on this late.

"Are you a Cubs fan?" she asked.

"Isn't everybody?"

"Oh yeah," she said, pointing to her shirt.

"Well, a lady with good taste in nightwear as well as in choosing a team."

Fiona flopped on the end of the couch to watch Soriano at bat.

"You smell like lemons and vanilla," Ted commented.

"Lemon rinse for my hair and vanilla bodywash." Fiona focused on Soriano's strikeout. She sat beside Ted and put her feet up as well, and they watched the game companionably. The tea tasted good on her dry throat, and she found herself yawning before the seventh inning.

"I can't believe how drowsy I am," she said. "Too much scary emotion in one day. Think I'll head to bed."

She rinsed out her tea cup and put it in the dishwasher and said good night.

"Leave your door open."

"I always sleep with my door closed."

"Not tonight. I need to hear into your bedroom."

Fiona put her hand on Ted's arm. "Look, I've been told that I snore sometimes. It's embarrassing. I don't want to deal with embarrassment on top of everything else."

Ted opened his mouth to argue, then snapped it shut when he saw that she looked woozy with fatigue and worry. If he pushed too hard, she'd be crying. He could tell. He gave in.

When Fiona fell into bed, she was sure she would fall asleep now. Wrong. She was wound up like a music box. She tossed. She turned. She stretched out flat, and willed herself to sleep. Her body wouldn't cooperate. She tried Ted's breathing exercises, and they helped a little. It seemed like a month ago that Tremayne rang her doorbell. Today's date was already a bad one for her. Now it had another strike against it. She tossed and turned some more. Entirely unbidden and unwanted, she thought back to the events of Jeb's death. What was the trigger for that? Probably today's stress? Or the fact that another man was sleeping in her town house?

30

It was two years ago on a Saturday, and Jeb was in D.C. covering a story. He was the anchor man for Channel 4 in Chicago, the same channel where she also worked as a newscaster. She was working on a big story and decided to drop in at the TV station, even though it was her day off.

As she entered the reception area of the TV station, Mary Adams, the receptionist looked as if she had seen a ghost. She screamed, "You're alive! You're alive!" She flew out from behind her desk and hugged Fiona.

Fiona patted Mary's shoulder. She noticed the receptionist's tear-blotched face, and she asked, puzzled, "Why did you say that?"

"We just received a news flash that Jeb and you were killed in a car accident outside Galena, Illinois."

"Obviously the report is faulty since I'm standing here in front of you."

"I wonder if it's false about Jeb's death, too," Mary said.

"Must be. He couldn't have been in a car accident in Galena. He's in D.C."

"Oh, thank God. We've been so upset."

"I'd better call Jeb and tell him what's going on," Fiona said, hitting the speed dial on her phone.

When a strange voice answered the phone, Fiona felt the first trickle of fear. "Excuse me, I must have the wrong number. I'm trying to reach Jeb Travis. I'm his wife. Is this his phone?"

"You said you're his wife?" the voice questioned.

"Yes. Who are you?"

"I'm the Galena County Sheriff," he answered, "Ma'am, tell me your name again."

"I'm Fiona Travis, the wife of Jeb Travis, and we live in Chicago."

"Ma'am, I hate to be the one to tell you this, but we have an accident victim here whose ID and cell phone indicate that he's Jeb Travis."

"Someone must have stolen his wallet and his cell. My husband is in D.C. I spoke to him there last night."

"The dead man looks like the picture on his driver's license," the sheriff persisted.

"Let me hang up and call his hotel," she said.

With shaking fingers, she dialed the number of the hotel in D.C. where Jeb always stayed. They said he was not booked there. Distraught, she called Jeb's cell again, and again reached the sheriff.

"Ma'am, I think you should come to Galena." he said.

Her sister, Regan, drove the car. "I refuse to cry," Fiona said to her. " It won't be Jeb. A woman was killed in the accident. They thought it was me. It can't be Jeb. He wouldn't do that. There's some mistake, a terrible mistake."

Regan kept reassuring her that it wouldn't be Jeb. Outside the sun blazed down, and there was a soft breeze. It was a day for going swimming or hiking. Not a day to deal with death.

When Fiona reached Galena, the sheriff took her to the morgue. When she saw that the dead man was really Jeb, she finally broke down. Regan held her tightly while Fiona sobbed.

"Why did you think that I was killed as well?" she asked the sheriff between sobs. She didn't really want to hear the answer.

"The couple registered as Mr. and Mrs. Jeb Travis. We don't know her identity yet. I know this is a bad time for you, but will you look at a picture of her? See if you can identify her?"

With tears streaming, Fiona nodded.

When she saw the picture, Fiona gasped, "I do know her," she said. "She's Florence Anders, a reporter from Madison, Wisconsin. Are you sure they registered as husband and wife?" she asked.

"I'm sorry, ma'am, but I'm sure. The owner of the bed and breakfast said they'd stayed there several times before."

Fiona used her fist to stifle the next sob. She turned to Regan. "Oh my God," she cried. "In one day, I find out that I'm a widow, and that my husband was also cheating on me."

"Cry your brains out and get it out of your system," Regan said, pragmatically, as she enveloped Fiona in a hug. "I certainly don't wish him dead, but it will be much easier not to have to divorce him."

Fiona wept. "I loved him. I thought he loved me. How could he sneak around and do this? How could I have been such a trusting idiot? And everything about this incident will become public knowledge because of our jobs. I can't even crawl into a cave and nurse my wounds." She tried to stop the tears from coming.

"I'm so sorry you have to go through this," Her sister held her and patted her back.

"I feel ashamed. I must be lacking in something if Jeb had to go to someone else."

"Whoa! Stop right there," Regan said, "Are you blaming yourself because your husband was fooling around? Put the blame where it belongs. He's an adulterer . . . and not just once. He broke his wedding vows."

"Do you think he fell in love?" Fiona asked. "Maybe he couldn't bear to tell me."

"Don't make an excuse for him. He promised to love you. Only you. Remember?"

"I remember. That's what hurts so much. I believed he loved me. Regan, I don't know if I can face my co-workers at the TV station. I feel so exposed."

"I know, honey." Regan reached over to squeeze her hand. "You can face them, and you will. And both Kailee and I will shore you up. We Morgan women hold our heads up. United we stand."

At the visitation and funeral service, Fiona fielded condolences from high TV dignitaries and Chicago officials to lowly janitors, knowing that all were aware of Jeb's infidelity. Some people avoided her, perhaps not knowing what to say.

At one point, Jeb's best friend came up to her, his eyes a little glassy, and reeking of liquor. He whispered in her ear, "None of them really mattered to him like you did."

"What?" she spat out louder than she intended, and the people around her looked over at her. She left the line, ushering him to a private corner. "What did you mean 'none of them?'" she hissed.

"I thought you knew that Jeb always liked to chase a skirt on the sly," he answered, reddening.

"Are you telling me that Jeb had affairs with other women before Florence?"

"A few. Look I was trying to make you feel better." His voice slurred on the words, and he smiled vacuously.

Fiona sat upright in bed. She couldn't believe she'd let herself re-live those painful days. What a waste of time! Since her experience with Jeb, she didn't trust any man. *If she could be that fooled by Jeb, how could she ever trust her instincts again?*

CHAPTER 10

It took Fiona another fifteen minutes to fall asleep. When she finally nodded off, she dreamed that Ralph Kendrick was chasing her through a dark, gloomy woods with a bloody rock in his hand. Her feet stumbled on heavy roots, and she pushed at branches as she tried to get away from him. When she glanced over her shoulder to see how close he was, she saw his pale blue, bulging eyes. Horns pushed out from his head, and smoke spewed out of his mouth. He raised the rock to smash her head.

Suddenly, the dream ended. Her eyes flared open. She thanked God when she realized it was only a dream, and she lay still as her heart beat slowed. But wait! Something wasn't right. Something had wakened her. Her eyes flared open, and her system buzzed onto red alert.

She was lying on her back, and she strained to listen for a sound. The clock radio said one ten. The bathroom door was ajar as she had left it, and the nightlight illuminated basic shapes in the bedroom. She stayed completely still and let her eyes travel around, but saw no one standing or crouching. Yet something was different. A smell. A whiff of . . . body odor?

When she saw the white curtains moving over the window at the end of her bed, her stomach clenched. That wasn't right. Ted had closed and locked the window. And the air conditioning wasn't on. She knew then that she wasn't alone.

Suddenly a large shape moved with a whoosh from the bottom of her bed, and a man's hard body landed on her, crouched on his knees. His hands flexed around Fiona's neck. She couldn't gather the air to scream, but, lightning quick, she stiffened the pointer and middle fingers on her right hand and aimed for his left eye as hard as she could, just as she'd been taught in self defense classes.

"Bitch," the attacker yelled and pulled back on his haunches, clutching his eye. Fiona screamed for Ted as she struggled to get all the way out from under the intruder. The bedroom door flew open, and the light went on.

Fiona saw Ted lunge forward and grab the intruder with both hands. He swung him off Fiona as if he was a rag doll. The intruder struggled like a mad tiger. Ted turned him and landed a powerful blow to the guy's stomach, and another blow to the man's face. The man crumpled to the floor.

In a blink, Ted flipped the intruder onto his stomach and secured the man's hands behind his back. The entire rescue took a minimum of moves. Ted wasn't even panting when he calmly told Fiona to get his handcuffs and cell phone from the coffee table in the living room.

Fiona's legs shook so badly she had to hang onto furniture as she walked. She found the items, and handed them to Ted. Ted cuffed the guy and rolled him back over to see what he looked like. In black shorts and T-shirt, the man's lanky body sported tattoos wherever skin showed, except for his face. His hooded, beady eyes gave him the look of a light-faced lizard. His left eye was also red and starting to swell from Fiona's attack. He definitely was not Ralph Kendrick.

Ted called 911, told them to contact Tremayne, and asked the attacker, "What's your name?"

"I want a lawyer," the intruder replied. "The bitch probably blinded me." He spat on Fiona's bedroom floor.

Still shaking from the scare, she huffed with anger at his defilement of her space.

"How much did Kendrick pay you for the kill?" Ted asked.

Fiona saw the injured man's eyes widen before he snarled once more that he wanted a lawyer. To her, the man's reaction was a sure clue that Kendrick or his accomplice had paid him to kill her. The thought was unnerving.

Ted read the man his rights as he rifled through the man's pockets. He found no ID, but did find a set of car keys.

"That's okay," said Ted. "As soon as they run your fingerprints, I'll lay money that you have a rap sheet a few yards long."

"Are you all right?" Ted asked Fiona. She stood near him with her arms crossed over her midriff so she could stop her muscles from shaking. She could feel tears leaking down her face, but she nodded her head.

Ted grabbed a box of Kleenex and handed her one.

"Do you think I'm safe now?" she asked hopefully.

"Not if Kendrick just hires another hitman," he answered.

"So, it's just like shooting ducks in a county fair shooting gallery," she said bitterly. "You get one down and another pops up. Unless we find Kendrick." The futility angered her.

Suddenly Fiona wheeled around and shouted at the man on the floor, "You know where Kendrick is, don't you? Tell me how to find him. My sisters are at risk from him. Where is he? And don't you dare spit on my floor again!"

The lizard man just looked at her with a stone-cold face.

Fiona threw her arms up in the air. She grabbed a pair of slacks and a sleeveless top and hurried to the bathroom to change before the police came.

Within minutes a squad car squealed to a stop outside. Fiona let them in. Her anger had ended her crying jag. She had enough presence to haul out a large coffee pot, and she concentrated on brewing coffee for the police and ambulance people. Tremayne arrived ten minutes later.

Paramedics came and treated the guy's eye and got him out of her house. She was relieved to see him go. Fiona recounted her fight with the man for Ted and Tremayne. Investigating the scene, the police found that the man had disabled her expensive alarm system. They also found plastic footies and a small toolkit waiting outside under the window. Tremayne and Ted agreed that, based on the man's ability to deactivate the alarm system, he probably had highly specialized knowledge of breaking and entering.

More police cars arrived. Some officers fanned out to look for the intruder's car. The guy's car keys indicated it was a Ford. Police found it parked two blocks away. More police vehicles arrived, and various technicians dusted Fiona's bedroom, measured, and collected evidence.

At one point, Fiona's adrenalin surge after the intrusion petered out, and she felt really tired. She went into the office closet, found a blow-up twin mattress and used a vacuum to inflate it.

Ted poked his head into the room. "What are you doing?"

"I can't go back in my bed where that smelly man jumped on me," she said, her lips trembling as she pointed to the air mattress. "I'll sleep in here the rest of tonight. But I need to take another shower first. This whole business makes me feel unspeakably dirty." She cringed just thinking about what happened.

"It's about three o'clock, and we'll need to get up by seven thirty to make the flight at ten. Maybe you'd be wise to skip the trip to Minneapolis tomorrow."

"I really want to go." She rubbed her two aching fingers. "The faster we get that info the better." She reached out to touch his arm. "Ted, I want to say thank you. I never could have held that guy off without your help. I'm really grateful."

"I'm glad I was here," he replied. "From now on, the bedroom door stays open, though."

"Uh-huh. What I don't get is why he would break in tonight. Wasn't he keeping track of me? Didn't he know you were here?"

"My best guess is that he followed you a few days before and probably needed to be someplace else during the day today. At the rate he's keeping his mouth shut, we may never know."

CHAPTER 11

When Ted's watch alarm went off at seven thirty, he rolled to a sitting position on the couch and rubbed his eyes. Damn! He'd only had a couple hours of sleep. It could be a long day.

He padded over to the open office door and rapped on the frame for Fiona. No sound. He rapped again and called her name. Still no sound. He looked inside and saw that she was sleeping on her side and breathing softly. When he saw that her hair was caught into a long braid, his mind jolted to the past. His wife, Lois, always braided her hair at night to prevent snarls. He used to enjoy unbraiding it before they made love in the morning. This was the first time since her death that he looked at a woman and felt a hankering for intimacy.

Of course, the similarity between the women ended there. Lois had dark hair and beautiful brown eyes. She was sweet-natured, painfully shy and unassuming, a homebody who was easy on the nerves. Fiona was blond and had bluish-green eyes. She was self assured and outgoing. She would keep a man on his toes. That might be interesting. He had to bend low over the air mattress to shake her awake.

"What?" she croaked, looking misty-eyed and disheveled. And sexy.

"Time to get ready for the airport, unless you want to stay here."

She jerked upright. "What time did the police leave?"

"About five."

"You must be exhausted."

"I'm okay. I'll grab a shower."

Fiona stumbled out of her bedroom, groggy, and in need of caffeine to get her body and brain going, especially after her experience with the intruder. She trudged to the kitchen and fixed a cup at her Keurig coffee machine. The aroma of vanilla biscotti filled the room and she sniffed deeply.

Ted came back out of the bathroom in an instant with a towel around his waist. "Got any soap that doesn't smell like a lady? I don't care to smell like a coconut, or something called brown sugar vanilla."

"Oh, um, let me look." She pawed through the linen closet, found a three-pack of Dial soap, and handed it to him, averting her eyes.

As he returned to the bathroom, Fiona shook herself, *For Pete's sake, I can go to any beach and see bare-chested men. I can't ask this one to keep his shirt on because he looks too sexy.* As she went to her closet, she wondered how to

37

dress to go to prison. After a few minutes, she set out a tan pantsuit with a black shell and plain black heels.

She could hear Ted's electric razor, so she took her clothes and her makeup and went to the small powder room off the kitchen, drinking her coffee as she went. She dressed, and applied her makeup in the cramped space.

When they both migrated to the kitchen, she said, "By the way, I tend to mutter to myself and move like a caterpillar until the second cup of coffee kicks in."

"Duly noted," he replied.

He let her be. She appreciated that. Jeb had been a rise and shine morning-jabberer, forever trying to get her to talk. She hated that. She set out bagels, yogurt, and cranberry juice. "Do you like instant oatmeal?" she asked. When he nodded, she set out the box, and he prepared it for himself.

They ate companionably at the small kitchen table in front of the sliding glass doors, sharing the newspaper.

When she finished eating, Fiona grabbed a watering can from under the sink and opened the sliding glass doors leading to the patio.

"Don't," Ted said.

"I'm just going to water my plants. It'll only take a minute."

"Negative. Especially if you do it every day. Someone could pick you off, just like that." He held out his hand. "Let me do the watering."

Fiona shrugged as she handed him the watering can, and she put their few dishes in the dishwasher.

Before they left the house, Ted checked his computer, hoping to have a lead on Sandy Johnson. "With a name like Johnson," he said, "looking for her is like looking for a grain of sugar in a saltshaker. I've narrowed the search to Caucasian females between the ages of thirty and thirty-five, who once lived in Minneapolis. I'm having no luck. Of course, she could be married, but even so I should be able to locate her."

"If you can't, hopefully Kendrick can't either."

"Another thing," Ted said. "I can come up with current information on Richard Clement, the new guy you met last week, but I can't find any background information on the man prior to his job at First Continental Bank here in Naperville."

"What does that mean?"

"It means that I can find no previous work or educational history, nor can I find any former residences. Has Clement ever come to your apartment?" Ted asked Fiona. "If I could get a fingerprint, I might get more information, just to rule out a hitman."

"No, he's never been here, but I can't believe that Rich could be a sinister person. He seems like a genuinely nice, straightforward guy."

"He very well could be," Ted replied patiently. "We just need to rule out any suspicion. When will you see him next?"

"Wednesday at noon. We're meeting at Malnati's for lunch."

"I know someone at Malnati's. I'll ask that the servers leave the dishes on the table until you and Rich leave. Detective Tremayne can arrange for someone from the PD to remove them and dust for fingerprints. I'd rather get the prints without Clement's knowledge. If we're dealing with an innocent man, we don't need to embarrass him. If he's not innocent, we need to know ASAP. Are you comfortable with the plan?" he looked toward Fiona.

"Not really," she admitted, "but I know you're just trying to protect me."

"Can you behave as you would normally?"

"Yes," she answered. "I'm sure I can, especially for an important reason like this." She pointed to the coffee table. "I see you have two guns," she said. "A big one, and a small one."

"Right, the larger gun is a Glock Forty It's my gun of choice. But on occasion, I may need a backup gun. That's the little S&W. I wear that above my ankle when I wear long pants."

Fiona shivered. "Seeing those guns brings back to mind the reality of my situation."

"Well. If I'm going to protect you, they become important."

When they pulled out of her driveway, Fiona rolled down the car window so she could smell the honeysuckles. Her neighborhood looked fresh and clean. Morning dew lay on the grass like a sprinkle of gaudy, tiny diamond chips. The three fountains across the street sent sun-kissed droplets shimmering back into the water. It was so unbelievable that a man sent to kill her could have walked down this same street just hours ago. She shivered.

As planned the day before, Ted drove inside the police department garage, and they left by another exit.

"So, your husband died two years ago," Ted said, as he threaded his way through the rush hour traffic on the way to Midway Airport.

"I'm sure that information was included in the file you have on me," Fiona said flatly. "He and his mistress were hit by a drunk driver as they walked along a road near their bed and breakfast in Galena."

"Then he was stupid as well as unlucky." Ted said, maneuvering onto the Stevenson

"Excuse me?"

"Any man who cheated on you must be an idiot."

"Thanks for the vote of confidence, but I was the idiot. I didn't have a clue, and I discovered afterward that he had affairs with other women as well," she said, proud of her matter-of-fact tone.

"I've known some excellent detectives who didn't know their own wives were cheating on them. And, some philanderers just like the scent of the hunt, like an eleven year old sneaking into a movie without paying, just for the thrill of getting by with something."

"Maybe."

"You shouldn't define your worth by a man who was a serial cheater."

"I don't . . . uh . . . well maybe. I thought it was me who was lacking, but my sisters shot that idea down."

"Good for them."

"Do you always ask so many blunt questions?"

"Only when I have to find out what makes you tick."

"I've given up resentments. I know they only hurt me. But I seriously question my ability to choose a life partner. And I don't want a relationship where I'd feel I have to check up on my husband every time he's out of sight."

"So you'll go through life lonely because you made one error in judgment?" He glanced over at her. "I was out of line there. I shouldn't have asked that. I have my own issues. My wife and I were college sweethearts. When she died in childbirth, I vowed I could never marry again and risk that kind of pain. Seems as if both you and I are damaged."

"I'm sorry about your wife."

"And I'm sorry about your husband. One thing I do know, when I was involved in the project at Quantico, it was damned lonely, not having a significant other to care whether I lived or died. I'm thinking it might be time to risk a little pain in my life. Being lonely can be painful, too."

"I suppose you're right."

"Why did you leave the Chicago station? Or is that another painful subject?"

"It's not painful, but it's complicated. I'd been thinking of doing something different even before Jeb's death. I felt bored constantly reporting about drive-by gang shootings and Chicago politics. I started to hope that we'd have a big tragedy that I could cover and demonstrate how good I was. That scared me a little. I mentioned it to Jeb, and he said that was part of being a reporter. I disliked the idea of being a newscaster who pastes a sorrowful look on her face when she's really excited to report a huge disaster."

"I can understand that."

"Yeah, well, Jeb loved all the attention and adulation. He was never happier than when he had fans wanting to treat him to a drink or begging for autographs. He'd sign those until his hand fell off if he thought the people were impressed by him. I found myself wanting privacy when I went to a restaurant . . . or used a ladies' room. I realized I didn't need the big time . . . or even want it any more. I was tired of the intensity and the scramble. I still wanted to be a reporter, but on a smaller scale."

"And?" he prompted.

"Two weeks after Jeb's death, the manager of Naperville's TV station, NKTV called me and offered me the newscaster position on a new daily news program at five in the afternoon, concentrating on southwest suburban news. He gave me free rein. I could take the program in several directions including interviews regarding history, or human interest stories, or just current events in Naperville. You know, telling people ahead of time about events and following up with pictures. He asked if I'd consider taking the job.

"I told him I'd think about it. My sisters grilled me mercilessly when I told them I might accept it. They said that they had never known me to back down from a difficult situation. Kailee was afraid I was giving up my life's dream. I told her I was just re-evaluating it a little. Regan asked if I was afraid of facing all the people in Chicago who now knew of Jeb's infidelity. I told her I already faced all of them at Jeb's wake and funeral. And, quite frankly, Jeb and I were already yesterday's news.

"The more we talked, the more I realized I really was excited about the hands on creative aspect of the Naperville thing. When Kailee and Regan realized that I wasn't just being a quitter, they backed me one hundred per cent.

"When I told my Chicago boss about my decision, he offered me more money to stay and told me to call him if I changed my mind. I haven't called him because I like what I do."

"Good for you."

CHAPTER 12

Fiona felt her neck and shoulders tighten when the pilot announced that they were ready to land in Minneapolis. The last time she left that city, her mother and the triplets accompanied their father's coffin on their way back to Naperville. It was a horrible time. Kendrick's trial ended in September, and her father died in October that year. Fiona's mother was grief-stricken. Fiona and her sisters weren't exactly grief-stricken, but they didn't know how his death would affect their lives. Fiona remembered that they all wished their father had never taken the temporary job transfer to Minneapolis in the first place. Thank God they hadn't sold the house in Naperville. The house represented something good and stable they could hang onto.

"Fiona, are you all right?" Ted asked, as he stood to leave the plane. "You look pale."

"I'm fine. But bad memories are rushing back."

"From the look on your face, they must have been painful."

Fiona shrugged, and they waited patiently to deplane. As they exited the walkway into the terminal, they saw a man carrying a sign with Ted's name on it.

"That'll be Detective Tim Brady, the one who handled Kendrick's case twenty years ago," Ted said. "He said he'd meet our plane if he could."

Fiona recognized the chubby, sandy-haired Irishman with the large ears and couldn't believe how little he had changed, even though he must be in his early sixties now.

As they walked through the airport toward his car, Brady looked closely at Fiona. "Your eyes are as pretty as ever. You've have grown up into one beautiful woman."

"A fearful woman," she replied. "Last night a man broke into my bedroom and tried to strangle me."

"Damn! Are you all right?"

"It was scary, but Ted was in the town house, and he saved me."

Brady looked at Ted. "Did you get anything out of him?"

"No, he lawyered up. He's a Chicago dirtbag with a long rap sheet. In my opinion, he's definitely Kendrick's hire, but he's not talking. At least not yet."

"Hopefully, we'll get Kendrick back behind bars soon before he can do any damage to you, Fiona, or anyone else," Brady replied. "Unfortunately, I was attending an out-of-town conference when Kendrick escaped, or I would have contacted you sooner. I've kept track of him even after all these years. And I've attended every parole meeting to make sure he stayed there. Until he killed another inmate. After that, his chance of parole became zilch."

A short drive in Brady's car took them to a two-story concrete building which housed his Minneapolis police department precinct. Brady led them to a conference room, barren of anything except a large table and six battle-scarred chairs. Tired looking blinds sagged at the windows, letting in puny slivers of light.

"How did Kendrick escape?" Fiona asked. "We heard he was in an accident on the way for medical testing. But how did he get away from the scene of the accident? Wasn't he in prison clothes?"

"Not for long," Brady said. "We know now that he went on foot for a half mile through a wooded area. Then he stopped at a farm where he broke a window in an outbuilding, took a long shard, and used it to terrorize a woman who was hanging clothes. He forced her into the kitchen where he changed his weapon to a long butcher knife. He stole clothes, a cell phone and took all her cash, about five hundred dollars. Then he made her go to the attic where he beat her unconscious. He took her car and dumped it about three miles away. That's where we think he probably stole another car. We're guessing he used the woman's cell phone to make contact with someone who picked him up. We tried calling her number, but he must have smashed her cell and tossed it."

"How could he know she could find him men's clothes?" Fiona asked. "She could have been a widow or something."

"Some of the clothes she was hanging on the line were men's jeans and shirts," Brady replied.

Fiona noticed that Brady still manipulated a pencil with his fingers like a small baton when he talked. She remembered him doing that years ago. She always wondered when he'd toss it in the air and catch it.

"Did Kendrick say anything to the woman?" Ted asked.

Brady hesitated."He said that five people will be sorry they ever crossed me."

"So he's still out to get us," Fiona said. "I was hoping he'd just leave the country."

"Was Kendrick ever under suspicion for anything other than the death of Rose Wilson?" Ted asked.

"We couldn't get our hands on his juvenile records, but neighbors reported seeing police activity at his house many times as he grew up. He was suspected of several instances of pet torture. From what the neighbors told us, he was a bully in the neighborhood from grade school on, but mostly involved in fist fights and barroom brawls, especially in Wisconsin where the drinking age was eighteen.

"A year before the incident with Miss Wilson, he came to our attention. Another young woman, Claire Mott, was raped and killed. We all felt that Kendrick was involved, but we never had enough evidence to take him to court, and Kendrick's lawyers pulled every trick in the bag to prevent that. There was no DNA testing back then, but we kept the evidence we had. If Kendrick ever gained parole, we'd reopen that case. My gut feeling said he killed Ms. Mott, too."

"Kendrick sounds like a piece of work," Ted said.

"He's one bad boy," Brady agreed. "He's been diagnosed with Psychopathic Personality Disorder. You familiar with that category?"

"Some," Ted said. "No remorse for breaking the law or hurting others."

"Exactly," Brady said. "Also enjoys manipulating others to do his dirty work, then sits back to see the results."

"Do you think he would hire others to do his killing?" Fiona asked.

"In a minute if he could access enough money," Brady said. "His family was wealthy at the time of his trial, but I don't know how he could access funds without leaving a paper trail. We always suspected that his father had some unsavory connections, but never could get proof. We've been running checks on Kendrick's lawyer and also on his mother. And on his father's friend, Joe Toro, who was Kendrick's only visitor after Ralph's father died."

"At least my sister and I have been warned. What about Tory and Sandy?"

"As soon as Tory returns to Minneapolis, we'll notify her. So far, we can't locate Sandy Johnson. We know she moved to Cleveland with her parents seven years ago, and her parents both died in a car accident five years ago. Evidently Sandy moved from Cleveland, but we don't know where."

The door to the conference room opened, and a police officer beckoned to Brady who excused himself and spoke quietly with the man at the door. Then he turned to Ted and Fiona.

"A homicide has just been reported. Gotta go. Sorry we didn't have more time. Officer Jeff Wax will drive you to the penitentiary and back. I'll try to touch base with you later."

As they traveled through the fertile, Midwest countryside, Fiona noticed that the rows of corn plants were about eight inches tall, already on their quest to be knee-high by the Fourth of July.

"Do you know any more about Psychopathic Personality Disorder?" Ted asked.

"No conscience," she said. "The individual has no conscience."

"Yeah, and no empathy for others." Ted took out his laptop. "I'm going to review info on PPD," he said. "I'll Google it."

"Good idea." Fiona pulled out her laptop as well. "I'll use a different search engine."

For the next fifteen minutes, they were busy. Then Ted closed his laptop. "Time for share and tell," he said.

"The individual not only has no remorse," Fiona said. "He also sees it as a weakness in others."

"He blames others and thinks people are out to get him."

"He manipulates and intimidates others," Fiona said. "Gets easily bored and causes trouble."

"A real charmer."

"A recipe for disaster."

"More like a recipe for murder."

CHAPTER 13

Fiona felt as if an ice cube skittered down her spine as she walked into the state prison. Chilling. As an experienced reporter, she quickly put on her game face. After submitting to a thorough search, she and Ted followed a guard who led them to the warden's office. Fiona felt more claustrophobic after each set of doors clanged shut behind them. Walls and floors were gray. She wondered if all prisons were gray. She doubted that tax payers would pay extra to hire someone to choose cheerful colors.

Warden Elmore looked like a well-toned walrus, meaty but not flabby, with a droopy moustache. He was all business as he ushered them into his utilitarian office, painted and furnished in more institutional gray. The room was clean and neat, with no amenities.

"We've been under siege here lately due to the accident and the repercussions of it. We have had funerals for two of our men, and we are doing everything possible to aid in the capture of each of the escaped convicts. So, what can I do for you?" Elmore asked.

"Was the accident a true accident, or do you suspect foul play?" Ted asked.

"I wish I knew," Elmore said. "We continue to view it as suspicious. Ten prisoners were traveling in a prison van to get medical treatment, along with an armed driver and an armed guard. All prisoners were handcuffed, and their legs were shackled. The two armed men were sitting in the front of the van and were killed from the impact. A prisoner must have taken their keys because six got away. The other four were in critical condition. Of the six who got away, two are still at large."

"Tell me anything you know about Kendrick. I need to understand who we're dealing with," Ted said.

"I was here when he was first incarcerated," Elmore said. "He had a pretty boy face and the personality of a poisonous snake. He was a rich, spoiled, arrogant man who alienated everyone who had to deal with him. He never showed remorse over killing Rose Wilson. He continually blamed the three ten year olds for lying about him.

"Prior to his arrest, Kendrick had a long history of anger management issues, poor impulse control, and physical violence before he ever arrived in prison. Our prison psychiatrist diagnosed Kendrick with Psychopathic Personality Disorder, with a background of physical abuse from his father. The doctor felt he could not benefit from treatment."

Although she was listening intently to Warden Elmore, Fiona spotted a fly trapped between the panes of the window behind Elmore. The fly buzzed back and forth and up and down trying to get out. Fiona felt like the fly, moving this way and that, trying this strategy and that, but still trapped in a dangerous situation with no way out. Someone had to open a window.

"Since he's been here, Kendrick ruined his chances of parole by starting more than fifteen brawls," Elmore continued. "Five years ago, he picked the wrong inmate and got cut on the right arm from the elbow to the wrist. In the last one, he killed a man. He claimed self defense, but twelve witnesses said different. The prisoners and staff hated him. If he had a soft side, we never saw it."

"I see," Ted said.

"What about his parents?" Fiona asked.

"His father died nine years ago. His mother is still alive, but she hasn't visited since Ralph's old man passed." The warden paused. "Ralph's mother, Frances, and I grew up in the same neighborhood in Minneapolis. She was my younger sister Jenny's friend. Frances was a laughing, sweet-natured girl. I lost track of her over the years. Jenny said Frances married a man with a bad reputation. Jenny and Frances met at Macy's one day when Ralph was about six. My sister invited Frances and Ralph to her home the following week.

"It was the visit from hell. Ralph pulled the heads off all my niece's Barbie dolls and broke my nephew's new electronic fire engine. Ralph also hit and kicked Frances when she admonished him. Frances was embarrassed and left money to pay for toys. There were no future meetings."

Elmore stirred in his chair and continued, "I had no contact with Frances Kendrick until her son was incarcerated here. I was amazed at the change in her. She looked like an abused wife, was skinny as a paper clip, and spacey, probably on drugs. Nine years later, Ralph's father died. About a year after that, she called me. She told me about years of physical and mental abuse from her husband. Ralph also abused her when he got big enough. She said she'd been receiving therapy and that she always felt guilty for Ralph's behavior. Her therapist helped her see that she was a victim of physical and mental abuse from both Ralph and his father. She was also a victim of her own unwillingness to leave a sick environment.

"Frances told me she was moving to Italy under a different name. She asked me to keep that info to myself, but she wanted me to contact her if Ralph ever escaped or got parole. She said she was afraid of him and would want to protect herself. She would even offer reward money for his capture."

Every new thing Fiona learned about Kendrick made her feel a little sicker inside. A man who could beat up on his own mother was just too awful. At least her testimony had prevented him for hurting other innocent people. Her heart went out to the poor woman hanging clothes in her own back yard the day of his escape. He needed to go back to prison. She wanted to have a part in putting him there.

47

Karen J. Gallahue

Ted interrupted the warden, "Fiona," he said. "You're looking pale. If this is upsetting to you, you could wait outside the office."

"No," said Fiona, "it upsets me to hear what a vile person Kendrick is, but I need to hear every bit of it."

The warden offered her water from a pitcher and glasses on a side table. Fiona gratefully took a few sips. "Please go on," she said.

"I called Mrs. Kendrick when Ralph escaped. She's hiring protection. She agreed to a tap on her phone, and she asked what she could do to aid in his recapture. We have notified the Italian police to keep an eye out for Kendrick. So far he hasn't shown up. She mentioned Ralph's obsession with killing the girls who testified against him, as well as Fiona's sisters, and she wanted me to warn you and ask if you and your sisters require funds to protect yourselves," Elmore said.

"Not at this point," Fiona said.

"Mrs. Kendrick said she wanted Ralph back in jail where he belongs. She didn't want him hurt, but she didn't want him to do more damage. She wants to set up a twenty-five thousand dollar reward for info leading to Ralph's capture, although she wants her donation kept anonymous. She repeated Ralph has always been relentless and ruthless when he bears a grudge."

Fiona looked at her lap and realized that she had shredded a Kleenex into a pile of white fuzz.

"Did his mother know if Kendrick would have access to money to hire assassins?" Ted asked.

"She said that when her husband's estate was settled, taxes were paid on three million dollars of income that could not be accounted for," said Elmore.

Ted whistled. "Possibly an off-shore account?"

"Who knows?" Elmore said.

"That should be worth a hell of a lot more now," Ted said.

Elmore shrugged.

Ted stirred. "Seems to me you could ask Mrs. Kendrick if she'll pop for a reward leading to the arrest of any person involved in a contract to kill any of the five women. I'd also like you to ask her to share any additional information about Ralph and his interests."

"I can ask her," Elmore said. "And I'll get back to you."

"Did her son have contacts outside of prison?" Fiona asked, "Like maybe people who knew his father?"

"Possibly. She said she was never privy to information about her husband's crooked business associates. But he used to spend time in his office with Ralph behind locked doors."

"What about Kendrick's visitors in prison?" Ted asked.

The warden said, "That's easy to answer. After his father died, he only had one, except for his lawyer. His name was Joe Toro, an associate of his father.

He showed up three or four times. He has been questioned and denies any knowledge of Ralph Kendrick's escape."

"So he would've had no peers who visited him?" Fiona asked.

"None," Elmore replied.

"What about inmates that he associated with?" Ted asked.

"He was a loner, but I can give you some time with a prisoner on either side of his cell."

"Good," replied Ted. "Did he talk at all with recent parolees?"

"I don't know how he would have, but parolees who left here in the last six months are being questioned as we speak," Elmore said. "There was always speculation about Ralph's father being mob-connected, or at least that he had some crooked business dealings, but his lawyer denies it."

"What kind of IQ did Kendrick have?" Fiona asked.

"Don't know," Elmore said, "but he was no dummy. He may not have been book smart, but he was definitely street smart."

"Did Kendrick use the computer at the prison?" Fiona asked.

"None of the maximum security convicts have access to computers."

He rose as he heard a knock on the door. "I told them to bring Kendrick's lawyer up when he arrived."

Kendrick's lawyer, Ed Tripanier, was a fat dumpling of a man, with three generously proportioned chins. He made a big production out of opening his brief case and shuffling papers. "I visited Ralph four times a year as the overseer of his inheritance. I am a reputable man. I don't know why you want to see me. I have not now or ever acted in Ralph's behalf to aid in his escape. I have already answered questions from Warden Elmore and the police."

"Can Kendrick access any accounts without going through you?" Ted asked.

"No, during his imprisonment, I held the only power of access," Tripanier said. "And he has not contacted me since his release."

"It was not a release; it was an escape," Ted said laconically.

"Yes, yes, of course."

Ted gave him a dark look. "Someone attempted to murder Fiona Morgan last night. If you know anything at all about that, you'd better come forth, or you'll be charged as an accessory."

"I know nothing about it," the lawyer said. His face flushed, and he shrugged. "I doubt that Kendrick will ever contact me. At the time of the settling of his father's estate, three million dollars was unaccounted for. It just disappeared."

"How could that happen?" Ted asked.

"We could only assume it disappeared into an offshore account," Tripanier said. "We ended up paying taxes on it before the estate was settled equally between Ralph and his mother. They each got ten million after taxes."

"That's a pretty good chunk of change," Ted said.

"Yes, but he has to go through me to access it, and, as an officer of the court, I'd turn him in, of course," Tripanier said smoothly. "I would surmise if Kendrick could access the three million, he would have done it already."

After asking a few more questions that the lawyer couldn't or wouldn't answer, Warden Elmore dismissed the lawyer and called for two inmates to be brought to a visitor's meeting room.

The first inmate, Manny Green, a bald, black man in his thirties, swaggered into the room. He whistled at Fiona. "So you're one of the girls who testified against him. He might change his mind if he could see you now."

Fiona tried not to shudder.

Manny continued, "Kendrick talked a lot about killing five women if he ever got out. Three who testified against him and two more because one was a triplet, and he didn't know which triplet testified. He always bragged that he was rich. Lotta good that did him here," he snorted.

"Can you describe Kendrick?" Ted asked.

"He was a mean sonofabitch." Nobody liked him. Nobody messed with him. He had a bad temper. We called him Mad Dog behind his back."

"How did Kendrick spend his day?" Fiona asked.

"Playing solitaire," Manny said. "I got sick of hearing him shuffle those damn cards over and over, night and day, night and day. And he was always clearing snot out of his throat. It was a goofy "aha-ahem" noise that drove us all crazy. Oh, and he spent a lot of time doing sit-ups and push-ups."

The second inmate, Joe Clark, was a tough looking man in his sixties with gray fuzz along sides of his bald head, sullen eyes, and a missing front tooth. When asked about Kendrick and how he got along with others, he said, "This ain't no pre-school. Everybody hated him. He was a mean fucker. Always boasting about his daddy's money and what he'd do with it when he got out. Hell, I don't know what world he lived in. He wasn't never going to get out after killing that prisoner in a fight he started. But he always blamed everything on someone else."

He looked at Fiona sharply. "If you was one of those who testified against him, you're definitely on his shitlist. If you was the triplet who testified, you'd better worry about your sisters, too."

"What about my mother?" Fiona asked. "Did he ever mention killing her or the parents of the other girls?"

"Never," Joe said. "Only the five women."

CHAPTER 14

A gray drizzle added to the melancholy of the afternoon as they left the prison, and Officer Wax drove them back to the Twin Cities. Fiona was very quiet, and Ted asked her if she was all right.

"Yeah. But thinking about Kendrick makes me feel dirty, like my mind needs a good, cleansing shower. And it's a sobering thought that such a vile human being wants me dead. Though I can't blame him in a way, living there." She glanced back at the penitentiary.

"His choice, not yours," Ted reminded her.

"Where do you think Kendrick is now?"

"If he's smart and has the right connections and an offshore account, he could be out of the country by now, sucking margaritas in a sunny place."

"How could he travel? I doubt he escaped with a passport in his pocket."

Ted cocked an eyebrow. "Money talks, and connections pay off. Since he's still at large, I figure Kendrick could have a new disguise and a passport to match it."

"And if he didn't leave the country?"

"If his grudge against you women is strong enough to compromise his safety, my guess is he's either in Minneapolis, or Chicago, or Naperville, or wherever Sandy Johnson is." replied Ted. "I think he'll want to gloat over every bit of news coverage. I also think he's probably staying at some expensive hotel where he can get room service. My guess is he has a helper, a liaison who can hire his hitmen."

"It worries me that he probably has access to a lot of money, so he could hire out the killings."

"Yeah, and we still don't know if he'll hire one hitman or more. Or, whether he'll hire high paid pros or thugs off the street. By the way, you asked good questions today."

"Thanks. It's part of my job to encourage people to give information. I never know when a tidbit of information can be an information treasure. You seem to size up people really well."

"It's part of being a cop."

"I always look at body language, and I thought I was a good judge of people until my fiasco with Jeb."

"An accomplished liar is a tough one for anyone to judge," Ted said. "I've met a few like that."

"Could you tell when they were lying?"

"Sometimes, if I observed them very carefully. One guy flapped his eyelids twice before he lied. One always stuck his right hand in his pocket. Things like that."

"Did you think anyone was lying today?"

"Tripanier. He was a little too smooth. But then, a lot of lawyers are." His cell phone rang. "It's Elmore," he said and put him on speaker phone.

"I spoke with Mrs. Kendrick," said Elmore. "She agreed to the second reward for anyone involved in a contract on the five women. When I asked about Ralph's other interests, she told me he liked horticulture classes in high school, and that his large hands were very gentle with plants and flowers. Also, he had joined the drama club in high school and had always liked experimenting with disguises."

Fiona and Ted looked at each other. "Too bad his hands weren't so gentle when he was torturing cats and raping and killing people," Fiona said.

"Go figure. That business about experimenting with disguises makes me wonder even more what he looks like now."

At that moment, Fiona's cell rang. It was Kailee. "What's this about an intruder?" she asked.

Fiona told her sister about last night's event and warned her to be extra careful.

"That's one sexy-looking guy you have watching over you," said Kailee. "I hear he's taking over as Chief of Police in Plainfield in a couple weeks."

"Right."

"That means Chief Hunky will be close by when this Kendrick thing is over."

"Your point?" Fiona wasn't going to share with her nosy sister that she found Chief Hunky . . . er, Ted, very attractive, especially since he was sitting in the car next to her.

Kailee laughed. "Oh, by the way, Justin and I are coming to Naperville the day after tomorrow for a doctor's appointment. Can you come for lunch at Mom's around noon?"

"That would be fine," Fiona said, after checking her schedule. They chatted for a few minutes and rang off.

Next, Ted's phone rang again. He put it on speaker when he saw it was Tremayne.

"Fiona's intruder's fingerprints were in the system as we suspected. We know now why he wasn't following you yesterday. He had an appointment with his parole officer at three and a family get-together at five. His name is Fred Ball, and he has a long history of criminal charges, including breaking and entering and assault. He just got out of jail a month ago. He'll be do-si-do-si-ing right back in. He still isn't admitting a tie with Kendrick. We'll be checking his movements for the last two weeks."

"Thanks for the info," Ted said as he hung up.

It was only three o'clock, and since their flight wasn't until six-thirty that evening, their driver, Officer Wax, suggested that they might want to have dinner at a restaurant at the Mall of America, just minutes from the airport. When they agreed, he recommended the Twin City Grill and dropped them at the entrance close to it.

As they walked into the Mall of America, they could hear the faint sounds of wheels and squeals off in the distance.

"That must be the roller coaster," Fiona said. "I know the mall has one."

"Want to scream your head off, and get rid of all your frustrations?" Ted asked. "We have plenty of time before our flight."

"That's bizarre. I hire you so that I won't be afraid, and then I pay to be afraid on a roller coaster. But in answer to your question, I'd love to go on it."

As they stepped into their roller coaster car, Ted put his left hand on the rail and his right arm securely around Fiona's waist. He could see that Fiona gave herself to the moment. With her hair streaming behind her, she shrieked to her heart's content. And he squeezed her to his heart's content.

When they got off, Fiona said, "That was great! For a few minutes I forgot what a mess I'm in. Thanks for suggesting it." She directed her razzle-dazzle smile in his direction.

"You're welcome," Ted said, smiling back. "Let's go eat."

They entered the Twin City Grill, a cozy place with mahogany paneling and dim lighting. The waitress directed them to an over-sized booth. Fiona noticed several black and white photographs of the Twin City area on the walls. The place offered a relaxing ambience after being in a police station and a penitentiary.

"Can I ask you a favor?" Fiona asked. "Could we not talk about Kendrick during dinner? I've had information about him up to my eyeballs today."

"Good idea. I'm starving. I hope you're hungry."

Fiona ordered a glass of white wine and the bleu cheese crusted filet mignon. Ted opted for a Heineken, and he chose the almond-crusted walleye. When the drinks came, Fiona took a satisfying sip, slid back in the booth, and stretched out her legs. "This is nice." She turned to Ted. "You know everything about me and my family. What about yours?"

He picked up his beer. "You've met my mother. My dad died when I was twenty. He was a career cop, a person who never quit wanting to help others. I have two brothers. One's an investment broker, who has given me several lucrative suggestions over the years. One's a priest, who watches out for my spiritual welfare."

"Does it bother you to talk about your wife?"

"For awhile it did, but it's easier now that time has gone by. Lois and I were high school sweethearts, and we had a good marriage. She had trouble getting pregnant, and she finally conceived about five years ago. She was so happy, but the whole pregnancy was touch and go. She went into early labor at six months, had complications, and died in childbirth. Our little boy was born prematurely and in critical condition. Billy was a tiny thing. He struggled to breathe even with all the hospital aids. He was two days old when he died."

Fiona put her hand over Ted's. "I'm so sorry for your loss. Did you go to Quantico soon after they died?"

"Yeah, everything here reminded me of Lois. I wanted a change of scene."

"Do you like to travel?" Fiona tried to talk about something less painful.

"I do, but I haven't visited many places. Although, I took a trip to Rome for a week after I left Quantico."

"I loved my visit to Rome two years ago, especially walking from the Spanish Steps to the Trevi Fountain, eating gelato and shopping along the way."

"I wouldn't know about shops, but I visited a lot of the important sites in Rome. My favorite was the Coliseum." He leaned forward. "Too bad we didn't listen to our mothers sooner. We could have been better acquainted by now. By the way, I'm sorry now that I turned down that opportunity to meet you, but I've had a few bad experiences with pushy media people in the past."

"The last date my mother encouraged was such a disaster that I swore . . . never again," Fiona replied. The conversation meandered through their tastes in book, movies, and music.

Fiona mentioned that she'd noticed that Ted spent every spare minute on his laptop. "Are you working on something special?" she asked.

"A friend in France gave me a highly sophisticated software program that can gather large amounts of information quickly, and it can access several data bases. I have several searches going on, including Joe Toro, Ed Tripanier, and Mrs. Kendrick. Also, Sandy Johnson, Ralph Kendrick, Kendrick Senior, and your new boy friend. I can find who are their friends, family, and business associates. I can find out what they buy, where they go. For instance, Joe Toro recently ordered sixty toss-away phones, and he has sixteen adult nephews. Any one of which could be helping Kendrick."

As they talked, Fiona decided that her sister's description of Ted as Chief Hunky was right-on. Not that he was traditionally handsome. Definitely ruggedly attractive, though, especially with those gray eyes that seemed to penetrate to your very inmost thoughts. He had what she defined as a Presence, definitely a male force to be reckoned with. The aura of a born leader. People deferred to him. He was articulate, but not a wordy man. Jeb had been a wizard with words, a born schmoozer, sometimes a little slick.

Ted had the physique and coordination of an athlete in his prime. He also had the unique ability to sit perfectly still. And he was comfortable in his own stillness. He did everything, including driving a car and buttering his roll, with an economy of movement. When he moved, he was totally coordinated.

"A penny for your thoughts," Ted said.

"They were about you," she said, feeling herself flush. "I was thinking how well-coordinated you are. You never move an unnecessary muscle. Most people tap a finger or make faces when they work. You never fidget or jiggle."

"I'd better not jiggle," he said with an amused smile.

"You know what I mean. You don't tap your foot or drum your fingers."

"Hours spent on surveillance taught me to sit still," he said, "especially when I wanted to blend into the background of a place."

"I suppose so."

"And, I had to learn to be well-coordinated," he said. "When I've been in dangerous situations I didn't have time to fiddle around. Anything else?"

"Yes. You're very neat about your personal space."

"When you've shared crowded quarters with others, you'd better be neat, or it can be chaotic. Soon it becomes second nature."

"So what have you noticed about me?" she asked, and then she thought, oh great. Now I sound like a teen-ager.

"You're a complete surprise. I knew you were beautiful before I met you. But, since you were a newscaster, I thought you'd be a pushy, non-stop talker. I'm glad that I was wrong. And I officially apologize for misjudging you. The fact is, I like the sound of your voice. It has a rich, smooth quality like real maple syrup. Even if you were a big talker, I'd like to listen to you."

"So my voice sounds like something you'd pour on waffles?"

"Definitely, but only the best quality," he answered with an upward twist of his lips. "Or maybe an expensive Kahlua. Would you prefer that?"

"At least Kahlua reminds me of something sexy, rather than sweet and clingy."

"There's no question about sexy. I've frowned at six or seven guys who wanted to get your attention just since we entered the mall."

"You're kidding."

"Not at all. You must be so used to it you don't even notice."

She figured there was no good response to that statement. "By the way, did I snore last night?"

"I wouldn't call it snoring. It was more like a kitten purring."

"Great," she reddened.

"I can handle it. The door stays open again tonight."

"I know. I know," she replied.

CHAPTER 15

Bloomington, Minnesota

Dusk was falling as Ted and Fiona called for a cab to take them to the airport. About the time their plane took off from the airport another woman entered the Mall.

When Tory Girard deplaned after her flight from Florida to Minneapolis, she figured she had time to run over to the Mall of America which was only minutes from the airport. She knew a little shopping would relax her after spending a week under her mother's roof.

Tory walked swiftly through the mall to the cosmetics counter at Macy's. She needed to get a good concealer. You would think at thirty I'd be too old for zits, she thought. She hoped she wasn't too late to get the free makeover. She was in the mood for some new ideas.

When the cosmetician finished her work of art, Tory smiled at herself in the mirror. She saw a pretty, dark-haired woman with a great complexion. Much better. She bought the concealer, as well as the foundation and powder. She couldn't make a decision between the Plum Apple and the Cherry Blossom lipsticks, so she bought both.

Macys had some great sales going on, so Tory stayed longer than she intended. She usually liked to get to the parking ramp when more people were around. As she approached the ramp entrance, she reached into her purse for her can of pepper spray. She believed in being prepared. She mentally kicked herself for not paying better attention when she parked her car. The parking ramp was as mammoth as the shopping mall. She knew she parked in the Alligator section, but where? She had to retrace her steps twice.

When she finally spotted her car, she popped the trunk quickly and set her packages inside. She clicked the unlock button, slid in, and quickly locked the door. As she pulled out of the ramp, she smiled at the attendant, paid her fee, tucked the receipt up her sleeve, and turned right out into traffic. It wasn't too busy at this hour. She smiled again. Finding such great bargains put her in a very good mood.

When she stopped at the next intersection, she checked her rear view mirror and choked on a scream. A person with a ski mask was rising from the floor of the back seat of her car. She hit the unlock button and prepared to flee from the car, but stopped short when she felt the cold nuzzle of a gun at the back of her neck. *Oh my God, he's going to kill me!*

"I don't want to kill you in heavy traffic," the man's voice grated behind her. "So messy. Keep driving."

"Please," Tory whimpered, "don't hurt me! I'll give you my money and my credit cards. You can have my car. Just let me go without hurting me!"

"Take a right at the next light. And, don't make any quick stops. My finger is on the trigger."

Tory could still feel the gun against her neck, and she obeyed several directions blindly.

When they reached a deserted warehouse area, the man said, "Turn the car off. Unfasten your gold necklace and hand it to me."

Her mind racing, Tory reached her hands back and undid the clasp of the unique necklace that had belonged to her great-grandmother. He grabbed the necklace from her hands. When she brought her hands back to the front, she pawed around for her can of pepper spray that should be next to her purse. When she felt the tin, she grasped it convulsively.

The man said, "Get out of the car."

Tory opened the car door with her left hand and stepped out. She whirled her body and sprayed in the direction of the voice with her right hand, catching him in the left eye with the spray.

"Now you've made me mad," the man snarled. Without wasting a second, he shot her twice in the chest. After she fell to the ground, he shot her again in the head. He used his foot to push her body further from the car and checked to make sure she had no other jewelry or ID.

His eye was killing him. He got back into her car and took off, squinting as he drove and cursing her. He parked the car back near the mall. After he removed his plastic slippers and gloves, he grabbed her purse and walked a block to where his rental car was parked. He drove to the airport, returned the car, and he went to the nearest men's room where he sluiced water on his eye for ten minutes. After that, he walked to the gate for the next departing flight to New York City.

CHAPTER 16

Naperville, Illinois

At two in the morning, a low-pitched moan coming from Fiona's bedroom disturbed Ted's sleep. He snapped up and off the couch and grabbed his Glock just as he heard a heart-stopping shriek. He flipped Fiona's bedroom light on and shouted, "Freeze!"

He saw Fiona thrashing on the bed as if she was fighting someone, but no one was there. He lowered his gun and placed it on her bedside table, just as she shouted a blood-chilling "No!"

Ted sat on the edge of her bed and gently touched her shoulders. "Fiona, wake up. You're having a nightmare."

She shoved herself away from him, yelling "No," her whole body trembling.

He reached for her again, trying to wake her. Her eyes flared open. "Thank God, it's you!" she cried and threw her arms around him. "It was a nightmare, a horrible one."

She was wearing a tank top, and he felt her softness against his bare chest. He patted her back in a paternal way, but his feelings weren't paternal at all. A gorgeous woman was hanging onto him in the middle of the night, and he didn't know what to do except to hang on to her right back. He could tell when she came to true consciousness because her body tensed, and she pulled away, embarrassed.

"Let me guess," he said soothingly, "Was it your Kendrick nightmare, back to haunt you?"

She twisted her hair and rocked herself. "You're right," she said shakily. "It was about him, but it was different. I dreamed I was mother to a boy with evil eyes. He was trying to chop the tail off a cat with an ax. I couldn't stop him. It was awful. I'm so glad you woke me up."

"You've had two long days of tension, which probably triggered the nightmare. Plus, it was chilling to hear about his relationship with his mother."

"The poor woman," she said quietly.

"Are you all right now?" he asked.

"Yes," she sank back on her pillow. "Thank you for the comfort. Is that part of your fee?"

"No, it isn't. It was entirely personal. Sleep well." He straightened her covers and pulled them over her. "See you in the morning."

"Yeah," her voice was already drowsy. "Thanks again."

Well, that was a far cry from his protective tasks on other occasions, he thought, as he settled back on the couch, wondering if he should interrupt her again so he could go through her bedroom to get to the bathroom with the shower. The cold shower.

Fiona snapped her eyes open as soon as Ted left the room. The terror of her nightmare disappeared like a black cloud. All she could think of was a bare-chested Ted clasping her close. In her bed, of all places! The problem was she liked the way he felt way too much. Who wouldn't? *He made her feel safe. But it was more than that. She respected him. But it was more than that. She was wildly attracted to him. There. She said it. How could she be thinking such things when her life was in danger?* She rolled over.

On her way to the kitchen the next morning, Fiona padded by the couch where Ted was on his back sleeping bare-chested, eyes closed, and breathing evenly. She paused for a moment thinking *six pack abs* until she heard, "Are you looking for something?" in a gravelly voice.

"I thought you were sound asleep," she could feel herself blushing.

"If I couldn't sense a presence coming near me while I'm sleeping, I could end up dead," he said, without opening his eyes.

"Oh, of course," she said and moved away quickly to the kitchen where she put water into her Keurig coffeemaker, added the single cup Dunkin' Donuts tub, and sat down with a thump. She remembered the feel of that hard chest when he comforted her last night. It was awesome. She heard Ted go out the front door to get the morning paper and took her cup to her bedroom where she changed to her navy gym shorts and matching sleeveless top for her workout. She grabbed another coffee. Nothing like a couple shots of caffeine to jumpstart a mushy brain.

While she waited for Ted to join her in the basement for their workout, Fiona called Regan to see how her family members were adjusting to their new home in Spain. Regan said she knew that an intruder had attacked Fiona, and she wanted Fiona to get on the next plane to Spain. Fiona thanked her and said that wasn't an option for her. Fiona ended the call sending big smacky kisses to her nephews over the phone.

She thought about what she and Ted had shared during the last two tension-packed days. During the frightening situations . . . make that terrifying situations . . . he was always steady, always in control of the situation. In addition to saving her life two nights ago, he seemed to get along with all types of people, including her family, coworkers, and law enforcement people. When he held her in his arms after the nightmare, she was well aware of how she felt about him as a sexually attractive man. She had hated it when he let her go. She felt embarrassed that he caught her ogling him this morning. *She's lucky he didn't run out the door to get away from the needy lady!*

Ted, wearing cut-off jeans and a sleeveless black Under Armour shirt, indicated that he was ready for the workout. He helped her take down the large black mat hanging from the wall in the basement.

"The first thing I need to do is teach you to trust me," he said.

"How?" Fiona asked, wrinkling her eyebrows.

"You stand with your back to me and let yourself fall backward. You'll trust that I'll catch you."

"I can't do that!"

"Yes, you can. I promise I'll catch you. You need to trust your protector."

"You're asking me to deliberately do a pratfall," she said, raising an eyebrow, "and risk serious injury to my body and my pride."

He laughed. "It's only a pratfall when you land on your butt. I'm going to catch you."

Fiona turned around so her back was facing Ted."I can't make my muscles do it," she said. "They won't cooperate."

"Pretend you're flopping backward onto a nice soft featherbed . . . which would be me."

Fiona closed her eyes and let herself go. Ted caught her easily. "See, it wasn't that hard."

"You're right, but you're no featherbed." she muttered.

He had her repeat the move until it became automatic. "Now, show me what you can remember from your self defense classes."

"Okay, but I don't want to hurt you," Fiona grinned.

"I'll risk it. Give it everything you've got."

He moved several steps behind her, then ran up, and grabbed her. She gave him a hard elbow to the stomach, stomped on his instep, and ran.

"Well done, Tiger," he said as he rubbed his flat stomach

Fiona smirked bigtime. "Why Tiger?"

"My family used to have a little tiger striped kitten. A sweet little thing. We called her Tiger, not because of her stripes, but because of her fearless personality. One day she met a big black Lab who growled at her. Instead of running, she faced him, hissed and actually tried to claw at him. When he lumbered away, she went back to licking her paws. Just now, you had the feisty look of our little cat."

"I wish I felt fearless."

"Act as if you're fearless. Sometimes you just have to do that."

"I'll try."

They spent the next half hour practicing a variety of moves. He showed her how to put a key between the forefinger and middle finger, make a fist and aim for the eyes. It was a variation on the move she'd used on the intruder.

"Don't disregard anyone because they look safe to you," cautioned Ted. "A killer could be man or woman, or even dressed as a policeman. Get used to me standing behind you with my hand on your shoulder. If I push down and or say drop, that's your cue to drop to the ground. We need to practice that. And never ignore the command!"

After five tries, Ted told her she had it right. Following that, they figured how to share the machines and began working out. Fiona had never seen her treadmill get such a workout. Ted did a fast run for thirty minutes, and the man still hadn't broken a sweat.

"By the way," Ted said, as they left the basement. "We need to talk about a Kevlar vest for you."

"I can't wear a bullet-proof vest. None of my clothes'll fit over it."

"You'll have to buy some that do. At least for some events."

"I'll look chubby."

"Looking chubby beats looking dead."

Fiona raised an eyebrow. "I'll wear one if you do. I don't want you to get shot either."

"If that's what it takes. I'll ask Tremayne to drop off a couple."

"I can hardly wait," Fiona grumped.

"Also, I was checking your schedule. I see you have a dinner dance and Silent Auction coming up at the Hotel Compagne. Your date is Grant Kilmer? I'll need to take his place as your escort. Will that be a problem?"

"No, Grant is an old friend, recently divorced. We both needed to attend the fund raiser because of our jobs. I'll call him and explain. You'll need to wear a tux, though. It's called a Gala for a reason. Do you have a tux?"

"No, but I can rent one."

" Okay, good. I promised to be the Mistress of Ceremonies for the Silent Auction which will follow the dinner and dancing."

"What's a Silent Auction?"

"Items donated by firms and individuals are displayed on long tables in a special room along the sides of the ballroom. Items can be worth anything from thirty dollars to a few thousand dollars. Every person gets a paddle number, and they can write the amount they bid next an item. If someone comes along and outbids them, they can always drop by again and raise their bid."

"What are the big ticket prizes?"

"I know one is a trip for four to Orlando to the new Harry Potter attraction."

"What charity gets the money?"

"An organization which offers activities for individuals with special needs. A lot of parents who have children with special needs choose to settle in Naperville because of the quality of school and recreation programs."

Fiona pulled off her sweaty headband and made her way to the shower. As she turned on the water and lifted her face to the spray, it blew her mind to think that while she was shampooing her hair, another human being could be plotting her death. Someone she didn't even know. At least in her nightmares about Kendrick, she knew the face of her bogeyman. Her pulse started beating faster just thinking about it. She needed to think of something else.

She had enough knowledge about defense moves to know that Ted excelled at them. Her respect for his expertise went up another notch. She wondered how it would work with him tagging along as she followed her schedule.

She was still getting accustomed to having a man in the house, and Ted was quite different from Jeb. Her husband had always looked perfect in public, but left an astonishing mess behind himself in the bathroom and bedroom. Wet towels on the bed. Underwear wherever he stepped out of them. Dirty socks under the bed. Whiskers and tooth paste in the sink.

No matter how many times she brought it up, Jeb would kiss her, promise to do better, and never do a damn thing about it. She should have figured out a long time ago that Jeb's promises in other areas of his life were worthless as well.

She should stop comparing the two men. But then, she really didn't know much about men. She never had a relationship with her father. He was too remote. She never had a brother or an uncle. She never had a live-in boy friend either before her marriage or after Jeb's death.

So many people said how charismatic and charming Jeb was. They wouldn't say that about Ted. He was articulate and direct. Period. It was kind of a relief. She'd better watch herself. Maybe Ted was looking good to her just because he was so different from Jeb.

Ted had worked with her to develop trust in him as her protector. She could do that. But in the area of her heart she sure didn't trust her judgment of men. So, if she couldn't trust herself, how could she trust a man again?

Except she couldn't forget last night. When she had the scary nightmare, his sturdy presence and reassuring words had cooled down the firestorm in her head.

CHAPTER 17

Near Wisconsin Dells

The hotel at the HoChunk Casino near the Wisconsin Dells was big enough for patrons to be anonymous. In room 614, a satisfied customer ordered steaks for breakfast from room service. And a pile of newspapers. He had just awakened, and Ralph Kendrick was a happy man. He finally felt free. He'd never go back to that fucking prison or that hole in the ground where he'd spent the last few days.

Jimmy Ponzo tried to talk him into leaving the country. No way. Not until the five women were dead. Then he'd leave.

Through Ponzo, Kendrick had now set up all five contracts. Five women would be dead by the end of the week, if not already. All he had to was sit back and enjoy the carnage. Finally, he would have his revenge.

He heard a knock at the hotel room door. When he heard Ponzo's voice, he removed the deadbolt and chain.

"Got bad news," Ponzo said as he entered the room. "Our hitman broke into Fiona Morgan's town house two nights ago and tried to strangle her. She poked him in the eye. She's still alive. He's in jail."

"Damn!" Ralph threw an empty beer can from last night across the room. "How could that happen? What kind of a *fucking asshole* is he? Will he talk?"

"He knows the rules. If he talks, he's a dead man."

"What about the others?"

"One dead in Minneapolis. Closing in on the third one."

"I just had an idea. Since I have to hire another hitman to kill Fiona Morgan, I want to make her sweat." He told Jimmy what he wanted.

When Ponzo said no way. Ralph snarled, "I'll pay you an extra ten thousand to get this done. Just do it!"

Ponzo threw up his hands and agreed.

CHAPTER 18

Fiona's cell phone rang just as she and Ted sat down to eat their breakfast of scrambled eggs and toast. She listened intently, said, "Gotcha" and turned to Ted. "Scratch the original plan for this morning. We have a breaking story here in Naperville. A small plane crashed into a three story building on Highway 59, several blocks south of 75th Street We have to shake a leg. Can you be ready in two minutes? We'll meet Charlie there."

Ted looked longingly at his eggs, grabbed a piece of toast and said, "I'll meet you in the car."

Fiona snatched lipstick, purse, cell phone, and I-Pad. They pulled out of the garage in record time.

"What happens to your planned agenda this morning?" he asked.

"I reschedule," she said, as she applied lipstick. "I forgot to tell you. I act as a stringer for our affiliate sister channel in Chicago. Charlie and I will put together a segment, and they'll put it on live during the day. Both my channel and theirs will run it at five. And again at six and ten."

While they drove, she notified the store where she had originally planned to tape a segment this morning. She also called a local author to delay the time of their interview. That would give her the window of time she'd probably need. By the time they reached the accident, she brushed through her hair and flew out of the car to hook up with Charlie.

Ted shadowed Fiona, always scanning for signs of danger. He was familiar with the area back from his days as a Naperville police officer. He could see the rear part of the plane wedged into the third story of the building. Surprisingly, it hadn't exploded on contact. Fiona talked to eyewitnesses and wrote down information. Charlie filmed the numerous rescue workers pulling up, as well as the damaged plane.

Within minutes Charlie and Fiona went on the air with her summary of current information. On camera, she also interviewed an onlooker who said the plane came from Aero Estates, which, Ted knew, was the subdivision right behind the fitness center where property owners had their own hangars and a small private airstrip. The onlooker said the plane didn't seem to have the lift it should.

When they finished the live segment, Fiona worked the crowd, gathering more information for the next segment. She learned that the pilot survived the crash, but was seriously injured. Charlie caught shots of the firemen using Stokes Litters to carefully remove him.

Fortunately no one else was injured. By this time, numerous other media vehicles arrived. Fiona found a neighbor of the pilot in the crowd and added another human interest segment for the next airing.

When they finally left the scene, Ted said, "It amazes me how you can gather bits and pieces of information and turn them into a succinct account on camera."

"My sisters say I have the gift of gab . . . words just spill out of my mouth." Fiona laughed. "I'm always relieved when the stories have good outcomes like this one when there are no fatalities."

"Where to now?" he asked.

"I'll call my author and tell her we're on our way."

Following that, Ted drove Fiona to the Naperville library, a state of the art facility which was repeatedly named the top library in the country for its sized city. Its brick front faced downtown on one side, and its soaring windows in the rear faced the activity of the Riverwalk where early blooming flowers looked as fresh, pretty, and perky as hundreds of teenagers getting ready for prom.

While Fiona researched a story about the Carillon, Naperville's controversial bell tower, Ted observed the incoming library patrons.

He saw young moms with their babies strapped across their fronts, shushing their toddlers, who trailed behind them and a number of "Q-tips," seniors who knew how to enjoy their retirement. And middle-aged men, just shortly past their prime and possibly unemployed if they were free at this hour. He concentrated on that group. He was trained to look for the unusual, but no one stood out.

When Fiona finished her research work, Ted asked her how her research went.

"I learned that the Carillon is almost ten feet taller than the Statue of Liberty and that on the top floor you can see the Chicago skyline on a clear day. I'm going to be in a friend's wedding which will take place at the base of the tower. Thought I'd also do a news segment about the tower down the line."

Ted trailed her across the street to Lou Malnati's restaurant for her twelve thirty lunch date with Rich Clement, the man she met a week ago. The pizzeria with red awnings now occupied Naperville's oldest fire station building and was chock-full of memorabilia. The place included the original brass pole, fire buckets, hoses, ladders, even the canvas circle used to catch jumpers. Malnati's also served a great deep dish Chicago pizza.

On this balmy May day, the fire doors were open, and patrons could sit outside and watch the shoppers as they headed to Talbots, the Gap, or Anderson's Bookshop. As prearranged for Fiona's safety, Ted had the waiter seat her at the east end of the outside dining area against a wall. Ted took the table next to her, so he could observe Clement when he joined her.

Before long, a good looking, mid-thirtyish man approached Fiona. She smiled, and he seated himself opposite her. Rich Clement was of average height, dressed in a trendy navy blue striped business suit, a white shirt and a red power tie. His hair was sun-bleached sandy, and he sported a thin designer moustache and a slender line of chin hair.

From their body language, Clement and Fiona seemed to have an easy relationship. The pair exchanged frequent smiles and laughter. When the couple left the restaurant, Ted exchanged glances with Detective Tremayne who was waiting inside the restaurant. Tremayne immediately motioned to a waiter to take the glass from Clement's iced tea. Tremayne placed the glass in a plastic bag and left for the police department. Ted unobtrusively followed Fiona to Anderson's Bookshop where she went as planned after saying goodbye to Clement.

As Fiona walked into the bookstore next door, she felt embarrassed and sort of cheap that she had participated in such a charade with Rich. He seemed to be too nice a guy to be treated in such an underhanded way. However, after meeting Ted, she couldn't remember what she saw in Rich in the first place. When he'd asked for a date for the following weekend, she had told him she already had plans. She walked over to the travel section to wait as planned for Ted to join her. She told him they needed to go to her town house to change clothes quickly for the next activity.

CHAPTER 19

"**Y**ou're going to love this next event," Fiona said, mischief twinkling in her eyes. She'd warned Ted ahead of time to wear washable older clothes, and she dressed in jean shorts and a navy cotton top.

"Why is that?" Ted asked suspiciously.

"It'll speak to the kid in you," she answered. "You've heard of hard news and soft news, right? This is what I call ultra-soft news, but, it's the best show in town. It was scheduled midweek because the kids are off school for Institute Day."

The event took place outside the Barn, a red brick building with a black mansard roof, one of the park district recreation centers.

Charlie met them at the site. "They oughta pay me double for this activity," he complained.

"Oh, come on, Charlie, be a sport." Fiona threw an arm around his shoulders.

As Ted scanned the area, he saw a big, shallow, oblong scooped—out mud hole which must have been sprayed generously by park district people. It looked like a huge puddle of dark chocolate pudding. Boys and girls between five and ten leaped around it with excitement, dressed in faded swim suits. Ted guessed that this was not an event for prissy kids, but there were only a few who looked reluctant.

Fiona grabbed her microphone, and Charlie filmed her opening words. "This is Fiona Morgan of Station NKTV news. We're here at the Naperville Park District's annual Mud Hole Event, considered to be the most down and dirty happening in town." She interviewed excited children and grinning park district employees.

Ted continued to scan the crowd of under a hundred, sixty of whom were kids. Parents and onlookers wore shorts and sleeveless tops. He saw no one who looked suspicious.

A Tug-of-War opened the activity. Organizers quickly lined up boys and girls to grasp the ends of a long rope which stretched over the Mud Hole. Grunts, groans, and shrieks filled the air as kids slipped and slid with mud squishing and oozing between their toes. Skinny arms and legs rapidly turned to deliciously dirty. Each kid became a slippery eel. After awhile, you could only see the whites of their eyes and their teeth, framed by big smiles.

Fiona kept up a running dialogue that described the kids as they smooshed and slopped during one mudhole activity after another. "Naperville boasts a variety of ethnic origins, but after a couple minutes in the mudhole only a loving mother would recognize her child . . . or want to." The last activity was a free for all.

Ted smiled and wondered how the parents got the filthy kids home. The next thing happened in the blink of an eye. Two over eager young boys rushed from behind Fiona to jump into the mudhole, somehow knocking Fiona off balance. She tossed her mike away only seconds before she sprawled face first into the oozy slime. Her cameraman was filming, and he caught her turning and laughing, with her thumbs in her ears, waggling her fingers at him. Next she grabbed two kids, threw her arms over their shoulders, and all three mugged for the camera, all dark-faced except for their white teeth and the whites of their eyes. Still scanning the area, Ted gave a hoot of laughter and went to the edge of the mudhole to offer her a hand out. He changed his mind when he saw the nasty smirk on her face.

Her laugh was rich and contagious. "Don't be silly. I'd only get you dirty."

She pulled herself out with a thwup of each leg, and grabbed a towel offered by a bystander. People clapped and someone shouted, "Way to go, Fiona!"

Charlie doubled over with laughter, but he straightened when Fiona tested the mike, and it still worked.

"I didn't know this event would be such hands-on entertainment," she said as she pushed her dirty hair out of her face. "I've heard of a pratfall, but I think that was a splatfall. The last time I had a mudbath, I had to pay a lot of money, and I didn't have nearly as much fun. This is Dirty Fiona broadcasting live for station NKTV."

She asked for the names of the two kids in the mudhole and the lady who gave her the towel, and she invited them to be on her five o'clock broadcast.

As she squished ahead of Ted to his car, he admired her shapely butt and wondered if she'd be such a good sport away from the camera. "Most women would be appalled to find themselves flat on their faces in the mud," he said as he spread out a plastic garbage bag on the front seat.

"Maybe." Fiona looked at him with a grin, "But after being so serious and scared, it just tickled my funny-bone that, for a few minutes, I didn't have to take myself so seriously."

"I like a woman who can laugh at herself." He glanced over at her, and in spite of the mud smudges on her face, he saw that killer smile and the twinkle in her eye that Kailee must have been talking about yesterday. With her shorts and top plastered to her body, he doubted that she even realized how seductive she looked.

"Although," he continued, "I have to say that when I came home that dirty, I ended up with extra chores or no TV. I can't believe that Naperville moms pay good money to the park district for their kids to get dirty."

68

While sluicing and wringing the mud out of her long blond hair before using the shampoo on it, Fiona thought how much she appreciated Ted's comments in the car. He could have thought she was just a clumsy bimbo. Instead, he liked that she could laugh at herself. And she had desperately needed a few laughs. Funny thing. Jeb had always preserved his dignity. He would've insisted on cutting that falling-in-the-mud footage from the show.

Fiona stepped into a slim, black skirt and adjusted the neck of a hot pink blouse for today's news show. She attached black chandelier earrings and stepped into black pumps. She joined Ted in the living room just as he got off his phone.

"That was Tremayne," he said. "The fingerprints from Richard Clement's glass of iced tea matched the fingerprint of a suspected embezzler from New Hampshire who disappeared while out on bail. He'll be extradited to New Hampshire. However, there was no information that would indicate he was a hired killer. Tremayne and I believe you are still at risk, and we need to proceed accordingly."

Fiona plunked into a rattan chair. "I feel terrible. If it wasn't for me, Rich would still be free."

"That's a very tender sentiment, but I doubt that you'd feel that way if he had embezzled *your* money."

Just then, Ted's cell phone rang again. He checked the caller ID and said, "It's Brady. I'll put him on speaker phone."

Brady's voice was loud and clear. "A woman's body was found this morning in a warehouse district in Minneapolis. Co-workers at Tory Girard's clinic have tentatively identified her as Ms. Girard."

"Oh, no, not Tory!" Fiona interrupted.

"Afraid so," Brady said. "I'm so sorry to have to give you this news. We're awaiting confirmation from dental records. She was stripped of jewelry and ID, and she was shot three times, apparently at that site and before midnight. We're looking for her car. It's not at the crime scene or at her apartment. We did find a parking receipt for the Mall of America up her sleeve that the killer must have missed. We'll be checking the mall and the area around it, including dozens of security cameras. I'm in a rush here, but I'll keep you posted. Stay safe." He rang off.

Face white and eyes wide, Fiona moaned, "Poor Tory. Oh my God, poor Tory. This happened last night? Maybe she was at the Mall of America when we were there. I feel as if someone just punched me in the stomach."

She clutched herself around the middle and rocked, tears streaming down her face. "How could that happen? She must have flown into Minneapolis yesterday. She probably didn't even know she was in danger. Which of us will be next?"

"Just remember. We're being proactive. And so are your sisters." Ted's voice hardened. "We know now he probably hired at least two killers. The man who attacked you two nights ago was in jail the night Tory died. And her death sounds like a professional hit to me."

He looked closer at her. "Fiona, put your head down between your knees and take some deep breaths. You'll get through this. I promise you."

"What if that was one of my sisters," she moaned.

"It wasn't." He knelt in front of her, put both hands on her shoulders, and said. "Fiona, don't wander off into 'what-if' land. Deal with the here and now. There's a saying I've heard. Don't fight the lion until the lion's in the living room. Make it part of your life for now. Can you do that?"

Fiona looked up into his steady gray eyes. "Is that what you do in your job?"

He nodded and checked his watch. "I'll need to grab a shower before we leave for the studio."

As a child (and one of a set of identical triplets) Fiona grew up in a house that was always clean, but often chaotic and cluttered. As she got older, she discovered she liked to read organizational how-to books. Each time she discovered a new tip, she'd incorporate the good idea into her life. She found it gave her a sense of control in her life. Right now, she needed some of that control. She opened her kitchen cupboard doors.

Later, when Ted walked into the small kitchen, several clean pots and pans decorated the counter. "I thought only little kids played with pots and pans," he said, as he made himself a cup of coffee.

"Hmph," she murmured.

"Let me guess," he said. "You're going to grab a spoon and play musical pots and pans."

"Wrong. When I feel upset, organizing comforts me," she replied. "See these five nesting kettles? You would think it would be best to store them one on top of the other. However I use the third one down almost every day. According to my latest organizational tip, number three kettle should stand alone. Now I can reach into the cupboard and grab it without digging for it. Voila! Efficient! Of course, to do that, I need to remove the bundt cake pan which I use twice a year. That will now go on a basement shelf."

Ted put his hands in palm up, stop mode and said, "Okay. Okay. Got it."

"How are your searches going?" Fiona asked as they went out the door to the garage. "What are you looking for now?"

"Movement of money, for one thing. I also want to continue to do research and flesh out Ralph Kendrick's profile."

"How will you do that?"

"I'm checking Ralph's yearbooks, calling old neighbors, his high school football coach. That type of thing. Sometimes one contact leads to another. I'll take Ralph's picture and try to guess what he might look like now. Two things he can't change too much are body build and height. Although he can wear elevator shoes. Or walk with a stoop. He can pad himself to look fatter. But he can't make himself thinner."

"That's a plus."

"With a soft ware program called Identikit, I can experiment with various hairstyles and colors, as well as facial hair. He could change the color of his eyes with contact lenses. If he uses facial putty, he could change his looks somewhat, but he probably hasn't had enough time to have plastic surgery of any kind."

"I never even thought of plastic surgery."

"Also, Kendrick has to have someone helping him. Someone who drives him when necessary, but more important, someone who brings him food and other necessities. Kendrick can't afford the luxury of shopping for himself. Too dangerous to be out in public. Why is this person helping? Probably being paid big money."

"But how is Kendrick getting access to the money?"

"I have no doubt that either Joe Toro or that slimy lawyer are involved, but they know how to do it anonymously. I've found no provable link to them. My research shows that Kendrick's dad's friend, Toro, is a successful real estate man who's active and respected in the community. Did he pick Ralph up . . . probably not . . . but he could have arranged it. Same with his lawyer.

"Someone picked him up and took him underground. And, the person that picked Ralph up didn't necessarily stay with him. He could have a second guy take over. One with contacts in major cities to hire hits. It's physically impossible to check hotels and motels throughout the country. But, for all we know, Kendrick could even be holed up with a hostage."

"I hope not."

"I try to put myself in Kendrick's mind. He was arrested at twenty. If he's not out of the country by now, revenge must be the thing that keeps him here. He may consider that more important than his own personal safety. During his growing up years, he had few restraints. He went from that atmosphere to the ultimate restraint: jail.

"After being incarcerated, He's going to want steaks, booze, maybe women. When he gets bored, he gets into trouble. He's probably getting bored."

On that sober note, they pulled into the parking lot at the studio.

CHAPTER 20

"Good evening, viewers. I'm Fiona Morgan reporting for NKTV in Naperville. Shortly before nine o'clock this morning, a small plane crashed into the Welborn Building in south Naperville, but we're happy to report, that, although injured, the pilot is in stable condition."

As Ted watched Fiona flash her beautiful smile, he felt proud of her. The next second, he wondered where that came from. Since when did he develop proprietary feelings for a person he was protecting? Actually, since he met Fiona Morgan. He liked her, and she intrigued him. Not only was she beautiful and intelligent; she was a feel-good type of person who had a knack of making others feel good, too. No one would ever call her a Pollyanna, though. She was too spunky and sassy for that. As he stood by the main door leading to the studio, he kept his eye on the other door at the far right.

He watched Fiona interview an aeronautical expert, regarding possible causes of the crash. Next, she covered the story of a lost child who was found unharmed after a three hour search. Ted saw that she followed the same format that she had two nights ago, going from main news stories to a discussion of the details of the latest local issues. Today that included last night's city council meeting, with its discussion of new roadway construction that affected north-south travel in Naperville. Next, Fiona spotlighted a local entrepreneur, an interview she had taped last week.

Following that, she welcomed a local author who was promoting her latest mystery. They moved to two easy chairs and drank coffee together. Fiona delicately extracted information from the woman like a hummingbird withdrawing nectar from a flower. Except Fiona was no bird-brained bimbo. She put the author at ease with her considerate, but thought provoking questions, and they chatted like friends.

When the interview finished, a young man gave sport updates for Naperville teams, and he also touched on weather for the immediate area. Fiona wound up the show with a listing of upcoming events. At the end, they played the tape and commentary from the Mudhole Event which generated laughs and whistles from the rest of the news team at the shot of Fiona coming out of the mudhole.

Fiona grinned as the inevitable, "Hey, we didn't know you were into mud wrestling" remarks flew around the studio.

On the way to the car, Fiona checked her I-Pad and said, "The Cubs are playing tonight. Want to order pizza and watch the game?"

Ted's smile was his answer. "We'd better pick it up on the way home," he said. "I don't want to take chances with someone tampering with a delivery order." When Fiona phoned in the order, she asked for pineapple and cheese on her half.

Ted said, "You've gotta be kidding. Pineapple on your pizza? That's like putting spaghetti sauce on ice cream."

Fiona laughed, "Live with it. They won't hurt your half."

When they arrived at the town house, she changed into jean shorts and her Cubs shirt, and she crammed a Cubs cap on her head.

"I didn't realize just how much time you have to spend preparing for each broadcast," Ted said, as they ate the pizza in front of the TV.

"Uh huh," she replied, savoring every bite. "I always research every person that I interview. Next month, Jenna and Laura Bush will be in town to promote their new children's book at Anderson's Bookshop. I try to read everything I can about my subjects, and I try to stay away from the same old standard questions."

"Anderson's can draw people like that to Naperville?"

"Yes. Tom Brokaw will be here next month, too, promoting his new book. I still have to read it before he comes. And also refresh my mind on his background."

"I also can't believe how many times you change clothes in a day."

"Well, today wasn't typical. I don't usually have a mudhole on my agenda."

Fiona noticed that Ted no longer sat gingerly on the white couch. He sprawled, and wasted no time arranging his stockinged feet on the coffee table after the pizza was gone.

"Did your father get you hooked on the Cubs?" Ted asked.

"No, my father wasn't into any sports. I had a boy friend in college who got me interested."

"You've never mentioned your dad. Were you close?"

"Not really. He had a brilliant mind for computers, but he didn't interact with us Trips at all. Mom said he didn't know how to. I know she was right, but it still hurt to feel ignored. He was always in another world in his head. One time, when I was seven, I fell off my bike just as he came home from work. I was squalling because I hurt my knee, and somehow I was stuck under the bike. I asked him to help me.

"'Uh, I'll get your mother,'" he said, as he walked past me into the house. Then he evidently forgot about me. A neighbor came along and untangled me."

"That must have been tough on a kid that age," said Ted. "Did your sisters feel ignored, too?"

"Oh, yeah. We each tried to get his attention when we were little. I'd try to chat him up. Regan tried tantrums. And Kailee tried to take his hand or crawl in his lap. By the time we were four or five, we didn't try anymore. Mom told us he showed his love for us by earning the money to have a nice home and plenty to eat. When we got older, she explained that he just didn't know how to socialize; and that he probably fit somewhere in the high end of the autism spectrum."

Ted's phone rang. When he heard Brady's voice, he put him on speaker.

"When we entered Ms. Girard's apartment, we found her mother's address and telephone number in Florida. Tory had been visiting her. Mrs. Girard was distraught, but according to her and Ms. Girard's co-workers Tory Girard always wore a distinctive heirloom necklace with a gold filigree chain and an antique gold coin. Ms. Girard even chose her wardrobe so that the necklace would look well. It was not on the body when it was discovered, nor in her car or her apartment. Tory's mother is positive she was wearing it when she left Florida. The word is out to pawnbrokers across the country to look for it."

"Thanks for the update," Ted said.

CHAPTER 21

During the game, Ted watched Fiona's face. It was mobile, expressive, and always intent. He felt comfortable around her. Hell, he felt happy and relaxed around her. It was a long time since he shared pizza with an attractive woman. A woman who was also a Cubs fan. A woman with a ready wit and a soul-touching smile.

The game was tied in the eighth inning when Soriano hit a grand slam homer. Fiona gave a whoop of delight and threw her arms around Ted in celebration. He tossed off her Cubs cap and pulled her closer. The kiss that followed started like a friendly smack, but it turned into much more as Ted tightened his arms around her. She melted against him and put her arms around his neck; he deepened the kiss. At one point, he drew back and ran his knuckle along the side of her face. Then he kissed her again, thoroughly.

As they came apart, Fiona asked, "What just happened here?" Sexual awareness crackled in the air around them.

Ted brushed some strands of hair behind her ear. "Something I've wanted to do since you walked into Quigley's Pub. I knew it would be good, kissing you. I had no idea it would be that good."

"Really?" she sounded amazed. "I thought you disliked me, at least at first."

"Is that right?" Ted reached for her again. "Let me show you how wrong you were."

"Um, Ted, I have to warn you, I don't do casual sex."

"I know."

"What do you mean you know?" Fiona's eyes widened.

"Your sister told me."

"My sister did what?" Fiona backed away. "Which one? Wait! I know. It would have to be Regan. Sometimes she crosses over the line."

"Just for the record, my feelings toward you aren't casual."

"What do you mean?"

"I think we have a lot of things in common. I want to explore a serious relationship with you. And I have some things going for me. I don't sneak around. I don't pretend. And I come with a guarantee. When I was married, I was a faithful husband."

Fiona snapped her eyes to his. "Oh, Ted. I don't know what to say."

"Don't say anything." He ran his finger along the side of her face. "My main job right now is to protect you, not to court you. But I want you to know it's on my mind."

"You hardly know me."

"After sharing some extreme conditions the past few days, I know some important things about you. I can't give you pretty words, and I tend to think in clichés, but I know you have grace under fire. You take care of your responsibilities in spite of a legitimate fear for your life. You're basically a considerate person. You don't take out your feelings on other people. I know you're brave and resourceful. You have the ability to laugh at yourself. You're fun to be with. I like a woman who can yell on a roller coaster. And did I mention sexy?"

"You think I'm sexy?"

"Sweetheart, when you raise an eyebrow or close a door, trust me, it's sexy. That's why I'll try to keep my hands off you until Kendrick is caught."

"You're joking with me."

"Definitely not. I say what I mean."

Before she got into bed that night, Fiona remembered buying Breathe Right tapes for her nose last fall. She found them in the medicine cabinet and put one on her nose to reduce snoring.

She was still shocked that she had thrown her arms around Ted. But his words washed away her embarrassment. He'd made it clear he was attracted to her. How could he be? She was a mess.

Her senses still reeled from those few seconds in Ted's arms that literally took her breath away. She knew she was attracted to him on a purely physical level, but those kisses were definitely special. Instead of being just a joyous celebration of a baseball score, they were more like a celebration of each other. The first kiss was more passionate, even exuberant, but the second one was a caring kind of kiss that grabbed her heart. She'd been clutching her distrust issues for a long time. Could she let them go?

After Jeb died, she'd had a flurry of date offers from men hoping to comfort the poor mistreated widow. Her sisters urged her to get out and date and show she didn't care about Jeb's fidelity. But she did care, and she'd needed to lick her wounds in private. She knew she and Jeb didn't have a perfect marriage, but she thought they were a pair.

When she did start dating, she hadn't been remotely interested in any man. Dates were superficial companionships, with surface flirting. She chose guys with little interest in settling down because she had no interest in pursuing a deeper relationship. Not after her experience with Jeb.

One thing she knew for sure. She needed to give Regan a piece of her mind. Some nerve she had, discussing Fiona's business. She was tempted to call her right now, but she was too tired to figure out what time it was in Spain.

She plumped her pillow and rolled over. Before she fell asleep, she realized that she hadn't thought of Ralph Kendrick for a few hours.

CHAPTER 22

As Ted rumbled the Mustang out of the garage the next morning, Fiona blinked at the bright sun, reached for her sunglasses, and rolled the car window down. A soft gentle rain had washed everything clean. Tiny shimmery raindrops, like baby fireflies, still lit the grass, and the air smelled fresh and pure, sweetened by the scent of the hearty honeysuckle bushes which separated each unit.

They had three appointments to keep today, followed by lunch at Fiona's mom's house. The first stop was at the home of a local author whose cookbook was just published. Marlys Price was a cheerful, motherly woman with an amazing sense of humor. She lived in an average colonial style house. Inside, her kitchen was way above average—a chef's dream of granite and stainless steel. Ms. Price kept Fiona and Ted laughing as she spoke of her recipes for seasonal desserts.

Their second stop was a shop called a boutique for little girls recently opened by a young Naperville entrepreneur. Charlie met them outside the door. Fiona saw the expressions on the two men's faces as they realized they were trespassing into pink tutu land. Fiona interviewed the owner, a thirty year old woman with red ringlets who was happy to have them showcase her wares. Two moms with pre-school daughters gave permissions for Charlie to film the young customers. As Ted escorted Fiona out of the shop, a little girl on the sidewalk called out, "Mama! Mama! I see words in the sky! Look up!"

Ted and Fiona looked up as well and saw a small red plane pulling a banner which said, *"Bye Bye, Fiona."*

Fiona's eyes widened. She drew in a sharp breath in outrage and burrowed her head against Ted's chest, shaking. Ted wrapped his arms around her, as he scanned the immediate area.

"What happened?" the little girl asked. "Did the sign in the sky scare her?"

"It surprised her," Ted said. "She'll be fine in a minute."

Fiona peeled herself away from Ted, and he tucked her into the car. "That bastard!" she muttered. "He's trying to demoralize me." She straightened her shoulders. "Damn if I let him!"

"Atta girl! Don't give him any brain time."

"Do you think everyone at the Plaza saw me clinging to you like Saran wrap?"

"I doubt it," he said, "But I was thinking that we fit together very well."

"You seem to know what to say to make me feel better." She gave him a shaky smile. "Thanks!"

"Listen," he said, "Kendrick just made a dumb-ass move." He phoned Tremayne and gave him the information about the sign. "Find out what airport that plane came out of, who hired it, etc. Maybe the trail will lead us to Kendrick."

"Do you really think it was a dumb move on Kendrick's part?" asked Fiona when Ted pushed the off button.

"Uh-huh, every time he makes a move, he threatens his own safety. Let's hope he really screwed up this time."

The third and last stop of the day was at a local magazine office. They wanted to feature Fiona in their next issue as one of Naperville's rising stars. Fiona posed for pictures and answered questions.

On the way to the car, Fiona said, "You know, I was just thinking, there are similarities in my job and yours."

"How can you say that?" Ted opened the car door for her.

"We're both trained to assess a person quickly and accurately. We both have to be aware of people's body language."

"You do gentle steering," Ted said. "I do insistent probing with a suspect. Although, with a witness, I'm gentler, unless the person is reluctant or antagonistic.

"Well, we both question people. In an interview, I try to get people to tell me their story."

"And in an interrogation, I try to get them to tell me their *true* story."

"The bottom line is that we both want information."

"You're not just patient when you interview. You have a genuine interest in the individual. People feel valued and special. When I interrogate, I have a genuine interest in justice for the safety of the public, as well as my fellow police officers."

As Ted and Fiona pulled up to her mom's house for lunch, Fiona spotted a slender young man shooting baskets in the driveway to the right of her mother's house, After years of compulsively shooting baskets, Michael Abbot was extremely proficient at the game. He was known for his three-pointers during his basketball games in the Special Olympics. He also diligently practiced his baseball pitching skills in the backyard with a pitching cage. He picked up something and trotted over as Fiona stepped from the car.

"Michael, it's good to see you," Fiona said. Although Michael turned his face to the side, he allowed her to give him sort of a hug. Fiona knew that that was as affectionate as the young man with autism could get. She introduced the two men.

"The Cubs are going to do well this year," Michael said, and he proceeded to give the names and statistics of all the new players. Fiona knew that Michael's mind contained a wealth of sports information and trivia. In areas of particular interest to him, he memorized facts quickly and accurately. He was a whiz with a computer as well.

"Look, Fiona," he said. "I have a new baseball that shows the speed when I throw it."

Fiona admired the ball and said to Ted, "Michael has always been like a younger brother to my sisters and me."

While they admired Michael's high-tech baseball, a horn beeped indicating Kailee and Justin had arrived. Fiona jumped involuntarily at the sound of the horn. She told herself to get a grip. The big topic at the Morgan house was what the obstetrician said about Kailee's baby, and she joined in. Once that information was shared, everyone chattered about the *Bye Bye, Fiona* sign. All morning, Kailee, Fiona, and their mother had fielded phone calls asking if the sign referred to Fiona Morgan. Their standard answer was that it was a joke.

After lunch they drank iced tea and relaxed around Barbara Morgan's kitchen table. The room was rich with memories for Fiona. Apart from the two years the family lived in the Bloomington suburb of Minneapolis, Fiona and her sisters had spent their childhoods, their teen years, and their young adult years in this one house.

The country blue cabinets sported white china knobs, only now her mother wiped off grandchildren's fingerprints rather than those of the Trips. The sturdy honey oak table matched the floors in the cozy kitchen. The triplet sisters completed many art projects at that table, from early attempts at fingerpainting to pencil sketches to calligraphy. Fiona loved the feel of the smooth shiny wood. It had been refinished at least three times that she could remember, and it still looked brand new.

Fiona remembered that before and after they returned from Minnesota, her mom and her sisters would sit around the same table, having a snack and talking over the day's events. Her father had never joined them because he didn't take part in chatty activities. But this was the place where they celebrated getting a part in a play, or commiserated over a close volleyball game, or discussed boys.

Mostly, they had healthy snacks, but every Tuesday, their mom made oatmeal chocolate chip cookies that were to die for. The spurt of melty chocolate chips oozing into their mouths as they bit into them still lingered in their memories.

After lunch, Ted and Justin went to the den, and the sisters migrated to the living room to sit on the squishy barrel-back blue chairs on either side of the open front windows. It was a warm day. Fiona wore a sundress, and Kailee wore shorts. A skittish little breeze pushed at the opened blue drapes and teased the ends of their hair. Kailee organized information for the psychology test she was giving her students tomorrow. Fiona used her laptop to Google for Jenna Bush's married name and did some research for her upcoming interview.

After ten minutes, Fiona said, "I hate this business with the airplane and the sign. It's like Kendrick is bragging that he knows where I live. I think he actually wants people to know he's after me. He's trying to rattle my cage, and I can't let him do that." She yanked the strands of hair near her left ear and gave them a good twist.

"I'm trying to keep from being too jittery about Kendrick's threats." Kailee set her pen down. "I have one test to give tomorrow morning. Then Justin's taking me away for a two week vacation. He won't tell me where; he doesn't want anyone to know. He's concerned for me and the safety of the baby."

"Good." Fiona stretched her arms. "I won't have to worry about you. It drives me nuts to think that you and Regan are in danger."

"I hate to leave you. Why don't you disappear, too?"

"I've thought of it. The thing is, I have Ted to protect me now . . . and the Naperville PD to back him up. If I went away, I'm afraid Kendrick'll just wait until I return. He's waited a lot of years to get me."

"Justin is hoping Kendrick will be caught soon."

"I sure hope so."

"Speaking of Ted, what's it like having Chief Hunky as a roommate?" Kailee changed the subject.

"He's actually easy to have, smart alec. He's neat, for one thing. Doesn't leave wet towels on the floor or dirty dishes lying around."

"I wasn't referring to his personal habits. Are you attracted to him?"

Fiona blinked. "Of course not. I'm paying him to be with me. Remember?"

"I always know when you're lying, Fiona. I can tell you like him. You blinked your eyes before you answered."

"It's a royal pain in the you-know-what to have a sister who's a psychologist." Fiona rolled her shoulders. "Let me get back to reading this stuff."

"Right. I need to get back to my stuff, too." Kailee smirked.

CHAPTER 23

The sisters worked companionably for another half hour until Kailee stretched and said, "I'm missing a notebook I need. I'm going to run out to my trunk and get it."

"You should call Justin to get it for you," Fiona reminded her.

"Don't be silly. It'll take me less than a minute."

Kailee flew out the door and ran to her car in the next second. Something nasty prickled down Fiona's spine, and she kept her eye on her fast moving sibling. She watched Kailee flip the trunk open and root in the trunk of her car which was parked in the driveway to the right of the front door.

At the same time, a black Honda Civic moved briskly into the small cul-de-sac. After Kailee grabbed her notebook, she slammed the trunk shut and started up the driveway. She couldn't see the gun being edged through the open window on the passenger side of the moving car.

But Fiona did.

In a horror-filled instant, she shrieked, "Oh my God! Kailee! No! A gun!"

As she shouted frantically, Fiona glimpsed Michael loping along between his house and her mom's. In the next nano-second, a shot was fired, hitting Kailee. She screamed in pain. As Fiona's sister fell to the ground, Michael aimed his new baseball toward the gun which looked to Fiona to be ready to fire again. Michael's baseball hit the gun dead-on. The gun did fire again, but it missed Kailee.

Fiona heard the shooter curse in Spanish, and the driver took off peeling rubber as the limp pieces of the baseball fell to the curb. Fiona shouted, "Ted, shots fired!" and dashed out the door to her sister.

"Kailee! Where did you get hit? " Fiona cried, as she crouched next to her sister who was bleeding onto the driveway. Ted and Justin must have heard Fiona scream, because she heard them come banging out the front door, right behind her.

Justin flew to Kailee and dropped to his knees. "Honey, you're bleeding. What happened? Where does it hurt?"

"Something hit me!" Kailee moaned. "In my leg. But it's just my leg, isn't it? The baby's okay. Right?" Her voice shook, and she looked up through her tears, which were falling fast.

Justin rolled her gently to see the wound.

Ted spoke up, his voice steady, "Looks like a superficial bullet wound, Kailee. I bet it hurts like hell, though. The bullet appears to have creased the outside of your right thigh. Your baby should be fine. Stand back," he motioned to the others. "We'll need to find the bullet." He immediately dialed for an ambulance and police.

Fiona said, "Someone shot Kailee, and Michael whipped his baseball at the gun and made the second shot go wild."

"The man shot my baseball!" shouted Michael. "The man shot my baseball! He ruined it!"

"Why were you outside?" Justin asked Kailee.

"I just needed my notebook," Kailee stuttered. "I should have called you first."

Justin hugged his wife. "Thank God you weren't killed!" He carefully picked her up and took her inside.

Fiona heard Ted calling on his cell for an ambulance and for an APB on the car. He asked Fiona for the make of the car, as he talked on the phone.

"It was a black Honda Civic."

"License number?"

"224-4417."

"Good girl! Any description of the shooter?" Ted asked.

"Not much. It happened so fast." She shivered. "The shooter was in the front passenger seat. He had shoulder length dark hair and a bushy, matching beard. I heard him curse in Spanish. I couldn't see the driver."

Ted passed on the information and warned that police officers should proceed with caution because the men were armed and dangerous.

Fiona called to Michael who was still standing in the driveway repeating that the man shot his baseball. "You just saved Kailee's life!"

She tried to hug Michael, who backed away, saying, "My baseball is ruined! It's the one that shows how fast I throw!"

"I'll buy you another one," Fiona promised. "You're a hero!"

"I am?" he asked, a little smile curling the corners of his mouth. "I'm a real hero? That's a good guy. Right?"

"Yes, you are," Fiona said. "And, thank God you're left handed and have such good aim!"

Ted said, "I need everyone to move into the house, so we can keep the crime scene intact. I need to find the two bullets. The shooter must have used a silencer on the gun. I didn't hear either shot from inside the house."

Fiona couldn't stop her lips from quivering. Ted walked over to her and put his arms around her. "Everyone's safe now," he murmured.

"We'll never be safe until Kendrick is back behind bars," she wept. "That should have been me."

"Bullshit! It shouldn't be either one of you. We're dealing with a crazy man. Hang in there. Every cop in Naperville is looking for that car now. I need you to go in and get me a couple baggies for the bullets so we can nail these guys. Are you up to that?"

Fiona nodded, left the circle of his arms, and ran to get the baggies. After she handed them to Ted, Fiona sat next to Kailee who was lying on the living room couch.

"I hear a siren. The ambulance will be here soon," she reassured her sister. "I feel so bad that you've been hurt. I'm so sorry this happened."

"Don't you dare be sorry, Fiona Marie. You didn't arrange this. Kendrick did, and we all know it."

"But you're bleeding. And you're in pain."

"You told me not to run out there. I did a stupid thing. Thank God, it's a minor injury."

"I want to come to the hospital with you . . . to make sure you're all right."

"You can't do anything there, Fiona. It's just a flesh wound. Justin will follow the ambulance and then take me home. Besides, you have a show at five."

"Will you call me from the ER?"

"Yes, Fiona, and quit feeling guilty. I mean it."

The sisters embraced as an ambulance screeched to a halt outside the Morgan house. The paramedics checked Kailee, put her on board and left for the hospital.

CHAPTER 24

O fficer Tom Parks was thinking about cutting his grass after work as he traveled east on 87th Street in his unmarked car. Just as he heard the APB, the lanky, forty year-old patrolman stopped for the light at Book Road. He couldn't believe his eyes when he spotted a black Honda Civic to his left turning east onto 87th ahead of him. Unfortunately, a large, white van turned as well, and he could only see the first three numbers of the Honda's License, 224. Since he wasn't far from Blackberry Court, it was enough to warrant following the car.

He radioed that he was heading east on 87th, tailing the suspicious Honda from behind the van. Two other squads checked in. One traveling south on Washington. One traveling north on Washington. Two other patrol cars radioed that they were heading in his direction.

Parks radioed, "The van ahead of me turned off on Gleneagles, and I can see the whole plate. It's 224-4417. Bingo!" He hit the lights and siren of his unmarked car, and his adrenalin soared. The Honda took off like a horse out of the gate.

"He's not pulling over. In pursuit. Eastbound on 87th. Approaching Modaff. He's pushing eighty."

Both the Honda and Parks blew the stop sign at Modaff. Now they were on a four lane road divided by a tree-lined meridian. Parks was glad to see a black and white squad pulling behind him. "If he's headed toward the Stevenson Expressway into Chicago, we can run him off the road at the dead-end on Washington. He's doing ninety now. He'll never make that right turn at this speed. My Crown Vic is keeping up, though."

Parks heard a voice crackling. "Squad 44 at Washington and 87th. All stoplights red. Intersection path clear. Squad 53 pulling up. Two squads, blocking lanes for turning."

"Passing Ring Road," Parks shouted, "Approaching Cedarbrook." He yelled "Holy shit!" when he saw a car deciding whether to pull out onto 87th from a side street. He laid on the air horn in addition to the siren. Thankfully, the car stopped dead.

Parks saw that the Honda was now approaching the dead end at Washington, another four lane thoroughfare. He started to brake his vehicle. The stoplight was on red, and squads blocked the turn lanes.

The Honda shimmied and wobbled as the driver initially tried to turn right toward the Stevenson Expressway, but he was forced to go straight to keep upright. After a horrendous squeal of brakes, the Honda sideswiped the stop light across the street. Metal on metal sent sparks flying. In the next second, the

Honda nosedived down a ten foot embankment, its front end finally pushing at a ninety year old oak tree.

Parks squealed to a stop in the middle of the intersection. Guns in hands, police officers flew out of squads, ready to give chase. Both front doors popped open on the Honda. Parks saw that Officer Ryan Mahoney was already on foot ahead of him, running to the Honda on the driver's side. The Honda driver emerged shooting wildly. One bullet grazed Mahoney in the left arm, just as Mahoney's bullet nailed the shooter in the left chest. The guy slumped to the ground. Parks hopped over a bush and veered to the right to chase the guy from the passenger side of the Honda, yelling, "Police! Stop, or I'll shoot!"

"They want them alive if possible," Pat Riley yelled, another cop who was panting, but keeping up to Parks. Parks nailed the fleeing suspect in the right upper arm, and the suspect's gun went flying. Riley tackled the suspect, who squealed like a stuck hog and writhed on the grass. The two police officers cuffed the suspect and patted him down.

While Riley read the shooter his rights, Parks ran to Mahoney who was holding his left upper arm and bleeding profusely. Parks saw two paramedics running to the scene, and he waved to one to help Mahoney. He waved the other one to the downed Honda driver. When the paramedic checked the suspect, he yelled to Parks that the man was dead.

The intersection became a cacophony of sound with continuous blaring of sirens as more squads, another ambulance, and a fire truck pulled up. Men shouted. More rescue vehicles stormed up. Paramedics dragged out gurneys and hurried toward the injured men. Police diverted traffic.

At the Walgreens store across the street, dozens of people gathered in the parking lot, gawked, and pointed.

Tremayne arrived at the scene, flagged Parks over, and asked for an update. They headed toward the paramedics pushing the shooter's gurney into an ambulance.

"What's your name, sir?" Tremayne asked the shooter.

The suspect said nothing.

Tremayne repeated the question in Spanish and noticed that the shooter evidently emptied his bladder in the excitement.

The suspect said nothing.

Officer Riley said, "According to his driver's license, he's Juan Santiago, address in Chicago.

"Who hired you?" Tremayne asked.

Santiago didn't answer.

Karen J. Gallahue

"You'll be recognized and identified by people as the shooter on Blackberry Court," Tremayne said. "It'll go easier for you if you cooperate and give the name of the person who hired you."

"I want a lawyer," Santiago said, in English.

Disgusted, Tremayne read him his rights before the paramedics slammed the doors on the ambulance and took off.

CHAPTER 25

B ack at the Morgan house, Fiona could hear first one siren, then others off in the distance. One squad car peeled into the cul-de-sac. The officer conferred with Ted and set up yellow tape around the curb. A shout went up when both bullets were found, one intact, one in pieces.

"Do you think the police will catch the shooter?" Fiona asked Ted.

"Let's hope we hear good news from Tremayne. When I just called him he was answering a call that, hopefully, was the Honda being pulled over. Hear all those sirens in the distance?"

Ten minutes later, Ted's cell rang. Ted listened to the message and relayed it to the Morgan family. "They got them," he said. "But it wasn't easy. When they were pulled over, both men came out shooting. The driver's dead. The shooter's injured. A police officer got winged, but he'll be okay."

"Did Kendrick hire them?" Fiona asked.

"The shooter isn't talking at this point. Maybe his lawyer can convince him that if he cooperates, he might get a lesser sentence. Tremayne says that, in his opinion, the shooter is no pro, more like a street thug. I'd like to know which of you Morgan women he was hired to kill."

Shortly after, as Ted passed Fiona in the foyer, he heard her say into her cell phone, "Send the mobile unit to Blackberry Court ASAP. We have a story." As she closed her cell and turned, Ted asked, "Who did you just call?"

"NKTV," she replied, "for my five o'clock show."

"Tell me what's going on."

"My job is to report the news," Fiona said. "It's what I do. I can't just ignore this incident. Besides, all the other media people will be arriving shortly. They all have contacts who listen to police scanners. I was only going to report what happened . . . that my sister was shot. I wasn't going to touch on Kendrick or the hitman business. But I can't keep ignoring things like this incident. I'd be out of a job."

"My job is to keep you alive. Once this incident turns into a media circus, that job will be a lot harder," Ted said, "My first responsibility is to keep you safe and aware of the dangers. Other hitmen may be out there, hopefully unaware that we're aware of them. Don't give them any information that you'll be sorry for later. Remember, the guy who tried to strangle you didn't know you had defensive training, and he didn't expect you to go for his eyes."

"I'll do my best, Ted, to report this accurately, without giving away too much."

"That's all I ask," he replied.

When Fiona's mother's phone rang, she answered it quickly. "It's Kailee," she said and put her on speaker phone.

Kailee's no-nonsense voice came over the line. "It was what we thought, a simple flesh wound. Most important, the baby's fine. When I fell to the ground, I didn't hurt anything. They stitched me, gave me some antibiotics, and said I'll be as good as new."

"Thank God!" Fiona exhaled a long breath.

"Justin and I are traveling back to DeKalb. He did some fancy driving and evaded some press people following us. He's been very busy on the phone. We're leaving the country immediately. I can't tell anyone where. And, Justin said, no phone calls while we're gone. He doesn't want me to be traced by anyone sinister. He'll give Mom the number of someone who can contact us in an emergency . . . or if Kendrick is apprehended."

"Good for Justin," Fiona said.

"I'd been arguing about going before the shooting. Now I agree with him. I don't want our baby hurt. I found a teacher who'll give my final exam tomorrow. And she'll grade it and submit results for me. But I feel like I'm bailing out on you. Don't do anything rash like I did."

"Trust me. I won't," Fiona assured her.

"Have a safe trip, honey," Barbara Morgan spoke up. "And take good care of that wound."

After they hung up, Fiona noticed the signs of strain showing on her mother's face. Lines around her eyes seemed deeper. Tears filled her eyes.

Mrs. Morgan said, "I wish I had never let you testify."

"You kept a killer off the street for twenty years. It was the right thing to do," Ted reminded her.

"That thought doesn't comfort me right now, not with all three of my daughters in danger."

"We'll get through this," Fiona hugged her mom. "Maybe the guy in the Honda will tell something that could lead the police to Kendrick. And I definitely learned a lesson. I won't be taking any unnecessary risks."

"I'll second that," Ted said.

Two hours later, Fiona and Ted entered the TV station. "Mr. Mackay wants to see you," Daphne said.

When Fiona and Ted reached Mackay's office, Fiona said to him, "Ted doesn't want me to mention my connection to this incident. I keep telling him I'm a reporter. It's what I do."

"I don't want unnecessary attention focused on her," Ted said.

"This is a situation that we can't just try to cover up," Mackay replied. "Fiona's home invasion is one thing. No one was injured. The culprit was caught. No other residents of Naperville were ever in danger. Today is different. Her sister was *shot*. A policeman has been *shot*. The Honda driver is *dead*. The alleged gunman has been *shot*. A police car chase took place on Naperville streets. I can't stifle other TV stations or the rest of the media. If we don't cover this truthfully. Fiona and I will be laughed out of the business."

"My first priority is Fiona's safety," Ted said.

"I appreciate that, but the truth is, I've already had calls from other stations. As soon as the news came over the police radio that a woman had been shot at the Morgan house here in Naperville, people made connections to Fiona. And they also wonder now what the real deal was three nights ago."

"Are you trying to say that the cat is already out of the bag?" Ted asked.

"I am definitely saying that. Loud and clear," said Mackay. "It's time we focused on airing information about reward money for the arrest and capture of Ralph Kendrick, or any hitman he contracts with. With one of my reporters at risk, I intend to get that ball rolling."

"We have an anonymous donor who is willing to pay twenty-five thousand dollars for that information," Fiona said.

"Great. Air that tonight." Mackay stood.

Fiona looked at Ted. "What do you say?"

"Apparently nothing at the moment. I understand you have to do this," he replied. "But I have a bad feeling about it."

"Point taken," Mackay said . "Get ready for your broadcast, Fiona. There's not much time."

CHAPTER 26

"Good afternoon, I'm Fiona Morgan with NKTV news. At two o'clock this afternoon, a young woman in Naperville was the target of a drive-by shooting by a man outside 708 Blackberry Court. I know this for a fact because my s-s-sister, Kailee Hughes," Fiona choked momentarily, "was the woman who was targeted."

Fiona paused for a second while her co-workers gasped in the background. "Fortunately, the gunman's first bullet only shot her in the leg. The second shot was deflected by a local hero, Michael Abbot. Following a car chase and outstanding police work, the driver of the car is dead, and the shooter is now in police custody.

"Unfortunately, a police officer, Patrolman Ryan Mahoney, was shot in the arm, but he is in stable condition. The driver of the shooter's car was shot and killed by police officers. The gunman, Juan Santiago, was shot in the arm, and he is in stable condition.

"This incident may be a direct result of a previous incident in my life twenty years ago." She paused. "At that time, I testified against a man named Ralph Kendrick when I saw him use a rock to crush a woman's skull in broad daylight in a Minneapolis public park. My two ten year old friends, Tory Girard and Sandy Johnson, were with me when we came to a clearing in the woods and saw this incident. They testified as well. At his trial, Kendrick made threats against all three of us. According to prison authorities, he has voiced those threats throughout his incarceration. Six days ago, Kendrick escaped from prison in Minnesota.

"Since that time, a home invader tried to strangle me three nights ago. Tory Girard was murdered two nights ago. I am one of identical triplets. I've discovered that Kendrick told cellmates that, because of sealed records, he doesn't know which of us testified, and that he'd have to arrange to kill all three of us if he ever got out of jail. My sister, Kailee, was shot today."

Fiona took a deep breath, and she clasped her hands together to try to stop her fingers from trembling. "I take this opportunity to make a public announcement to Ralph Kendrick who is still at large. Stay away from my sisters. I'm the one who testified. Your grudge is with me, not them. I was the Morgan triplet that helped to put you behind bars. I know you want me dead, but I am just as determined to see you back behind bars."

Fiona paused while a picture of Ralph Kendrick flashed on the screen. "This is a recent photo of Ralph Kendrick. He is probably armed, and he's a dangerous man. He killed another inmate while he was in prison. Don't try to deal with him. But if you have any information about him please contact police.

"An anonymous donor is offering a twenty-five thousand dollar reward for information leading to Kendrick's capture and return to prison. Another twenty-five thousand dollars reward is being offered for information leading to the capture of anyone offering or accepting a contract from Kendrick for any of the five women he may be targeting."

"And, to Sandy Johnson, wherever you are. As the third witness twenty years ago, take steps to protect yourself. "

Fiona continued with the rest of the news. When the telecast ended, she saw Ted raise one eyebrow and give her a speaking glance. She strode over to him, moving up close, so that she was toe-to-toe with him. She could see the muscle twitching in his jaw.

Ted wasted no words. "What were you thinking?" he said in a terse whisper.

Fiona's turquoise eyes flashed to green, but her voice shook. "Before you start yelling at me, let me explain. I couldn't live with myself if one of my sisters was injured or killed. Please say you understand. I'm so scared that you'll fire me as your client!"

"We'll talk after we leave here," he said.

It took several minutes to leave the studio because Fiona's co-workers stopped to commiserate with her dilemma and offer wishes for her safety. She appreciated that Ted didn't lambaste her in front of her colleagues, but she also wasn't in a rush to bear the force of his anger. She extended the chit-chat, until Ted finally pointed his finger at his watch and nodded toward the door.

When they reached her car, he snapped, "What part of don't give away unnecessary information didn't you understand? What if Kendrick tries to hurt you even more by deliberately attacking your sisters before he comes after you?"

"He can't if he can't get to them," she replied. "Kailee and Regan will both be far away as soon as Justin and Kailee leave Illinois."

"You realize you practically dared him to come after you?" He heaved a sigh and started up the car. "You certainly will have caught Kendrick's attention if he was watching."

"I did the only thing I could." The militant gleam in her eyes belied any sense of remorse.

"Kendrick probably won't be watching this channel, but all the major channels will be running that segment on the six o'clock and later newscasts. My sisters should be safe now," said Fiona. That's the main thing."

Ted grimaced, "You have no idea what you may have unleashed on you and your sisters."

"And I say it would have been unleashed anyway."

"Whatever," Ted sighed in disgust. "The damage is done."

"Will you still continue to protect me?" Fiona worried her tongue from one side of her mouth to the other.

91

"Yeah, damn it. But I think I need a roll of tape for your mouth."

"People have been telling me that for years."

"I can't imagine why." He changed the subject. "Want to pick up something to eat for dinner?"

Fiona fell back against the seat in relief. She had been pretty worried about his reaction. "If you'll eat chicken breasts, baked potatoes, and salad, I can rustle up some food for us at the town house."

"A home-cooked meal?"

"Home-nuked is more like it. I'll defrost the chicken breasts in the microwave, and I can grill them on my George Foreman grill. It's the kind you can set on a counter. And I can microwave the potatoes."

"Sounds like a plan," said Ted.

Fifteen minutes later, as they drove down the street to Fiona's house, Ted groaned. "The vultures have arrived," he said, as he pointed to the small battalion of media vans flanking her house. Groups of three or four people stood near her front lawn. They all surged toward the car when they saw them coming.

"Fiona! Fiona! Over here!" Several voices sounded out as Ted grimly continued to inch his way onto her driveway and into the attached garage. He had to keep tapping his horn to let people know he was coming. I hate this monkey business, he thought sourly. When he finally got the car into the garage, reporters swarmed around the vehicle.

"Hey Fiona, you're one of us. Give us something."

"I just said all that I can," she replied.

"Did you keep in touch with Tory Girard and Sandy Johnson after you left Minneapolis?"

"No. I think we all wanted to forget that summer."

Ted stepped out of the car, holding up his badge. "Right now you're all trespassing onto private property. I wouldn't want to have to arrest one of Ms. Morgan's friends."

The reporters backed off a few inches.

"I can call for backup, or you can politely move off personal property," he said, giving them a stone cold look that could shrivel an ordinary man. People muttered but moved back out of the garage. Ted hit the button for the overhead garage door, and it clanged down.

"You still look grim," Fiona commented as they entered her kitchen. "I thought you weren't mad at me."

"I'm not. I'm thinking of strategies to keep you safe, . . . other than dropping you into a cell at the Naperville PD. You practically said, 'Here I am, Kendrick. Come and get me.'"

"Isn't it a good thing . . . to draw a killer out?"

Ted gave her a long look. "If he were the actual killer, maybe yes. But he may have the resources to hire as many hitmen as he needs. As long as his money lasts. Just to make sure you're eliminated."

"I'm still not sorry I spoke out. I mentioned that I couldn't live with myself if one of my sisters were harmed. Well, I think I'm responsible for my father's death already. I couldn't chance another."

CHAPTER 27

New York City, 9:30 p.m.

On Manhattan's west side, Sandy Johnson smiled across the table at her new boyfriend. Although they only met a week ago, they'd already gone out three times. Armand Fortuna was so easy to talk to, and they enjoyed the same things.

Armand was good looking, too, with thick black hair. And he had some class. His manners were excellent, and he was thoughtful. He always opened doors for her and treated her as if she were special. Today he brought her a bouquet of jonquils. She knew he got them at the little kiosk near the restaurant, but at least he thought of it.

As they stepped from the ambiance of the small, cozy Italian restaurant, Armand asked, "How about inviting me back to your place?"

Sandy smiled and bobbed her head. Armand took her hand, and they walked along companionably. Although it was after ten, other couples strolled along as well, either walking their dogs, or just meandering home. Several shops and restaurants had their black wrought iron grills in place, but many other bars and restaurants still had beckoning lights. Everything looked quaint and charming to Sandy on this romantic evening. She looked sideways and admired Armand's lean build, his pencil-thin moustache, and his short goatee. She wasn't too crazy about his pony tail and ear-ring, but maybe she could get him to change that.

When they reached her apartment, she used her key to enter the ancient brick building. As they stepped into the shabby, but clean foyer, she checked her mail and led Armand to the elevator which wheezed and rattled on its way to the sixth floor.

Sandy hoped that Armand would like the black, white, and tan color scheme in her apartment. Three black, squishy bean bags clustered near the tan couch with the plain lines, surrounding the brick and black wood coffee table. Other bricks held up black wood shelving which housed her books and her flat screen TV, a new purchase.

After Armand admired her place, Sandy excused herself to use the tiny bathroom, where she freshened her lipstick, fluffed her hair, and sprayed on some more Tommy Girl perfume. When she returned, she found Armand gazing out the window.

She said, "I'll make us some coffee now," and she walked into the pocket sized kitchen. When she reached up for the special coffee beans, she sensed that Armand was right behind her. She smiled and wondered if he would put his arms around her waist.

In a nanosecond her smile vanished as Armand pulled a heavy wire tight around her neck. Coffee beans shot around the floor like marbles as Sandy Johnson sank to the floor, lifeless.

Fortuna carefully removed Sandy's jewelry . . . a topaz ring, a gold necklace, and her Kenneth Cole watch. Fortuna had put on plastic gloves while Sandy was prettying herself in the bathroom, so there was no worry that fingerprints would be left behind.

After snapping off the lights and carefully clicking the door lock, Fortuna left Sandy's apartment and ambled unhurriedly down the street for two blocks, turning into a lively bar. Stepping into a unisex bathroom and locking the door, Sandy's killer removed the plastic gloves, pulled off the goatee and mustache, removed the ponytail ring, and fluffed her long black hair. After applying lipstick and eye makeup, she sauntered through the bar and out to the street. When she reached her hotel, she spent the rest of the evening applying bright red polish to her fingernails. At ten o'clock she called a cab for JFK.

CHAPTER 28

Naperville

"**W**hat do you mean you caused your father's death?" Ted asked Fiona.

"I remember overhearing him and my mother arguing during the trial," Fiona said, as she took the frozen chicken breasts out of their wrappers and put them in the microwave on Defrost. "He never wanted me to testify. He hated any arguments or confrontation. He didn't want the stress and the aggravation of the trial.

"My mother insisted that it was the right thing to do. And that the police needed my account as well as ToryGirard's and Sandy Johnson's, to put Kendrick behind bars. Brady told her that police suspected Kendrick of another woman's murder as well, so our testimony was really important.

"My father often went riding alone at night, especially if he had a computer problem to figure out. A month after the trial ended, he took the car out at midnight and never came back. He was hit by a train at a railroad crossing."

"Surely you don't feel responsible for that!"

"Yes, I did. And I still do. The train engineer saw him; he had time to move off the tracks, but he didn't."

"Some people freeze with fear and can't move."

"Either way, he's dead." Fiona twisted her hair.

"Surely not because of you, though. If Kendrick's trial triggered it, which I doubt, do you know what other stresses your father might have been under? You were just a little kid! You did the right thing to testify. At least you put Kendrick behind bars where he couldn't kill another innocent woman. How would you like to have that on your conscience?"

"I guess I needed to be reminded of that."

"Does your mother know how you feel?"

"No, since she wanted me to testify, I couldn't bring it up. It would sound like I was blaming her."

"So instead, you took all the blame on yourself. That's a cruel and unnecessary burden for a kid. You should discuss this with your mother, and soon."

Fiona looked at him thoughtfully. "I also felt guilty that I didn't miss him after he died."

"If he didn't develop a close relationship with you, your feelings were pretty natural. It sounds to me as if you've had some pretty undependable men in your life. First, your father. Then your skirt-chasing husband. There are plenty of dependable men out there, you know." He stopped for a second and turned to her. "Including me."

She looked up quickly, wariness in her eyes. "I'm sure there are. I just don't trust my judgment enough to be able to make a commitment. My mistake with Jeb was horrendous."

"It's in the past. You're wiser now."

Ted's phone rang, and he put Tremayne on speaker.

"The shooter, Juan Santiago, has talked to his lawyer, who has pointed out the value of divulging information for a lesser sentence. Santiago says he doesn't know the name of the man who hired him. But he was paid to kill Kailee, not Fiona. The man who paid him was taller than him, over six feet, with an average body build. They met at night outside the back door of a bar on the south side, but the guy had a ski mask on. Santiago couldn't even tell his nationality."

"Well, we know now that Kendrick's definitely targeting all the Morgan sisters," Ted said.

"Yup, and now we know for sure Kendrick has an accomplice," Tremayne added. "Kendrick is five foot ten. The guy who paid Santiago was over six feet."

Later, as Ted flipped channels on the TV, he heard, "Coming up. You'll hear about Fiona Morgan, a young Midwestern news broadcaster, who caught the nation's attention this afternoon when she reported on her news show that an escaped convict is trying to kill her and her triplet sisters."

Ted called Fiona to the living room, and they watched the screen together. Priscilla Blake, a national network broadcaster, reviewed the information about Kendrick, his threats to kill five women, and the events of the past week.

"In conclusion," Blake said, "three nights ago, a home intruder attempted to strangle Fiona Morgan in her own bed. That person was arrested and refuses to say who hired him. *Is that incident a coincidence?*

"Two nights ago one of the three girls who witnessed the murder of Rose Wilson, Tory Girard from Minneapolis, was shot and killed after her car was hijacked from the Mall of America. *Is that a coincidence?*

"As to the shooting of Kailee Hughes, Naperville is an upscale Chicago suburb which has never had a drive-by shooting. *Is that a coincidence?*"

Ms. Blake showed the segment where Fiona sent an urgent message to the escaped Ralph Kendrick, stating that she was the triplet who witnessed the murder and telling him to leave her sisters alone. Ms. Blake also mentioned the reward and sent the message to Fiona that her fellow broadcasters are pulling for her.

When the program ended, Ted said nothing for a moment, but Fiona could see his jaw muscle tighten. Finally, he spoke, "So much for damage control. Now we're in for it."

She heard him call Tremayne to update him and also asked for a police officer to be stationed out in front of Fiona's house.

Fiona looked at Ted's grim face and said, "Maybe this publicity isn't a bad thing. National attention will be focused on Kendrick's vendetta. Ms. Blake showed a picture of him. Can't we use the media for the good? Why can't we provide pictures of what Ralph might look like in disguise and make them available as well?"

"I can do that right now. We could post them on your website. Would other members of the media accept them, too?"

"Some will. Some won't. It's worth a try."

They moved to her office, and posted the pictures on her website. As they finished, he was bending over her slightly watching the computer screen. When she tried to stand, she stumbled into his chest. His arms went around her quickly to balance her. They stayed there and tightened.

She looked up and saw that his gray eyes were almost soot color. He raised his left eyebrow, but didn't release her. Their mouths joined together as if they were magnets, both responding to their gravitational field. He deepened the kiss, and her arms went around his neck.

"Do you have any idea how hard it is to keep my hands off you?" Ted asked as he turned his face to talk into her ear.

"Even when I don't agree with you on something?"

"Especially then. When you finished your show today, you were magnificent. Your eyes shot sparks at me that almost singed my chest hair. I'll give you credit. You're a woman of your convictions. Misguided though they be at times," he added.

"Now you spoiled it," she complained. "Why don't we go back to where you said it was hard to keep your hands off me?"

He lowered his lips to hers. "I'll show you, instead."

When they finally broke apart, it took her awhile to catch her breath. "I'm so glad you're here for me."

"You're a pretty special lady." He stepped away. "You've had quite a day, and it's getting late." He kissed her on the top of her head and said, "Hopefully, tomorrow will be a quieter day."

CHAPTER 29

Near Wisconsin Dells

S urrounded by empty beer cans, potato chip and popcorn bags, and dirty
socks, Ralph Kendrick watched TV in the Hochunk Hotel room while Jimmy
Ponzo grumbled about the mess in the place.

"Shit! Get a load of this!" Ralph said as he took a deep slug of beer. "Look,
Ponzo, I'm on national TV. It's that Fiona Morgan broad. She's talking about
me."

"Damn! That's the last thing we want."

"Whaddaya mean? She's making me famous."

They focused their attention on Priscilla Blake's broadcast when she aired
Fiona's segment.

"We should have left the country instead of hanging around like this," Ponzo
said.

"Wait a minute." Ralph shouted and threw a sneaker at the TV. "Hey, what's
this? She's threatening me! She has the balls to threaten me? She claims she was
the triplet who testified. Like I'd believe her?" He listened in disbelief as Ms.
Blake talked of reward money

Ralph saw Ponzo's face turn white when he heard the part about reward
money for anyone assisting Kendrick. Kendrick threw another tennis shoe across
the room, knocking a lamp to the floor.

"Cut it out. We don't want management checking on us. You're half in the
bag."

"I think better when I'm drunk."

"Nobody thinks better drunk."

"Are you some kind of expert?" Ralph sneered as he awkwardly reached for
his beer again and upset a giant bag of popcorn, scattering the contents.

"Look what you did now. You're such a slob."

"Clean it up," said Ralph.

"You clean it up."

"Listen up, Ponzo. My old man told me he set up an account with the
Corporation. You're being paid well to look out for me now. Clean up the damn
popcorn."

"If I left you, you'd be a dead man."

"Hell, I was thinking about contacting that Priscilla Blake chick. Bet she'd
give me TV time. I could tell her my side."

"You do that and you'll be back in the slammer so fast, you won't know what hit you. All those fights in prison must have creamed your brain. You gotta keep a low profile or you're gonna be either in jail or dead."

"You're right. But I need all five women dead before I can leave the country."

Ralph knew he needed Ponzo for that. But when he was sipping tequila someplace warm, maybe he'd just get rid of the smart-mouthed pest.

CHAPTER 30

Naperville, Illinois

The next morning, Fiona woke up, remembered the predicament she was in, and stuck her head under her pillow like she did when she was a child. *It was so scary to be the target of a hitman.* Just thinking of the incident with the lizard man who tried to strangle her was enough to make her sweat all over again. And if Ted hadn't been there, she just might have been dead already.

She uncovered her head and put her legs on the floor. She wasn't a child any more. And she'd better follow Ted's advice to be proactive in keeping herself alive. Today she'd really work hard on the defense moves with Ted.

The news of Tory's death still boggled her mind. She remembered Tory from when they were ten years old. She'd had a wonderful belly laugh. Sometimes, Fiona and Sandy would burst out laughing just from the sound of Tory's rich cackle. Tory was a nice girl and fun to be with. She should not be dead. It was an obscenity that she was killed in the prime of her life. And by an unfeeling monster who didn't even know her. Who killed her for the money.

Was that same person coming after her next? If he didn't, someone else would. And she wouldn't even know what he looked like. That was part of the anxiety. At least, in her nightmares about Kendrick, she knew what he looked like.

Yesterday, as she and Ted went from one activity to another, it had been on her mind all the time. Ted thought she was brave. Hah! That was a laugh! Even when she focused on stuff like the mudhole and her news broadcast, the feeling of fear was right there like a canker sore, waiting to get her attention.

In all her life, she never thought she'd be putting on a bulletproof vest before she stepped outside her house.

When Ted went out the front door of Fiona's town house to get the morning newspaper, he saw six media vans, plus assorted photographers and reporters milling around nearby. And a catering truck as well. He swore under his breath as they started yelling questions at him and said, "No comment." He gave the door an extra jerk with his wrist as he closed it, and he grumbled on his way to the coffee pot.

"What's up?" Fiona asked when she heard him muttering.

Ted rolled his eyes, "The media people outside look like fleas ready to jump all over a dog's back. And the dog was me."

"Maybe they'll help protect me from Kendrick," Fiona said, hopefulness shining from her eyes. "You know, safety in numbers."

"Or, how about this? All an assassin needs to do is grab a camera and masquerade as a media person."

"Oh, I hadn't thought of that," she said, crestfallen.

"I even saw a catering truck out there."

"Really?" She flushed.

"Don't tell me you ordered it." His eyebrows shot up to his hairline.

"Okay, I won't tell you that."

"Why didn't you just invite them all inside for their refreshments," he groaned.

"It's just doughnuts and coffee. Ted, they're my fellow press people."

"You're just encouraging them to hang around."

"They're going to hang around regardless . . . as long as I'm news. I might as well make them comfortable. I know that some step over the line, but even police departments have pushy people . . . people that step over the line. Or are corrupt."

Ted snorted.

Fiona continued, "The media spotlights what's happening. Without media focusing on them a lot of evil people, including dictators, murderers, and thieves would be unstoppable. People want news. They expect to know what's going on, locally, nationally, and internationally."

"They cross over the line of propriety, intruding on people's fear and grief. They enjoy putting people on pedestals and then knocking them off."

Fiona's eyes flashed. "Don't blame the hardworking, capable, sensitive people for the pushy few." She placed her hands on her hips.

Ted hesitated momentarily and looked down at her. "I observed an incident a couple years ago. I was in a crowd of people, ready to pull the trigger on an assassin to prevent him from shooting a minor dignitary. A reporter jostled me. I couldn't take the shot in time. The person I was protecting took a bullet in the chest. Fortunately, he survived."

Fiona sucked in her breath and laid her hand on his arm. "No wonder you feel so strongly. Did the reporter know what happened?"

"No, she was too busy trying to get close to the fallen guy."

"Did you file a report or anything?"

"I tried. They told me it would be too hard to prove."

"I'm sorry that happened." She put her hand on his arm and squeezed gently. Ted squeezed her back and said, "So am I."

"So that's when you developed your ugly eye for the press?" She tried to lighten the mood.

"Pardon me?"

"Your ugly eye. I've seen you flash it at the media. They all fall back when you do."

"You're supposed to be hustling past them, not checking my face".

"Point taken. Let's table this discussion."

They headed to the basement for their workouts. Over the past few days, they developed a routine where they drank coffee, exercised first, then practiced self defense skills. Following that they showered and had breakfast. As Ted stepped onto the elliptical and turned on MSNBC, Fiona started her run on the treadmill. Suddenly she heard a commentator interrupt the program with an incoming story. "MSNBC has breaking news from the US embassy in Barcelona, Spain, where an explosion as occurred in its building."

Fiona's stomach clenched, and she shouted, "Oh no! Ted, look!"

Instantly they shut off their machines and riveted their attention to the screen. "Early reports indicated injuries and possible deaths," the newscaster said.

"Oh no!" moaned Fiona, as she frantically grabbed her cell phone and dialed Regan. When she heard the voice mail robot, she tried texting. No answer. She tried Regan's husband's number. Again, a voice mail message. She texted him. No answer.

She realized she was panting and tried to catch her breath. "What time is it there?" she asked Ted.

"Probably around two in the afternoon."

The TV showed canned pictures of the embassy before it switched to a shot of pandemonium, presumably outside the building. Emergency lights flashed from several vehicles. People rushed in and out of the building.

"Tell me that Kendrick couldn't be involved with this," Fiona whispered.

"I doubt very much that this is his work." Ted bounced from one news channel to another trying to get more information.

"I'm so scared! I don't think I can stand it if Kendrick hurt Regan or her family or anyone else at that embassy."

"As I recall, the Barcelona area has had its share of threats from the Basque movement," Ted reassured her. "It could be them, or some nut, or some freak accident."

Fiona's phone rang. She grabbed it and said, "Regan?"

"Sorry, it's Mom. Have you seen the news?"

"Yes, but I can't reach Regan." They agreed to call each other if they heard anything.

After she closed her phone, Fiona's legs gave way, and she sank bonelessly to the rubber surface of the treadmill. She put her hands over her face and sobbed, "I'm living in fight or flight mode, only things aren't happening to me. They're happening to other people. Every time I turn around, something bad happens to someone I know, and I think it could have been me. I feel half guilty that they got hurt and I didn't."

Ted sat next to her on the treadmill and put his arms around her. She clung to him. "You're as white as a styrofoam cup." He stroked her hair back. "First of all, we don't know the facts. Don't expect the worst. You're not responsible for Kendrick's actions.

"And secondly, don't do anything reckless. Relax yourself. Let me do my job to protect you. I'll be covering your backside. The best way to fight Kendrick today is to follow your schedule in a reasonable way and keep fit to protect yourself. Send up some prayers for you and your sisters. But don't fight the lion till the lion's in the living room."

"I'm so worried about Regan and her family. Especially after hearing about Tory being murdered."

"We're just going to take the waiting one minute at a time for now. Just remember you had no control over Tory Girard's death. And, unfortunately, she didn't know she was in danger from Kendrick. You do. Get your treadmill going again. Focus your energy. Give yourself a super workout. I'll keep switching from one newsroom to another." He helped her to stand up.

Fiona skipped any warm-up and went straight to a fast walk followed by a run, while Ted worked the TV control from the elliptical. Her heart pumped, and her legs ached.

The event continued to receive coverage, but the information trickling in was mostly a rehash of what they'd heard already. Fiona prayed fiercely for her relatives as she pounded away on the treadmill. Sweat trickled down the side of her face.

Finally, a TV station had something new. The announcer said they had received the information that a reception for new employees and their families had been scheduled for that day. Fiona groaned, and her stomach clenched again.

"They're in the building, even the kids. It's worse than I thought." Like a mantra, she repeated, "God, please have Regan call. Please have them be safe." Tendrils of hair slipped out of her pony tail.

When her cell phone finally rang, she clicked off the treadmill and almost dropped the phone in her hurry to answer it. "Relax," her mom's voice was clear and steady as she said, "Regan and her family are all safe. They weren't in the part of the building where the blast occurred. Some group in Spain has already claimed responsibility, so it wasn't connected to Kendrick. You can relax, honey."

Fiona murmured, "Thanks, Mom, I'll get back to you later." After she closed her phone, she just stood there on the silent treadmill. Tears slipped down her face.

Ted came to her side. "Are you all right? I thought you sounded relieved when you hung up."

"I'm all right," she blubbered. "They're okay, and it wasn't Kendrick."

"Good," he said, helping her step off the machine.

"I've broken down more in the last few days than I have in a lifetime. I guess I have the curse of the Finnerty tears after all."

"What's that?"

"Women on my mom's side cry at the drop of a hat. Including Regan and Kailee. They say their bladders are too close to their eyes. I thought I escaped it. But I guess I was wrong."

"It's hard to be under siege. Not just you, but your sisters, too. We'll skip the self defense workout today. Come on upstairs. A little breakfast and you'll feel better."

"I think I worked up an appetite for pancakes, and I need to be doing something. I'll grab the special mix from my mom and rustle up a few. You can shower first."

CHAPTER 31

"Those were delicious pancakes." Ted pushed his long frame away from the table.

"Glad you liked them. It's a secret Morgan recipe," she said, clearing the breakfast table, while Ted watered her plants on the patio. She felt almost slap-happy with relief after the terrible worry about Regan.

She saw Ted answer his phone out on the patio, and she heard him say, "Let me step inside and put you on speaker, so Fiona can hear this. Will you repeat what you just said?" He motioned to Fiona and said, "It's Brady from Minneapolis. Why don't you sit down at the kitchen table with me."

Fiona sat down gingerly on the edge of a kitchen chair. She could tell by the seriousness of Ted's face that this probably wouldn't be good news.

Brady wasted no time. "New York City had a murder yesterday. Name Mary Sandra Johnson, but everyone called her Sandy. Age thirty, Caucasian female."

"Oh, no!" Fiona gasped.

"Did she ever live in Minneapolis?" Ted asked

"According to friends, yes."

"Did she ever testify at the trial of Ralph Kendrick?" Fiona's voice trembled.

"According to friends, she testified at some trial when she was a kid, but they don't remember the name," Brady replied. "It sounds like our woman, though."

"They don't have much," he continued. "Miss Johnson was found strangled in her apartment. She did not have a roommate. No rape was involved. No sign of forced entry. They assume she let her killer in. Her purse and some jewelry were taken, but probably only to make it look like a robbery."

"What was the date and time of the murder?" Ted asked.

"Ten thirty p.m. yesterday."

"How and when was her body discovered?"

"By a work associate and her landlord this morning. Seems Miss Johnson was well-liked and conscientious. When she didn't show up for an important meeting, her co-workers made several phone calls and just got her machine. Finally, one of them came to her apartment, contacted the landlord, and they went in. They found her in her kitchen. Looked like she had been reaching up to get something out of the cupboard. The strangler must have come up behind her. Neighbors heard no unusual noises."

Fiona choked, "That's awful!" She twisted her hair as she listened intently. Then she caught herself and folded her hands carefully on the table. Ted immediately covered her hands with one of his. The warmth of his calloused hand and the gentle sensory pressure from his touch helped her concentrate on what she was hearing.

Brady continued, "Her co-workers said that Miss Johnson had talked about a new boy friend. She apparently met him at a bookstore. No one knew which one. They had several meetings at coffee shops. We've shown her picture around the neighborhood. No one remembers seeing her with a man. Except for one place. They remembered Miss Johnson. They described the man with her as medium height, coal black hair tied back into a ponytail, goatee and moustache. So far, he hasn't come forth. However, we have a security tape of a guy with that description going up with Ms. Johnson and coming back down by himself."

"So it probably was a professional hit," Ted said.

"Afraid so," Brady said. "But this MO is different from that of Tory Girard's killer. I doubt that it was the same killer."

"Thanks for the heads up. Keep us posted." Ted hung up. He looked across the table at Fiona and took both her hands in his. "Tiger, I wish I could protect you from such bad news."

"You can't." She clutched his hands. "I can't seem to register the fact that both Tory and Sandy are dead. I'm the only one left who testified. Sandy mustn't have known about Kendrick. She wasn't on red alert as she should have been. And nobody knew her first name was really Mary. Ted, I'm so glad you're here with me. I know I'm safer than Tory and Sandy were. And, for right now, my sisters are safe and forewarned. I've got to hang on to that."

Ted looked at her closely. "You sound as if you're okay. But, are you? This was tough news to hear."

"I think I'm okay. I just feel overwhelmed."

After the call, Fiona finished cleaning the kitchen and went into the office to pay some bills. She needed to pay her property tax bill. Where was it? She couldn't find it. She looked frantically in all the obvious places. Her fingers shook. *Get a grip*, she told herself. *I wouldn't have thrown the damned bill out. It was too important.* It had to be here somewhere. She didn't need this frustration. Her stomach clenched. She forced herself to sit back in her chair. Feeling so jittery she wanted to slap herself, she took a deep breath and tried again. Voila! The bill was stuck to her gas bill. She paid the bill and went into her bedroom. *What was the matter with her?* It was ridiculous to get so upset over something that wasn't life-threatening. She took another deep breath.

Shortly after, the sound of a hammer banging began in her closet.

Ted followed the noise. "What are you doing? I thought maybe you were boarding up your windows."

"No, I had a few minutes. I'm pounding cup hooks into the panel of wood in my closet."

"And that would be for . . . ?"

"My necklaces. I can hang them individually and group them by gold, silver, or color." With her tongue between her teeth, Fiona prepared to pound the next one in.

"Can I help?" he asked.

"No thanks, I'm banging away a few aggressions as well."

"Whatever works," he replied.

CHAPTER 32

The rest of Fiona's day breezed by quickly. She didn't have time to think of the terror she had felt in the morning. She had four appointments for interviews at the studio, and she met Charlie twice. Once for a terrible five car accident. Once for a goose nesting on someone's balcony. She also attended a Chamber of Commerce meeting, resulting in a promise from her to do a short segment on the Naperville Riverwalk which now was five miles long.

As she shot into the TV station for her five o'clock show, the press pelted her with questions. She tried to answer a few.

"Where is your sister, Kailee?"

"I don't know. She and her husband do not want to be traced for obvious reasons."

"Why don't you do that? Just disappear?"

"I'm being well-protected. I want to see Kendrick caught."

"Is Regan safe in Spain?"

"I surely hope so.

"Were you worried when the news about the embassy explosion hit the news?

"Of course. I was terrified, then very relieved that they were all right. And that Kendrick wasn't involved."

"How is your mother holding up?"

"She's doing as well as can be expected."

"Did your father commit suicide?"

She blinked her eyes and wondered where that came from. "No comment," she replied as she entered the station and closed the door.

That evening, during her five o'clock broadcast, Fiona mentioned the death of Mary Sandra Johnson, in New York City. She also mentioned that various policemen had tried to notify Ms. Johnson of the danger, but they only knew her as Sandra Johnson, and they could not locate her address. Her legal name was Mary Sandra Johnson.

As they left the studio, she fielded another flurry of questions from the press.

"How does it feel to be the only remaining witness to Kendrick's murder of Rose Wilson?"

"Exactly how you would feel if you were in my shoes," she replied. "I am luckier than Tory or Sandy because I know someone is after me, with intent to kill. I can take reasonable precautions."

"Give an example of reasonable precautions."

109

She explained how she changed her exercise routine and how she avoided any activity that was routine when she could. "I don't stop at Starbuck's at the same time each morning. I can still go there, but not at the same time."

"Can you still go grocery shopping or out to eat?"

"Yes, as long as it's not predictable. Only one more question," she said and pointed to a lanky black man from Chicago whom she respected.

"How did the fact that you saw Rose Wilson murdered affect your life?" he asked.

"It gave me a bald glimpse of evil at an early age. Also, when it came time for me and my sisters to choose extra-curricular activities, Regan chose dance lessons, Kailee chose volleyball, and I chose karate classes. I wanted to be able to protect myself."

On the way home from the broadcast, Fiona filled Ted in on the wedding shower she would be attending that night. She also talked about the dates for the upcoming wedding rehearsal, the wedding ceremony itself, and the reception. The rehearsal and ceremony would take place outside at the base of the Carillon.

"I'll have to wear a vest for these functions, won't I?" she asked.

"Not for the shower, the rehearsal dinner, or the wedding reception," he replied. "However, you'll need to wear one at the wedding rehearsal and also at the actual ceremony, since they'll both be out in the open, and we can't control the environment as well. You know, if it was up to me, you'd be in full body armor twenty-four/seven."

"I'll have to have another fitting for my bridesmaid dress." I'm hoping Kendrick'll be back behind bars by the time of the wedding."

"Tell me about the wedding party."

"Annie McElroy, the bride, was my roommate at college and a very dear friend. She's marrying Tom Conrad, a fireman. The groomsman assigned to me happens to be a cop. His name is Dave Barrett. You might know him."

Ted shook his head.

"Annie's sister will be the maid of honor. And there's one other bridesmaid besides me."

They had a quick supper. As she scraped the dishes into the garbage disposal after eating, Fiona wished she could take all her scary thoughts about Kendrick and his cohorts and shove them down the disposal, pulverizing them into nothing with a turn of the switch.

On the way to the bridal shower, Ted said, "I always thought of Naperville as a city of cookie cutter subdivisions, four or five styles in a specified area, each with its own name and neighborhood swimming pool. I'm surprised to see these big mansions tucked in here and there, between much more modest homes."

"Tear-downs have become popular anywhere that has a close location to the downtown area."

"I wonder how the neighborhood residents feel about the big houses mushrooming up next door to them."

"Probably increases their own resale."

When they arrived, Ted saw that a cop in an unmarked police car was in place out front, and he knew another police officer would patrol around the house on foot during the shower.

At the door, Fiona introduced Ted to the bride, Annie McElroy, who was a tall, slender, titian-haired woman with laughing brown eyes and a big smile. "Don't worry, Ted, you won't have to sit with the ladies. The men are hanging out in the den. But you'll be able to see Fiona from there."

To Ted's eye, the living room and dining room were strewn with white decorations . . . crepe paper streamers, wedding bells, whatever . . . all girlie stuff. He was relieved when the groom came forward to usher him to the den off the living room where a few guys would be watching the Cub's game. It was a perfect spot for Ted. With the door ajar, he could follow the game and keep an eye on Fiona at the same time.

He could hear the laughter and the camaraderie of the women. Ted could see that Fiona was relaxed and enjoying herself. Her eyes sparkled. You'd never know she was afraid for her life. She needed more time like that. By the ooohs and aahs and razzing remarks, he could tell when the bride opened a personal item.

He chatted with the groom, a local fire fighter, and spoke with Dave Barrett, the groomsman who was assigned to Fiona. He was also a Naperville police officer. Dave offered to let Ted replace him for the ceremony if he needed to be closer to Fiona. Ted told him he'd be glad to have him protect Fiona, as that would free Ted up to patrol the area and check out guests.

Fiona told Annie that she would have to wear a bulletproof vest for the outdoor parts of the wedding ceremony. "If you would rather I not be in the wedding, I would understand."

"Don't be silly. Just as long as you're there."

On the way home from the shower, Ted said, "Just before we left, I spoke with Katie Archer, a police woman who'll be attending the wedding. I asked her to cover the room where you females of the wedding party will be getting ready prior to the ceremony. I figured you'd rather have her there than me."

Fiona laughed. "You mean the intrepid Ted Collier is afraid of being alone with a bunch of females?"

"No, I just don't want to get kicked out by a bunch of ladies set on being beautiful."

"Hmph."

"Seriously, I can serve you better at that time by making sure the outside environment is safe for you."

"I know," she placed her hand on his. "And I appreciate that."

"You girls must have given your mother a few gray hairs when you all started to date. Did she have to install three phone lines?"

"We did give her a hard time and no, she didn't install more phones, which was the cause of many arguments. She stood her ground, and phone calls were limited to ten minutes. We all needed braces at the same time. We all got driver's licenses at the same time. And we had to share one car for the three of us. And we all went to different schools, from junior high through college.

"She spent a lot of time chauffeuring us around because we were all in different activities. Thank God, our father left her well off financially. She never really blew money. But we lived comfortably. After the Kendrick incident, as I told the press today, I was dead set on becoming skilled in self defense. I never wanted to allow a man to overpower me without a fight on my part. I taught a lot of moves to my sisters over the years, too. As I mentioned earlier, we still meet every once in awhile to refresh our skills.

"While Regan and Kailee were involved in school activities of dance team and volleyball player, I worked on the high school newspaper. I worked my way up from covering various school activities to a regular column where I interviewed a person of interest."

"Did you three go to different colleges, too?"

"Yup. Regan went to the U of I and majored in French and Spanish. Kailee went to DePaul and majored in psychology. I went to Northwestern where I majored in Broadcast Journalism. But even though we were apart, we always talked daily, often more than once.

"In general, we're all outgoing. Regan is great at making small talk. I'm the blabber-mouth. Kailee is more of an observer, but then she comes up with some really good comments."

"How about dating? Did you ever triple date?"

"The only time we did was at a football game. We were all there with our dates, and at an agreed time during the game, we three girls headed for the rest room. When we got back to our dates, we each had switched places. Since we had worn different clothes and had different hair styles, our dates all looked confused. Two of the guys got a kick out of it. One guy evidently felt threatened, and he got ticked off. He was my date, and he never asked me out again."

As they drove by Gartner Plaza, Ted said, "When I was in Quantico, I used to dream about Colonial Café's chocolate peanut butter ice cream."

"Why don't we stop at Colonial and get some. I like that flavor, too."

They ordered two quarts of the hand-packed ice cream and headed for home. After they ran the gauntlet of more media people outside her town house, Ted did his usual routine safety check on the main floor and down the basement before Fiona could go beyond the kitchen.

After changing into comfortable clothes, they spooned the ice cream into bowls, and Fiona said, "I told Annie that I had reservations about being in her wedding. That I didn't want anyone to be hurt if someone came after me."

"What did she say?"

"She got very teary and repeated how much she wanted me in her wedding. I introduced her to her future husband, and that means a lot to her. She also said that if Kendrick isn't caught by then, we can always have the ceremony in the Visitor's Center. That's where it would be held if it rained, and the reception will be there, as well. Part of the reason they chose the Carillon was that the guests could be entertained while they waited between the ceremony and the reception. They can tour the tower, go for a stroll along the Riverwalk, or even take a paddle-boat ride at the quarry. And I could stay in the Center."

"Is the place big enough to hold the ceremony inside?"

"Apparently," she responded, as she sat cross-legged on the couch and dug into the ice cream. They looked at each other and smacked their lips after the first spoonful.

"Delicious," Ted said, fervently, as he flipped the TV on to CNN.

A picture of Fiona appeared on the screen and riveted their attention. Ted started to change the channel, but Fiona asked him to wait. "I want to hear what they're saying."

The announcer said, "Fiona Morgan is the only witness left alive of the three girls who testified at Kendrick's trial. Tory Girard was hijacked and shot. Sandy Johnson was strangled in her own home. So far Ralph Kendrick is still at large." The newscaster showed various pictures of what he could look like. She also mentioned the reward money for anyone who aided in his capture.

"Turn it off, please. For a few hours tonight, I forgot about my situation," Fiona said, "But I'm bumping up against reality again." She heaved a big sigh.

Putting his empty bowl on the coffee table, Ted put his arm around her. "Put it out of your mind," he ordered. "Don't give Kendrick any mind-space."

"I try not to, but it's really hard to ignore the possibility of a killer around every corner."

"That's part of my job. Let me do that." Ted turned her toward him and angled his mouth over hers. Their kiss was hot . . . a mating of mouths and a promise of more. They pulled apart and looked in each other's eyes.

"You're trembling," Ted said.

"You do that to me," Fiona smiled.

"You have a smile that could light up Broadway."

"Enough to make you want to break into song?"

"Not hardly. But I like the little smile crinkles at the corners of your eyes."

"I'll say it again. I don't know what I'd do if you weren't here with me."

CHAPTER 33

The next morning, Ted offered to make his special cheese omelet after their workout. He was removing it from the pan when Fiona returned from her shower.

"Hungry?" he asked as she sat down at the table with the perky daisy centerpiece.

"Yeah," she said as she tucked her fork into the eggs. "Delicious! By the way, today's calendar saying was: *Don't sit in a mental mud puddle.* Seems appropriate, especially after my recent mudhole experience! I'm not going to let Kendrick cause me to do that."

"Atta girl." Ted placed a couple strips of bacon on her plate.

As she took a bite of the bacon, Fiona said, "I don't often eat this. Too fattening. I forgot how good it tastes. How did you know to have the omelet ready just in time?"

"I've noticed you usually take fifteen minutes for a shower."

"You really are observant. And how long does it take for me to apply my makeup?"

"Ten minutes, give or take a little."

"I repeat, you are really observant."

"Speaking of that," said Ted as he glanced toward the front window. "The newshounds are gone."

"Doesn't surprise me. I just got a text from a contact that shots were fired at a McDonalds in Downers Grove, and there's a hostage situation. Ben Hamilton is covering it."

"So, our carrion are flying off to better prey."

"Excuse me, they *are* my peers."

"Do you hate missing the excitement of something big?"

"I guess my nose will always twitch at the scent of a story. But I have enough excitement in my life right now."

When Fiona's cell rang, she listened, said okay, and rang off. "That was Mr. Mackay." She put their dishes in the dishwasher. "His plane's been delayed, and he won't be back in time for the staff meeting at one-fifteen today. He asked me to run the meeting."

"Is that a big deal?"

"No, he said the agenda is on his desk. I've done it before. I'd better make sure I get there on time. And I'll have to endure stink-eye looks from Ben Hamilton. The last time I ran a meeting, he said he should have been the one selected. I told him to take it up with Mr. Mackay, not me."

"He's the pretty boy who does the morning show. Right?"

114

"That would be him. He's my cross to bear. At least I don't have to co-anchor with him." She checked her I-Pad. "I need to set up a meeting later today with two women to debate the pros and cons of Naperville now being an Edge City."

"What the hell is an Edge City?" he asked.

"It's a grouping of business, shopping, and entertainment venues outside a bigger city," she replied. "Which also means that we don't have to go into Chicago for our entertainment. Of course if we do, it's only thirty-five minutes away on the express train."

"I've noticed that Potter's and Bar Louie's are more crowded at night."

"And they're not the only ones. Downtown Naperville has become quite a suburban gathering place. I can think of at least fifteen popular night spots alone, let alone all variety of restaurants."

They chatted companionably and shared the newspaper.

CHAPTER 34

A s she left Ted's air conditioned car outside the studio, hot air smacked Fiona in the face like a moistened washcloth, handed out after a meal in a fancy restaurant. She knew the temperature was in the mid-nineties, but the humidity caused a palpable heaviness in the air that made her hair stick to the back of her neck. She'd heard that thunderstorms were in the forecast, and she thought she heard a faint rumble off to the west.

"Oh, good," she said to Ted, "did you hear that thunder? Maybe a little rain will cool us off."

Daphne waved her black-tipped fingernails at them as they entered the TV station. "Mike says we're in for some really bad weather."

"I hope it chases off the humidity," Fiona said. "I wilt in this weather."

"Not me." Daphne flapped her eyelashes at Ted like window shades zipping up and down. "I'm like a jungle flower. I just blossom in the heat."

Fiona rolled her eyes and picked up the folders for the meeting. She saw Mike Brown, the station's head technician, come in, and she introduced him to Ted. A short, wiry guy with a bowlegged gait, Mike wore his standard uniform, battered Nikes, white socks almost up to his knees, tan cargo shorts, and a white T-shirt. Gray frizz edged his bald head, and a gold hoop clutched his right ear. He spoke with a southern drawl and told Ted, "I may talk slow, but I don't think slow."

"I'll remember that," Ted replied.

Ben Hamilton stopped by and said, "Everyone is in the staff room. Where's Mackay?"

"He's delayed and asked me to run the meeting." Fiona said.

"Oh," Ben scowled.

Fiona darted a glance at Ted, and his mouth twitched. "We're on our way," she said.

As they walked down the hall and entered a room with a large bank of plate glass windows on the side facing Chicago Avenue, they saw a flicker of lightning and heard a belt of thunder. They could see that the sky was darkening.

Fiona introduced Ted to several people he hadn't met yet. He made sure she stood in a place safe from a sniper's shot.

"There's a tornado warning for the next hour," Mike reported as he checked his BlackBerry.

"This room isn't the best place for shelter in a storm," Ted said. "Do you have an emergency plan?"

Nobody knew.

"We'd need an inside wall that's away from any windows," Ted said.

"That would be the storage room," Fiona said. "It's in the center of the building. We'd probably have to move some stuff out of the way to fit all of us in."

"Lead the way," Ted said. "I always like to be proactive.

Ted and Fiona, along with several others, removed boxes of toilet paper, paper towels, office supplies, and they wheeled out extra office chairs.

When they returned to the conference room, the wind seemed to be picking up. Fiona saw a Styrofoam cup fly past the window. She opened the meeting, using a flip chart to show scheduling for the next week. At one point her words were interrupted when they heard a crash against the side of the building.

"Must be getting windier," Ted said. "That was a shopping cart that hit your building."

Lightning flashed. The thunder that followed was louder and closer. The sky darkened more by the second. Flyers and plastic bags sailed by the window. A child's beach ball skittered by, two feet off the ground.

"Those are butt-kicking clouds," Mike drawled as he peered out.

When more debris from the parking lot flew by, Daphne said, "It's like a giant leaf blower, whooshing and pushing the stuff ahead of it."

As the meeting progressed, the sky darkened by shades from gray to dark and then to an eerie greenish black. When the wind ripped off the large sign for the strip mall and sent it sailing down the street, Ted said, "It's time to move to the storage room."

In the next second, they heard the strident wail of the tornado siren as it reached its eerie crescendo and wavered back down. No one argued.

"Grab a heavy book or something to protect your head, and get down low in the storage room," Ted instructed. He closed the doors of the conference room as they left it. He also closed the door of the storage room after the last one hurried in.

When Fiona knelt down next to Ted, he reached for her hand. His grip was warm and firm."This is where duck and cover works well," he said.

Fiona's nerves jangled, and it felt as if he was transmitting his steadiness to her where his warm fingers met her clammy hands. Her reporter's brain registered that this was not the kind of fear that she'd been living with. Revulsion was mixed up in her fear of Kendrick. Awe was mixed in her fear of nature gone wacko, as objects thudded against the building, and the winds outside sounded like a fast train chugging through Naperville.

"We'll be fine," Ted said, reassuringly. "It should only take a few minutes. These things generally go through quickly. His tone continued, calm and steady. Fiona took a deep breath and felt her body stop quivering. Suddenly the wind sounded louder, like a stampede of cattle right over their heads.

CHAPTER 35

Ted placed himself over Fiona, and she was glad to have his large body shielding hers. In the midst of her terror, she could smell his woodsy aftershave. She also wondered if this is what he felt when he was involved in a dangerous police action.

Next, they heard thuds, and thumps, and the crashing of glass. Ted said "I think the conference room windows went. Good thing we're out of there."

Fiona's throat filled with the metallic taste of fear. After the next thump, Daphne let out a blood curdling scream. "Oh, my God! I have to get out of here!"

"No, you don't," Ted answered calmly. "Your best protection is right here."

All around them noises filled the air. Wild winds. Thunder. More glass smashing. A thud as something heavy hit the side of the building. Next, with a wrenching roar, the winds tore off part of the north half of the TV station roof. Without a roof for protection, rain pelted all of them. Daphne continued to scream.

Someone yelled, "Put a sock in it, Daphne!"

She yelled even louder.

Fiona clenched her teeth together so she wouldn't scream like Daphne.

Just when she didn't think the noise outside could get any louder, the wind lessened. People bobbed their heads up and started breathing easier. Even Daphne was quiet.

Ted said, "I think we've seen the worst of it." He pulled back from his crouched position over Fiona. "I'm going to check out the situation."

"I'm coming with you," she replied. "I'd feel safer right behind you."

They opened the door from the storage room and crossed the hall to the conference room. As he opened the door, Fiona grabbed Ted's arm. "Look! There's a tree branch on the conference table, and you were right. The windows are gone!"

Shards of broken glass crunched under their feet, as they rushed to the gaping window and looked out. Rubble littered Chicago Avenue. A huge uprooted tree covered all four lanes of traffic. Downed wires sputtered like crazy Fourth of July sparklers.

"The roof's damaged at that elementary school across the street. Are kids still in school at this time of day?" Ted asked.

Fiona checked her watch. It was one fifty. "Yes! Dear God! Yes, they are! School doesn't let out until three o'clock."

"I've had some paramedic training. I need to get over there pronto." He gave her a quick glance. "You should be safe here now. But those kids might need urgent help."

"I wouldn't have it any other way, but I'm right behind you."

Ted gestured to the others who clustered behind them. "The school personnel across the street may need some help. I need volunteers who can follow directions. If children have been injured, and the place is unstable, you could do more harm than good."

Mike Brown and Charlie Hunt offered to come. Ben Hamilton said, "I wouldn't want to hurt someone. I'll broadcast." He signaled his cameraman, a droopy, large-nosed man.

Ted alerted Tremayne about the damaged school, and he and Fiona took off running, weaving in and out through rubble and abandoned cars on Chicago Avenue, and skirting the downed wires. It was unnaturally silent. No traffic moved on the street. No birds twittered. As they neared the school, they could see that parts of the right side of the school's roof was gone, and they could hear the terrible screams and shouts of frantic children.

They ran even faster. On the sidewalk leading to the school, they found a young girl with blond hair, about ten. She had a huge gash in her head, and her brown eyes were lifeless. Ted quickly checked for a pulse and shook his head. A few feet from the girl, they spied a woman, also dead, whose arms were outstretched toward the child.

Ted motioned the others to follow him toward the screaming inside. They ran through an outer classroom that was devastated. When they reached an inner wall, Ted climbed over five feet of rubble from a partially buckled wall to get into the school. Charlie gave Fiona a knee up, and Ted pulled her in.

CHAPTER 36

Fiona's eyes flared wide as she saw the scene of devastation. Children moaned and cried and whimpered. Some screamed hysterically. They were trapped under all kinds of rubble, including tables, concrete blocks, chairs, school desks, even a neon sign.

A large cabinet teetered on top of an adult, presumably a teacher, who was on her stomach over children who were crying and struggling to get out from her dead weight. Mike and Charlie removed the cabinet. Ted checked the woman. She was dead. He and Fiona gently moved her to release the children beneath her. They appeared uninjured. Another woman was unconscious nearby.

Ted's eyes swept the area, and he looked toward part of the roof that was still there, which was creaking ominously."We need to get all ambulatory kids out quickly, before the rest of that roof goes."

"We also need to set up a triage. Critical cases here," he pointed, "Moderate injuries here." Another point. "Send those who have only bumps and bruises over by the wall where we came in. Remove items such as school desks and concrete blocks. Don't move any large object or unstable pile of rubble without checking with me. They may be like pick-up sticks. Remove one, and the rest may topple. In some cases the rubble may be providing a tourniquet of sorts. We don't want to move them and then lose them. If anyone is bleeding profusely, call me." He looked up at the damaged roof which creaked above them. "We need to work quickly. That roof is very unstable."

A woman yelled from an inside wall where there was an opening up near the ceiling, "Can anyone hear me? I'm the principal. I've called 911. Kindergarten through second grade are okay. How about the children in there?"

"We have a serious situation here," Ted responded. "Send rescue workers to the playground side on the east side of the building."

"Right away," she replied.

"Get all children moved out of the school. The building may be unstable," Ted said.

"We're doing that," she answered.

Just then Ben and his cameraman, Phil, clambered into the area.

"Get outside," Ted said, "unless you're helping."

"You can't tell me what to do," Ben snapped.

Ted glared, not wasting any more time on Ben. When he spotted a boy trying to pull a shard from a mirror out of his leg, he yelled, "Don't do that!" but it was too late. Blood spurted from the boy's thigh. As he took off his belt, Ted called, "Fiona, can you monitor a tourniquet?"

"Just tell me what to do."

He showed her how tight to make the tourniquet. "Hopefully the paramedics will arrive before we need to loosen it. Call me if you see any change."

"What's your name?" Fiona asked the boy with the suffering eyes.

"Danny," he whispered through dry lips.

"Well, Danny, we're here to take care of you until the paramedics get here. You're very brave, and the storm is over."

Fiona's nose twitched at the smells. Blood. Urine. Sweat. Dust. So much dust! It clogged her nose and made her eyes water. While she held the tourniquet, she saw Ted, Mike, and Charlie remove a variety of objects covering the children. Ted directed them to the far corner of the room where a large oak teacher desk covered several children. A bicycle was lodged and crushed under the desk. After they carefully removed the items, two children walked away unscathed. Three more had serious injuries. Ted then directed the three men to clear a path in the rubble, so walking children could be moved into a safe area.

As Ted and Charlie tried to get a refrigerator off children, Ted yelled at Hamilton to help.

Ben shouted, "I'm here to report, not save people."

Ted yelled, "*Put the damned mike down and get over here now!* And get your cameraman over here, too!"

Something in Ted's tone got through to Ben. He and his cameraman pitched in.

With the extra help, they were able to remove the refrigerator. Ted quickly checked the children. Three were injured, but not critically.

A woman crawled over the wall where they had entered the school. "I'm the school health tech. Where can I help? The woman had a gash in her arm and one on her forehead. Ted pointed to Fiona and the tourniquet.

Fiona went back to digging out children from under school desks and rubble. At a nod from Ted, Fiona and Charlie lifted another bike off two unconscious girls. Fiona saw Ted move a bookcase off four children in the corner. Two children walked away scared, but only scraped. One had a broken leg. One had a nasty head wound. All the children were covered with dust from concrete chunks and dust from the swirling winds of the tornado.

A young boy with curly hair said, "I think my friend, Pat, is under that stuff in the corner." He pointed to a pile of rubble mixed with school desks.

Ted said, "Thanks, kid, and shot over to the area.

Everyone's head snapped up when the sound of part of the ceiling collapsing echoed through the room "Hey Mike, Fiona, Charlie. I need to tell you that his ceiling could collapse at any time. I can't guarantee your safety. You may want to leave while you can."

"Not while kids are still trapped," Fiona said. "I stay."

Mike and Charlie nodded in agreement.

Ben and his cameraman disappeared back outside.

A little girl sobbed, "The books. The books came flying at us and hurting us."

"We need to get as many children out of here as possible before the rest of the roof goes," Ted said. "Charlie, get outside the place where we came in, so you can help them out. Fiona, get the children in a line, and help them get up to Charlie."

Fiona found a chair to place near the opening. Using it, she could boost the children out to Charlie. There was still so much crying and moaning that she had to shout to be heard. Using the tune "*Row, Row, Row your Boat*," she got a few to sing with her.

"Move, Move, Move your Legs,
Quickly, Where She Guides.
Quick-a-ly, Quick-a-ly, Quick-a-ly, Quick-a-ly.
We'll be Soon Outside."

Within a minute, other children joined in singing and formed a line to leave the area. The whole atmosphere in the area became more positive. When Ted looked over and gave her a thumbs up, Fiona beamed as she kept on singing.

CHAPTER 37

Before long, Fiona's arms ached almost to the point of numbness, but she worked tirelessly; it felt as if she'd been lifting children for hours. Some scrambled up like little monkeys. Others were like dead weights. Some needed careful handling because of injuries.

Dust clogged her nose. Grit filled her mouth. She kept the children singing and moving out, but her throat kept getting croakier. Just when she didn't think she could lift another child, she heard the welcome sound of a siren, no, lots of sirens. Getting louder, too.

Children clapped and screamed when they heard the rescue vehicles screech to a halt outside. As paramedics rushed to the opening in the wall, Fiona could hear Ben ask, "What took you so long to get here?"

One paramedic said tersely, "Blocked roads."

"Move out of our way!" ordered another. "Where's Ted Collier?"

"He's inside here," Fiona shouted through the opening.

"What do you have?" the paramedic asked, climbing over the rubble and into the school.

"We have an unstable roof," Ted said. "We've evacuated as many as we could. We have twelve critical." He pointed to their location. "A femoral artery needs immediate attention." He pointed to Danny.

He indicated where the moderate injuries were, and said the minor injuries were mostly outside.

"Three boys are still trapped under debris in the far left corner. We couldn't touch the pile for fear it would collapse," Ted indicated the location . . .

After he briefed the rescue workers, Ted said, "Now that you pros are here, we'll get out of your way." He signaled to Fiona, Charlie, and Mike.

The adrenalin surge that had kept Fiona working tirelessly fizzled out as she and Ted plodded back across Chicago Avenue to the TV station. She felt bone weary. Her throat was still full of grit, and her eyes stung. She shoved her dirty hair back off her face and checked her watch. The tornado had plowed through at one forty. It was now only two twenty. It had felt like a lifetime working in the rubble.

On Chicago Avenue a city crew was already repairing downed wires. Another crew was sawing the huge tree blocking the road. Apart from the sounds of the saws, the usually busy street seemed weird without traffic noise. Detritus littered the area . . . a bike in a tree, garbage cans, overturned shopping carts.

When they got to the station, Fiona saw that other than partial damage to the roof and the conference room, and some rain damage to objects in the storage room, all major equipment was okay. They'd had a power outage for fifteen minutes, but the generator took over, and the afternoon exercise program was being aired as scheduled.

A wide-smiling Ben Hamilton grabbed her arm when he saw her. "I have my uncle's authority to pre-empt your newscast at five," he said.

"Why?" she asked tiredly.

"I told him about my footage. This is my big chance!" he exclaimed. "Of course, I'll turn to you at one point. You can give statistics, number of children enrolled at the school. That kind of stuff."

"Whatever," Fiona said as she stumbled toward the bathroom.

Ted grabbed her arm. "You're going to let him do that?"

"It's called nepotism," she replied. "His uncle owns the station."

Fiona grabbed the change of clothes she always kept at the station, black slacks and a black silk top. When she saw herself in the mirror of the station's small bathroom, she shook her head. She looked pretty much like she did coming out of the mud hole the other day. She thanked God for the small shower stall in the bathroom. She used a wad of paper towels to clean her face, arms, and hands before she even got under the water. In the shower, Fiona scrubbed to remove the grime, and she cried for the children who were hurt, as well as for their families waiting in fear to find out if their children were safe. She cried for the dead child and teachers. When she dried herself off, she felt much better.

She realized that if the tornado had veered just a little more south, the station would have been demolished, and people would have been digging her out of the rubble. She sent up a prayer of thanks. She wondered how the principal was doing. Getting every child reunited with their parents would be a logistical nightmare. Every family would have a tornado story after today. Most would have happy endings.

When she left the shower, she didn't feel like a new woman, but at least she was a clean one. The only thing she could do with her hair was put it into a high ponytail. It hurt to lift her arms to do that. Ted was waiting for her when she emerged from the bathroom. He decided to use the shower as well even though he'd have to put his dirty clothes back on. A wilted Daphne came over and apologized for screaming so much.

Fiona had precious little time to prepare for the broadcast at five, but she set to work at her computer and Googled information on the school, its enrollment, name of the principal, etc. She also looked up information on recent tornados in the area. She jotted notes on what she had seen and focused on what she'd cover. Soon it was showtime.

Ted and Fiona stood by as Ben opened the newscast. He was bursting with importance.

"My name is Ben Hamilton, Channel NKTV newsman. Instead of regular programming, the next half hour will deal entirely with the vicious tornado that slammed through Naperville, cutting a swath along Chicago Avenue from Loomis Street to Route 53.

"The Channel NKTV station is located on the south side of Chicago Avenue directly across the street from the Susan B. Anthony Elementary School which was badly hit by today's tornado. Ted Collier, former Naperville police officer was visiting the NKTV studio when the storm hit. He put himself in harm's way when he led members of Channel NKTV's staff to save the lives of children trapped in the rubble of their school where walls had collapsed and part of the roof was torn off. Our local hero provided help at the school until emergency crews could get there.

Fiona could see a muscle twitch in Ted's jaw, and his tan face turned a dark red, a good indication to her that he was seething.

Ben continued, "Ted is in the studio right now. Let me introduce him."

Ted shook his head vehemently.

Ben kept prodding, "Don't be shy. We're all friends here." He walked over and shoved the mike under Ted's nose.

Ted finally took the mike. "I'm not shy, and I'm not a hero. I happened to be across the street when the school was damaged, and I have the training necessary for this type of rescue. Real heroes are the policemen and firemen who overcame downed power lines and trees blocking roads to get to the school as quickly as they could. Real heroes are the teachers who covered children with their own bodies when the tornado hit. Or the health technician who managed a tourniquet on a boy's leg even though she was injured herself.

"Real heroes are the three members of Channel NKTV, Fiona Morgan, Mike Brown, and Charlie Hunt, who, under dangerous and unstable conditions, worked swiftly and efficiently under my direction until the rescue units arrived." He thrust the mike at Ben and walked to the back of the room.

Ben's demeanor was sober, but he could not contain the excitement in his voice as he said, "The following scenes were recorded minutes after the tornado passed through. Some scenes are graphic, and viewer discretion is advised."

The cameras rolled. The initial scene showed the devastation, the chaos, and the pitiful screaming of the children. From that point on, Fiona could not believe that Hamilton could be so crass, or that he had not edited his tape. Footage showed Ted and Mike grunting and straining to get the refrigerator off the children. It showed Ted yelling at Hamilton to help. It showed Ben's response, "I'm here to report, not save people."

It showed Ted yelling at him and the cameraman.

Next, it showed Ben telling a child to get out of his way, so he could get close to Ted and Mike as they removed debris off another child. It showed Fiona lifting children over the rubble, so she could assist each one out to Charlie. Fiona could hear the *Row, Row Your Boat* song. Fiona saw film of a husky paramedic

Karen J. Gallahue

telling Ben to get out of their way. When Ben didn't move, the rescue worker put his huge hands on the reporter and lifted him bodily and placed him to the side.

Fiona looked over at her boss. His face showed his disbelief and rage. After further footage, more rescue people arrived. Ben handed the mike to Fiona for a few words.

She said, "The hearts and prayers of the staff at Channel NKTV go out to the children who were frightened and hurt during the five minutes of fury that was today's tornado, and to their families who spent agonizing time waiting to hear if their children were all safe. We also extend our sympathy to the families of the ten year old girl who bolted from the safe area, and to the teacher who tried to save her. Both were killed. The teacher's name has been released. She is Nancy Alslip, and she has taught third grade in District 203 for ten years. Another teacher was also killed as she covered children with her body when the storm passed through. Her name has not yet been released. No other children were killed.

"The Susan B. Anthony School has an enrollment of three hundred seventy-five students. At program time, all kindergarten, and first and second grade children were safe. Fifth graders who were trapped in their classroom only suffered minor injuries. The third and fourth grade areas were hit the hardest, and several students were injured. School officials are trying to reunite children with their families at either the school or the Emergency Room at Edward Hospital."

Fiona concluded her broadcast with information about tornadoes. When she finished, Ben took the mike and asked, "Is it true that Ted Collier is your boy friend as well as your twenty—four hour bodyguard?" He shoved the mike back in her face.

Fiona's eyes flashed, but she answered coolly. "That's a personal question, unrelated to the event." She shot the mike back to him. When the program ended, Gordon Mackay roared, "You're fired, Hamilton! Pack up your stuff and get out of here, and take your cameraman with you!"

CHAPTER 38

Ben, flushed with elation over the program, couldn't believe Gordon's words. He was totally shocked and completely oblivious to his misconduct.

"What? Why? What did she say about me?" he asked, pointing to Fiona. "I gave her boy friend credit."

"This has nothing to do with Fiona or Ted," Mackay said. "I've received complaints about you from the school's principal, the fire chief, and the police chief, who by the way, has threatened to arrest you for obstruction of a rescue in progress. You asked inappropriate questions of men who were trying to do their jobs. And this footage shows how little you understand the ethics of broadcast journalism."

"You can't fire me. My uncle won't stand for it," Hamilton blustered, his face suffused with red.

"Your uncle just called. He agrees with me. If you aren't out of here in ten minutes, I'll call the police."

Ben finally got the message. He threw the folders in his hand on the floor and stalked to his office. Mike started clapping. One by one the others joined him. In a few short months, Hamilton had brought dissension and rancor into their studio. No one would miss him.

"It's a good thing you fired him." Ted's lips twitched. "Now I won't have to arrest myself for assaulting him."

"Why did you let Hamilton take over your program?" Mike asked Fiona.

"He said he had the okay from his uncle."

"He lied," Mackay said. "He never talked to his uncle. I've been keeping a file on him. This was the last straw. I'll have Maureen Foster replace him for tomorrow morning's show." He picked up his ringing cell phone and listened. When he hung up, he said, "The roof of the school completely collapsed ten minutes ago. All the children were already out." He looked at Fiona, Ted, Charlie, and Mike. "The rescue workers all thank you."

As Fiona and Ted left the studio, she said, "I don't know about you, but my mouth is as dry as dust in a drought. I can hardly wait to get home and drink a gallon of water."

"A cold beer or two would do the trick for me."

As they traveled back to her place, Fiona couldn't believe that only a few blocks away from Chicago Avenue, the neighborhoods were untouched by the tornado. She turned to Ted. "I'm sorry about Ben. I could tell you were furious about him calling you a hero. He thought you would be happy to have the adulation."

"He thought wrong. He's a human irritant, a first class jerk. The last thing we need is for attention to be drawn to me when I'm trying to protect you. I should have shoved his mike down his puny throat."

"You were amazing, the way you organized others and saved the children. You're pretty impressive."

"I just happened to have the training."

"And you didn't hesitate to use it," she replied. "Thank God for that or Danny could have bled to death."

"Which one was Danny?"

"The one with the nasty femoral artery injury."

"Not all civilians could pitch in and follow directions like you did. Your demeanor calmed the children. I couldn't believe how the screaming stopped when you got the kids singing. That was a stroke of genius."

"Thanks," Fiona beamed. "Were you reminded of being in a tricky cop situation when that tornado went through?"

"A little. Today it was a case of nature gone wild. It's actually easier to deal with that than where it's a case of human beings gone wild, coldly causing devastation and death to other innocent human beings."

"Yeah, I see your point." As they drove from the studio, they could see that the most dramatic damage seemed to be in a straight line down Chicago Avenue. The sidelying streets had wind damage of various levels but no large trees uprooted or roofs off.

"I hope my town house is okay," Fiona said, looking out the window.

When they got to her street, she saw several weeping willow branches down by the pond but nothing horrendous. The sun was back out, and the three water fountains in the pond across the street from her house still shot their water up high as if nothing had happened earlier that afternoon. Her front yard was strewn with twigs and good-sized branches. Flower pots from the front stoop had scattered all their dirt and flowers, and they laid empty and rolling on the grass, but the wrought iron chairs on her the stoop hadn't been budged.

They pulled directly into the garage, bypassing the media people who were back again, and who tried to stop the car.

They entered the house and looked out the back sliding glass door. Fiona's table umbrella was sticking upside down in the middle of a large bush, looking like a reverse lollipop. The safety glass on her round table was shattered. Fortunately, there were no large shards.

Fiona sighed. "I don't think I can move to clean up. I can barely lift my arms."

"You go on in," Ted said. "Give me a half hour. I'll get the front yard back to normal before I take a shower. The back can wait until tomorrow."

"Sounds like a plan. I have a chicken and wild rice casserole in the freezer. I'll pop it into the oven."

When Ted opened the garage door to take out a recycling bags and garbage bags, the members of the press started their questions.

"Tell us about saving the kids."

"No comment. Got work to do. Wanta help?"

Several reporters and photographers shrugged, but a couple young guys came forward "Why not? Have to be here anyway."

"I never worked with a hero before," said a tall, guy with a blond ponytail.

Ted grunted. "I only did what I was trained to do."

"Yeah, but when we heard the roof caved in shortly after you left the school, they said if you hadn't helped when you did, there would have been many more fatalities," a short, skinny frizzy-haired guy said.

Ted grunted again as he lifted a large branch to take out to the curb.

"Can you tell us what project you were involved in when you were at Quantico?"

"No." Ted filled yard bags with small branches and twigs

When they finished raking, Ted shook the hands of the two young men and said, "I'll remember your help."

When he got inside, he grabbed a beer and headed for the shower . . . finally. He could smell something good in the house, and he was really hungry.

By the time he came back to the kitchen, Fiona had set the table, warmed up some crescent rolls and made a salad, to go with the casserole.

After dinner they sat together on the couch. Ted said, "Here, sit in front of me on the couch, between my legs."

"What?"

The side of his mouth twitched. "I noticed that you're rubbing your neck a lot. Thought I'd give you a neck and back rub."

"That would be wonderful. I think I must have strained my neck and shoulders when I helped the children out."

After a few rubs, Fiona said, "I knew you were a man of many talents. I didn't know you were a skillful masseuse as well. I just might start purring."

Ted didn't reply, but used his thumbs and fingers to find all the achy spots.

As Fiona flipped channels on the TV, she saw a picture of herself on the screen and stopped. "Let's see what Ms. Blake has to say tonight."

The broadcaster gave a brief review of the program the night before and said, "Today Fiona Morgan faced a different kind of danger. When a vicious tornado ripped through her hometown of Naperville, Illinois, severely damaging a school, Fiona and her bodyguard were first on the scene. According to reports . . . ," Ms. Blake went on to describe the trapped children and the unstable ceiling. She ended with "According to firefighters and police who were delayed by blocked roads, Ted and Fiona saved many children's lives."

"She didn't mention Mike or Charlie," Fiona said.

Next, Ms. Blake said, "The body count of the five women Kendrick allegedly promised to have killed remains one dead in New York City, one dead in Minneapolis. Of the Morgan triplets, Kailee Hughes has reportedly left the country after someone attempted to shoot her. Regan Daly is also out of the country. Fiona survived an attempted strangulation during a home invasion. As of now, unless Kendrick sends assassins overseas, Fiona remains the focus of his revenge here in the United States.

"Yesterday we showed photos of Ralph Kendrick in various disguises. Police departments in New York, Minneapolis, and Chicago have been deluged by possible sightings. We will show a variety of photos again." She also mentioned reward money.

Fiona shut the TV off and said, "Turn about is fair play. My turn to rub your back."

"That's not necessary."

"Of course not. It's a perk. All of us Trips give great backrubs. We've practiced on each other." She kneaded his neck muscles. "You did a lot of heavy lifting today. Wasn't that something when that brawny fireman manually lifted Ben Hamilton out of the way?"

"I would have applauded if I hadn't had my hands full."

"I keep thinking of the little girl that died. What a nightmare for the parents!"

"I can't imagine it. I thought it was bad to lose an infant. How much worse to lose a child you've raised and loved for ten years."

"I agree. Well, at least we didn't come face to face with any of Kendrick's hired thugs. That was a relief."

Ted felt Fiona's hands stop moving. He turned to look at her and saw that she was literally falling asleep. He moved and said, "It's time for us to go to our respective beds, Tiger." He lifted the nodding Fiona and gently set her on her bed. He was going to kiss her good night, but she already rolled over, fast asleep.

CHAPTER 39

Fiona groaned as she moved her neck from side to side. She tried to get comfortable while she worked at home to prepare for her five o'clock show this afternoon. She ached from head to toe after yesterday's workout, but especially her arms from lifting the children. Her throat still felt dry and scratchy.

She tapped her web of contacts at City Hall, the police department, fire department, and schools as well as the internet for information on yesterday's tornado. She prepared bios for the two teachers who died, all heroines who tried to save their students. She also collected information on Amanda Cutter, the ten year old child who bolted out of the school. According to Fiona's contacts, Amanda's mother said her daughter, who was an only child, had always suffered from a fear of loud noises and storms.

Three children who survived the damage at the school went home to find their houses demolished. Seventy children were treated at the hospital and sent home. Twenty were hospitalized overnight, but were in stable condition.

Fiona also received a call from the principal of the school and the mayor. Both thanked her for her efforts the day before and were planning a ceremony to honor and thank her, Ted, Charlie, Mike, and the police and firemen who came to help.

Ted went outside to clean up the detritus in Fiona's back yard. At least he could work in the back without the media bothering him. As he swept up the smashed glass from the patio table, he thought about Fiona. She was a class act. It was a given that she was beautiful and intelligent, and that there were strong sexual sparks between them. But he was more and more impressed with her character. She was a brave woman with a tender heart.

At the mudhole, she showed a sense of humor, and the ability to laugh at herself. At the school yesterday, she showed grit. Not only did she follow directions. She also showed genuine caring for the injured children. Her soft voice and gentle hands comforted and soothed.

As he plucked the umbrella out of its nest in the bush, he put it back in its holder. It worked! It must have gone into that bush straight as an arrow. He knew Fiona had a feisty side, but he liked that. She had stood toe-to-toe with him after the broadcast following the drive-by shooting.

He felt strongly that he wanted to protect her, not just as a bodyguard. She was a woman who deserved to be cherished. He realized he wanted to be the one to do that. He doubted that she had been with another man since her husband died.

As he raked small twigs and branches and set flower pots back on the patio, the thought of the murders of Tory and Sandy made his blood run cold. He couldn't jeopardize Fiona's safety by mooning over her like a teenager. He needed to focus all the time on protecting her.

Ben Hamilton's idiot question about whether he was Fiona's twenty-four hour body guard could cause a problem. The assassin would now recognize him. There was nothing to do about that. No way was he handing over her protection to another person.

Neither he nor Fiona believed in short term affairs. Fiona needed a long term lover. Him. First he'd better save her life. Next, he'd better marry her. He couldn't push too hard. She'd shy away, and he didn't want to complicate the present situation. She had enough to deal with. He was considered by others as a competent, even brilliant, strategist. He needed to put those talents to use in his personal life. He needed to show her by patience and determination that she could trust a man enough to marry him.

When Kendrick was dead or behind bars, he could court Fiona properly. That was a given. He didn't want to take advantage of such a vulnerable woman. But he hoped they'd have a short engagement. Very short.

He surveyed the back yard. It was back in order again, except for getting a new patio table. He figured it was time to take a shower.

As Fiona tore lettuce and sliced green peppers for a lunch salad, she had a good view of the back of Ted's head as he sat on the couch working at his laptop. A few threads of silver laced his thick black hair. Although it had a definite wave, his hair was tamed into a conservative cut. The set of his shoulders below his well-shaped head gave him a noble look, one you might see on a Grecian bust. His neck set just right on his wide shoulders. It wasn't too long or too stubby. I'm getting fanciful, she thought. Well, at least it's better than thinking about Kendrick's mean-looking eyes.

While they ate lunch, Fiona asked, "Have you ever heard the phrase Fem in Jeop?"

"No. Let me guess. Woman in danger?"

"Right. It refers to thrillers with the leading lady always in constant danger, as in Women in Jeopardy. I like to read those books, but I sure don't like living them one bit."

"As I recall, even thrillers have happy outcomes to satisfy the readers. We have to make sure that happens here."

"Hopefully."

"How did you arrange to get me a seat at your table tonight?" Ted asked.

"I called Bob Kilmer, my original date and explained the situation to him. He was very nice about it."

"You two go out much?"

"No, he's recovering from a divorce. We're just friends."

"From my research on him, his divorce was final a year ago," Ted said.

"Yeah? Well, like I said, we're just friends."

Later, as Ted backed out of the garage, the media horde ascended on the car, shouting questions at Fiona.

"Can you describe your feelings while you rescued children, knowing that the roof could cave in at any time?"

"I was entirely focused on lifting children up and out of there. My fear was that I might not be quick enough."

"Have parents called to thank you for rescuing their child?"

"Many have called the TV station."

"Have you heard that the city of Naperville wants to honor you and Ted?"

"No."

"Is Ted Collier living with you?"

"It's what a bodyguard does."

"Any romance here?"

"He's been hired as my bodyguard. I met him the day I hired him."

"Too much information," Ted muttered, edging Fiona to move on.

CHAPTER 40

"So, according to the schedule, we have dinner, dancing, and a silent auction tonight," Ted said, as he drove to Fiona's townhouse from the TV station after her broadcast.

"Right."

"Do you like social activities like this?"

"In moderation, yeah," she said. "I enjoy dancing. I even enjoy a little schmoozing and trolling for big spenders to buy NKTV commercial time. But I also value my quiet time. Probably because I spend so much time talking during my job hours. What about you?"

"On a scale of one to ten, tonight would probably be a three."

"That bad, huh?"

"I'll survive."

Ted's phone rang, and he took the call. When he hung up, he said, "New York police now suspect that Sandy's killer might be a woman."

"How did they come to that conclusion?"

"They've been re-checking surveillance cameras. Apparently, there are none on individual floors, just at the main lobby elevators and staircases. They were puzzled, because they saw Sandy and her supposed killer get on the elevator to go up, but only he come back down. After studying the way the individual walked, they're wondering if he was actually a woman. They'll send us a copy of the tape."

Later, Fiona took special pains as she prepared for the night. She luxuriated in a scented bubble bath. Apart from the sit-down dinner, she knew that she would be on her feet . . . in three inch heels . . . for most of the evening. She spent a half hour fixing her hair in a "messy bun," the latest hairdo according to her hair stylist. It looked a lot simpler to do than it was, by the time she had teased out a few blond tendrils here and there. Her black, strappy heels set off the black, form-fitting, long dress with a neckline that drifted off one shoulder and had a slit up one leg. As she put the finishing touches on her makeup, she realized that she placed more value on how Ted thought she looked rather than anyone else at the party.

When she finally emerged into the living room, Ted said, "Once again, you clean up nice, Ms. Morgan."

"And you as well, Mr. Collier," she replied. His rented tux looked as if it had been made for him. It fit perfectly, and it enhanced his dark hair and gray eyes.

She was surprised that a rugged man like him could look so good in a tux. For just a second, she thought he'd make a great-looking bridegroom. *Where did that come from?*

"Good thing I didn't insist on the Kevlar vest," he said, eyeing the black dress.

"I can't imagine that Kendrick would pay two hundred fifty a plate and a tux rental to send a hitman to the Gala."

"Unfortunately, we can't assume anything connected with him." Ted escorted her out to the car. They planned to arrive a half hour early so that Ted could satisfy himself that the setup was safe for Fiona.

When they left the town house, Ted heard the car engines starting up and down the street as the media cars and vans prepared to follow them. At times like this, he was really glad they had an attached garage, but backing up was always dicey. He hated when newspeople ran alongside the car, trying to shout questions. When they finally exited the subdivision, he exhaled.

Fiona looked his way and said, "I feel like a mama duck, with all my little ducklings scrambling to keep up with me."

Ted grunted. "I see them as a swarm of mosquitoes trying to get at you. No offense to your profession. But some of those people have no manners and no fear."

"There are always a handful who step over the line," she admitted.

He swore as a media van passed them on the right trying to get a picture of Fiona.

When they reached the Hotel Compagne, Fiona led Ted through the stunning honey colored marble lobby to the huge Main Ballroom where the cocktail party and dinner would take place. Round tables for twelve filled the massive room, with room for a small dance floor in the middle. A podium stood at the far end of the dance floor. Ted estimated that there must be seating for four hundred people. The room smelled like lemon polish and spring flowers. Chandeliers sparkled. Pale pink tablecloths and pastel flower centerpieces signaled that spring was here. A fancy spread.

Along the outer sides of the room Ted saw six long, draped conference tables loaded with items of all kinds, including a number of gift certificates.

"These items range from twenty dollars to five thousand or more," Fiona said.

Ted saw everything from perfume to golf clubs. "So, how does this auction work?"

"Each guest gets a paddle number, and each item has a sheet for bidding. If a guest sees an item he'd like, he writes his paddle number with the amount he wants to offer. Throughout the evening, people will place their bids on the sheet belonging to chosen items. And if someone outbids them, they can make other bids."

"Got it," Ted said. "Is that where you'll stand as you announce the silent auction winners?" He pointed to the far end of the room where a podium stood with its microphone in view.

"Yes, but first they'll have cocktails from seven-thirty until eight-thirty. Then dinner will be served. After dinner, they'll have dancing until eleven. At that point the lights will go back up, and the Silent Auction will be announced."

For the next half hour, Fiona familiarized herself with the items that she would be auctioning while Ted checked out the area and talked to hotel security personnel.

Ted stayed by Fiona's side during the cocktail party before dinner. He noticed that she had kind words for everyone as she moved among the beautifully dressed people. She air-kissed and shook hands with them. He also noted how often she steered the conversational focus to the other person. He figured she must have a phenomenal memory because she remembered attendees' names as well as the names of their children, what sport the kids played, even what college they were attending. As they mingled, Ted saw Detective Tremayne enter the large room.

Ted greeted him. "I'm surprised to see you here. I didn't know detectives could afford these pricey events."

"Only when their mothers are on the steering committee," Tremayne answered smoothly, looking far too cosmopolitan in his perfect-fitting tuxedo for Ted's taste. When Fiona turned to greet Tremayne, Ted saw the other man look at her with frank approval.

"Charisma and class," Tremayne commented. "What a combination. I'll be glad to help protect you tonight. Will you save me the second dance?"

Fiona nodded, and Ted swallowed the reply he wanted to make.

For dinner, they sat at the round tables of twelve. Robert Kilmer, Fiona's original date, sat at her left and Ted at her right. Kilmer didn't bring another date. He was a JFK junior look-alike, a big handsome man.

When he was introduced to Ted, he said, "So you're the one she dumped me for tonight." Ted kept his face impassive. There was nothing platonic in the way Kilmer looked at Fiona. And the look he gave Ted was pure dislike. Fiona was wrong about Kilmer not caring for her in a personal way.

Fiona tapped Ted's arm. "See that woman in the bright green gown at the next table? She's an *Enquirer* reporter. Wonder who and what she paid for the ticket. I thought they were all sold out."

"Money talks," he replied.

After the dinner, various people at the head table made remarks and announcements at the podium where Fiona would stand when she managed the Silent Auction. When they finished, dancing began.

Ted thought he'd be Fiona's partner for the first dance. Wrong. Kilmer beat him to the punch by asking Fiona to dance before Ted even got his mouth open. Unfortunately, Ted couldn't discourage it. He stood to one side, watching over Fiona like a predatory animal watches his next meal. He also kept the entire room under surveillance. It was a slow dance, and he itched to hold her himself. Then, before Kilmer brought her back to the table, Tremayne tapped Fiona for the second dance. It was a tango, and only five or six brave couples stayed out on the floor. Tremayne knew all the moves, and Fiona never missed his cues.

When Ted finally got to dance with her, the glance between them was electric, and he almost purred when he heard her breath hitch as he took her into his arms.

As Fiona joined Ted on the dance floor, she felt as if she was floating; her only anchors to earth were his hands on her. He danced with the same effortless economy of movement that he did everything else. He was so damned smooth! He guided her through the dance moves as assertively as he guided her in their daily activities. She was afraid to look up into his eyes, afraid he'd recognize how much she was beginning to care for him.

She had never felt she could depend on a man before. Her father was like a puff of smoke when she needed him, and Jeb reminded her of the Rock of Gibraltar, which she visited one year. She was shocked to find that the landmark was riddled with holes and caves. Some rock!

Unfortunately, that was the last dance she could enjoy with Ted. She had escorts lined up for the rest of the dances. On the plus side, she was able to land a sizable account for NKTV.

At ten forty-five, hotel employees turned lights back on over the dance floor. People returned to their tables in preparation for the Silent Auction.

Fiona stood at a podium in front of black velvet curtains. Earlier, Ted had checked the area behind the podium and saw a two-foot space behind the curtains. A hotel employee told him it was just dead space, not used for anything. He checked it again and set a chair immediately behind Fiona to the right and sat down, his face impassive. He figured people might wonder what he was doing there. Let them. His job was to watch them and protect Fiona.

When Fiona opened the Silent Auction, she thanked contributors for the donated gifts and prepared to name the winning paddle numbers for the items of the Silent Auction. She started with the smaller items. The first one was a basket of scented goodies from Bed, Bath and Beyond.

Fiona looked so elegant standing there in her wisp of a black dress. Yet Ted knew that with a grin and a Cubs cap, she could look completely different, down to earth, and appealing in a more approachable way. For right now, though, she entertained the audience with light humor and witty remarks as each person claimed his or her prize.

After a half hour of handing out items, Fiona could see people moving to the edge of their seats, and she could feel the level of tension and anticipation rising as she got closer to the larger ticket items. She reached for the next item, a certificate for a year's membership at a pricey local health club.

Without any warning, the lights went out. It was dark as a moonless midnight except for the exit lights. Ted immediately shouted, "Down, Fiona!"

CHAPTER 41

Panic sluiced through Fiona's system. She dropped to the floor and crawled away from the podium on all fours. She heard a thunk and a thud, followed by grunts. She figured it was Ted and someone else fighting. But who? Where did the person come from?

She heard another noise that sounded like a fist hitting bone, probably a face. She could sense movement, with more thuds and grunts. When someone trounced on her foot, she grimaced in pain. She scurried further away, staying low. In the next instant, the podium crashed over and landed where she'd been.

When the lights went out, at first there had been a hush, then murmuring. After the podium fell, someone shouted, "What's going on?"

Another person yelled, "I hear sounds of fighting."

"Turn the damn lights on!" shouted another voice.

A woman's voice shrilled, "Let's get out of here."

Someone shouted, "Open the doors!"

Fiona could hear rustling and sounds of some people bumping into tables. Someone opened an exit door. It didn't help much. Only the exit lights were on in the halls as well. Fiona wondered if Ted needed her help, but she couldn't even see where he was.

Just then the lights snapped back on. Fiona blinked to adjust her eyes. In that moment she saw John Tremayne talking on his cell and hurtling toward her as if he were a football receiver headed toward the goal line.

"Are you all right, Fiona?" he shouted.

"Yes, but Ted . . ." She cut herself off as she saw Ted heave a powerful blow into the belly of a man wearing a ski mask and dressed in maintenance worker coveralls. After a loud "oof," the man crumpled. Ted flipped the person onto his stomach, and secured both the man's hands behind his back. The man continued to struggle like a beached bass. Ted grabbed his gun, and the man stopped moving.

"Got handcuffs?" Ted asked Tremayne.

"Nope, but squads're on the way. I'll take over with him." Tremayne pulled a gun from under his trouser cuff.

"Be careful," Ted cautioned. "He's a tough customer." He pointed to a long, slim knife lying on the floor. "This guy lunged toward Fiona with that in his hand." He looked around quickly to assure himself that Fiona was okay.

Someone in the audience shouted, "Look, there's a knife on the floor!"

"And one man's wearing a ski mask!" a woman squeaked.

At first, Fiona's eyes were shocked and uncomprehending. When she saw the length of the knife, she shuddered. It was a long, ugly murderous-looking object. *That was supposed to kill her!*

"We'll probably find a maintenance man trussed up some place." Ted pulled off the man's ski mask. "Let's see what we have here."

Fiona saw that the alleged attacker was a wiry, tough looking man with a nose that looked broken and bloody, a pimply complexion, a scar down the left side of his face, and a diamond earring in his right ear.

"He had to have an accomplice to douse the lights. Nobody should leave this room," Ted said.

"I agree." Tremayne handed the gun to Ted and went to the fallen podium He pulled out a microphone that actually still worked.

"Ladies and Gentlemen, I'm Lieutenant John Tremayne from the Naperville Police Department. We have had an incident that is now under control. Please be seated immediately in the exact same seats where you sat before. Let us know if someone is missing from your table. Since we now have a crime scene, we ask for your patience as we request that no one leave the room."

General groaning and grumbling erupted, but people moved to sit back down in their chairs. Fiona saw the Enquirer reporter snapping pictures with her cell phone, as well as representatives from the *Naperville Sun*, the *Glancer* magazine, and *Positively Naperville*.

"Are you all right?" Ted asked Fiona.

"I'm a little shook up," she admitted. "How did you know to tell me to drop?"

"I'm glad I was sitting behind you. I could sense his presence as soon as the lights went out. I deflected his upraised arm just as he was bringing it down to stab you. If you hadn't dropped on cue, he might have killed you. He was one tough customer to subdue, though. Solid muscle, and knew every dirty trick in the book. I'd think I had him, but he'd keep coming back."

Fiona couldn't get her mind around the fact that the pimple-faced man actually planned to kill her. It felt surreal. One minute she was handing over a set of golf clubs, and the next minute she was down on her knees and dodging a podium.

Just then three policemen arrived in the ballroom. Tremayne yelled to them to bring him handcuffs. The police officers cuffed the attacker and read him his rights.

Tremayne said to the thug, "I'd suggest you cooperate fully. A room full of people witnessed Collier take you down."

"He was mistaken. I did nothing!" the man muttered.

"Does a maintenance man always wear plastic gloves and a ski mask to a ballroom?" Tremayne asked. "I don't think so."

"You've got the wrong man."

"What job would have you working at midnight in a ballroom with a knife in your hand?" Ted asked.

"I want a lawyer." The man's right eye was puffing up. Blood continued to leak from his nose.

"Of course. I wonder how many maintenance men need lawyers on a Saturday night at this hotel," Tremayne said. "We already know who hired you. Trust me. He'll let you fry." He touched the embroidered name on the coveralls. "Is your name Riley? Or will we find Riley trussed up somewhere. He better not be hurt."

More police surged into the room, as well as hotel security.

"Where's the location of the main switch?" Ted asked.

The hotel manager quickly gave the information.

"We need your men and police officers to find a maintenance man named Riley," Ted said. "He may be hurt, so be quick about it."

"Ted, are you really okay? Fiona asked. "You've got a scrape on your cheekbone. Are you hurt anywhere else?"

"I'm fine. I was worried about you when the podium went over."

"I was far enough away," she replied.

CHAPTER 42

At that moment, Tremayne's mother sailed toward them, looking like a dressed-up battleship in gray lace over silk. Her huge bosom quivered as she lamented the incident that interrupted her party. She bee-lined for her son. "We must continue with the Silent Auction," she said.

"This is a crime scene," Tremayne answered.

"Well, put your tape up at the north end of the room where the podium was," she said reasonably, training her silver lidded eyes on her son, "and let us continue on at the south side of the room with a new podium. The hotel people surely can find another podium." She looked balefully at the overturned one, which had an ugly crack in it. "Then everyone can just stay seated and turn in the opposite direction."

Tremayne looked at Ted, and they nodded their heads.

Tremayne said, "It's doable. My men can take people for questioning into the adjoining conference room, and the guests can return to their seats when they're done. Also, we'll get a handle on who's missing, because some may have left when the lights were out."

"I don't know if Fiona is up to it," Ted said. "She just had an attempt on her life."

"I, uh, well, yes, I'm good to go," Fiona stammered. "It'll take my mind off what just happened here."

"Oh, thank you, Fiona." Mrs. Tremayne smiled and took her hands. "I know you can do it. It would be almost impossible to match the items with the winners . . . and also collect the money . . . if we couldn't finish the program."

"She'll need to give her statement to the police officers before she emcees," Tremayne reminded his mother.

"Oh, very well," she replied. "We'll wait till she's ready."

More police officers entered the room by that time. Within minutes, the police taped off the part of the room around and behind the podium that remained a crime scene. A new podium was placed at the entry area of the room.

Tremayne stepped up to it and said, "We have had an incident here, but everything is under control, and the person involved has been arrested." He explained that the police needed to question each of them for a few minutes in the adjoining conference room while the Silent Auction continued, and he asked for their patience and cooperation.

As he turned to leave the podium, an attendee called out, "Can you tell us what the incident was?"

Another man asked, "Was Fiona Morgan the intended victim?"

"Why do you have to question us?" asked a third person.

"Ladies and Gentlemen, this is not a press conference." Tremayne moved back to the podium. "But I can say this. An unidentified man allegedly attempted to stab Fiona Morgan from a hiding place behind the podium. He may have an accomplice who turned out the lights. You may have important information and not know it. Has anyone asked questions about tonight's event and whether Fiona Morgan would be here? Have you seen something or heard something that now seems suspicious? Please share any pertinent information when you're questioned."

When Tremayne left the podium, a police officer approached him. "We found the maintenance man in his underwear in a storage closet. He's unconscious, probably from a blow to the back of his head. He can't tell us a thing."

After giving a statement to a police officer, Fiona clicked her backbone into place and stepped behind the newly located podium to continue with the Silent Auction. She tried to overcome a feeling of dizziness and rapid, shallow breathing, which, she vaguely remembered, were symptoms of shock.

As she raked her eyes over the crowd, the sweet smells of the table flowers and the variety of expensive colognes and perfumes suddenly clogged her nose. She thought wildly, "I can't do this! *That awful-looking man just tried to kill me . . . cold-bloodedly . . . for a few bucks.*"

She caught the concerned look in Ted's eyes as he sat in the front row, and she gave him a shaky smile. After she took a deep breath, her professional personna stepped in. After adjusting her microphone she reached for the interrupted item, a year's membership at a trendy health center and said, "The interruption is over. Thank you for your patience. We are just getting to some of the biggest prizes of the evening."

Although she was aware of the slight trembling of her lips and the fine tremoring of her hands as she made announcements and handed out items and certificates, she soldiered through. It took awhile to get the momentum going, and she could hear the underlying whispering between people in the audience and murmuring from the police interview area. Eventually, she drew the attention of most of the group, and she continued with the program. After awhile she began to feel a numbness throughout her body, and she had to consciously stiffen her leg muscles to keep a standing position.

The last two items were the big ones, a trip San Francisco for five days, and a Disney cruise. Each winning bidder received a loud round of applause. Finally, the show was over.

As she left the podium, Fiona put one foot after another carefully. She felt like a punchy prize fighter leaving the ring. Ted met her as she left the podium and cupped her elbow more firmly than usual. She leaned into him gratefully to offset her rubbery legs. Ted motioned to Tremayne, and he sent two police officers to help them get outside.

As the three men escorted her through the crowd, Fiona overheard one woman trill excitedly, "I think in the future I'll check ahead to see if Fiona Morgan will be present at my next event. Being near her could prove to be dangerous."

Fiona's cheeks burned. "Did you hear that? Am I going to become a pariah in my own town because of Kendrick?"

"No, you're not," he reassured her. "And you were magnificent at the podium."

She huffed, and they inched their way along the congested hall. Evidently people were too curious to leave. The closer Ted and Fiona got to the lobby, the more press people were in the crowd. "Give us a break, Fiona! Remember, you're one of us," a short reporter who worked for a rival TV station yelled.

"How could a man stab you in front of an audience?" shouted a photographer, snapping Fiona's picture.

"As you can see, I'm happy to report I'm not injured," she replied.

"Are you beginning to feel like Pauline?"

"What?"

"You know, the Perils of Pauline, the oldtime movie."

"Oh, please," Fiona muttered.

"How do you feel now?"

"I'm tired, and my feet are killing me."

People were jammed together in the hotel lobby. Fiona felt as if she and Ted and the two police officers were like four crayons trying to push into an already full box of twenty-four. They nudged forward a few inches at a time, then back a couple. Ted and the police officer shouted "Coming through!" but the noise level was so high, few heard them. Media people were pushing to get into the lobby from outside, which added to the traffic jam.

When they finally made it outside, Fiona took a deep breath of fresh air.

"I gave Tremayne our valet ticket, and he sent someone to get our car, so it should be out here," Ted said as they inched to the curb.

"Thank God," said Fiona as someone stepped on her toes. Her strappy heels provided no protection, and she hopped on her other foot.

Within minutes, Ted maneuvered her into the car. Before he left, he asked one of the policemen to give them a head start from the press cars lined up behind them.

CHAPTER 43

Ted looked over at Fiona and immediately pulled to the right down a side street and stopped the car.

"Is something wrong?" Fiona asked.

Ted unsnapped his seat belt and grazed his knuckle down the side of her face. "Nothing's wrong, Tiger" he murmured. "You looked so forlorn just now. I've been wanting to hold you ever since that dirtbag tried to stab you." He hugged her close. "I'm so sorry for what you had to endure for the past couple hours. And I realized how devastated I'd have been if that guy had hurt you."

"Oh, Ted," she reached up to kiss him. "I don't remember a time when I needed a hug like I do right now. Foiling these assassins is like sewing buttons on a balloon. The job never gets done."

As headlights loomed behind them, Ted reluctantly let Fiona go. "It didn't take the media long to find us. We'd better head for your house." He straightened and pulled back onto the street. They drove in silence for awhile.

Fiona's stomach growled.

Ted looked over at her. "Are you hungry?"

She nodded her head.

"I can't believe I'm saying this, but can you believe I'm starving?" she asked.

"So am I."

"I shouldn't be after that beautiful dinner, but I was too keyed up to eat much. And at least you got a workout. I didn't."

"Sweetheart, what you were doing would have been a workout for most other people. You did a great job, by the way." He turned to smile at her.

"Thanks. I felt a little wobbly at first, but it got easier. What did you think of John Tremayne's mother?"

"I'd say that the lady is used to getting her own way."

"She sure knew how to make people hop to attention."

"Now I know why John's probably still unmarried. She'd be a forbidding mother-in-law."

"I'm glad we could finish the presentation. It would have been a horrible job to track people down for their checks."

"You said you're hungry. At this hour, our choices are probably fast food only."

They opted for the best in comfort food . . . Big Macs, chocolate shakes and fries. The cavalcade of media followed them right past the takeout window.

When a reporter ran up to the window and asked Fiona what she'd ordered, Ted shook his head.

At the town house, they inched their way toward the garage with media vans and cars ready to pounce on them.

Fiona said, "I want so say a few words before we go in."

Ted shrugged. "Just don't give too much information. If you're going to talk to them, remind them that an assassin could pose as one of their group. If they see someone they don't recognize, ask a cop to check the person out."

Fiona passed on the message.

One of the reporters called out. "We'll put it on the air that we're monitoring our group. That might deter someone from even thinking of it."

Fiona thanked them. When they finally got inside the town house, Ted took his dinner jacket and tie off. Fiona removed her heels and wriggled her toes gratefully. They both dug into the food.

"So what do you think about the guy with the knife?" Fiona asked, taking a sip of her chocolate shake. "Will he implicate Kendrick? Give us info about him?"

"Hard to tell. But he can't explain away why his coveralls bear the name Riley, the man he attacked and beat unconscious."

"How did he know that I was going to be there tonight? He must have spent time at the hotel to know where I'd be standing and when."

"Probably he's been checking your schedule. A question here. An overheard conversation there. He could easily have contacted one of the planners. His questions would have been carefully worded, like he was a big fan of yours."

"I wonder if the police will find his accomplice. Someone had to turn out the lights. And what about the Enquirer reporter snagging a ticket to the party and sitting so close to us?"

"Nothing surprises me."

After they tossed the remains of their impromptu meal into the trash, Fiona said, "I could barely move before. Now I seem to have a new burst of energy."

"I was hoping so. I have a request to make. I only had one dance with you tonight. I'd like one more while you're still wearing that great black dress."

"With pleasure if I don't have to put those heels back on." She was surprised at his request and secretly delighted.

Ted went to Fiona's stereo and fiddled around till he found *Strangers in the Night*, the oldie they had danced to at the Gala. He dimmed a few lights and folded back the area rug to give them space on the hardwood floor.

When he took her in his arms, Fiona forgot all the events of that evening and concentrated on his presence. He held her lightly, and they moved in harmony to the haunting strains of the music.

When the song ended, Fiona said, "M-m-m. More."

"I was hoping you'd say that."

Ted selected a few more songs. His arm went further around her waist, and she placed her arms around his neck. They danced for several minutes.

Eventually, they just stood together as one, rocking and moving only a little. Somehow, imperceptibly, it seemed, their bodies inched closer.

When Fiona felt the evidence of Ted's arousal, she tried to pull back. "He's going to want to go all the way," she thought.

"No, I'm not," Ted said as he reeled her back in.

"What? Are you reading my mind?"

"No, I'm not. But I'm guessing you're thinking I want to have sex with you. You'd be right. I obviously do. But I'm not some randy adolescent who needs instant gratification. I told you I wouldn't rush you."

"The thing is, I have some sexual issues." Her cheeks reddened.

"I figured that," he replied.

"How?"

"I'm guessing Jeb's behavior made you doubt yourself as a sexual partner."

Fiona let out a breath with a whoosh. "Wow, you don't pull any punches." She twisted the strands of her hair. "You're right. I never again want to suffer the humiliation of being not good enough in that area."

"I'm no behavior specialist, but over the years I've figured the skirt-chasing adulterers lack something. And just might be poor lovers themselves."

"Kailee tried to tell me that."

"It's time you believed your sister. And I have a plan to help you with that."

"You sound like a battle strategist."

"Maybe so. I think of it more like an important objective to be reached. Taking advantage of a woman terrified for her life is not in my plan. Courting you is. I want to win your trust. And your heart."

All the while they talked, they had moved imperceptibly to the music in the background which now ended. Keeping one arm securely around her waist, Ted used his other hand to cradle her head. And he kissed her. It started as a delicate brushing of his lips against hers. It ended as a searching, probing emotional explosion for both of them.

Ted looked down at her with lowered eyelids. "Between us, we have enough electricity to light up a casino. It won't be much longer," he whispered. "Kendrick will be dead or back behind bars again. I'll be able to prove to you what a sexy temptress you are."

"The only man I was ever with was Jeb, and he never made me feel the way you do. You've tapped into feelings I never knew I had."

"We're both in unfamiliar territory. I was just a boy when I married Lois. I do know you take my breath away. I know I'm into commitment. And I hope you're thinking in that direction. But we'll just take it one step at a time."

Karen J. Gallahue

Later, as she tried to fall asleep, Fiona's thoughts kept drifting to Ted. He certainly made her pulse beat faster. And she continued to be impressed with him as a human being. Today she saw him again as a born leader, a man who was used to putting his life on the line for others, a man people could depend upon and trust with their lives. She caught herself and realized what she had just thought. A man she could trust. For the first time since Jeb died, she found a man she could trust. She knew this to the depth of her soul. *It scared her witless.*

CHAPTER 44

Fiona groaned as she woke up and rolled over the next morning. Her body ached from her neck down to the arches of her feet. Probably still some residual aches from lifting the children during the tornado. Probably some from wearing those three inch heels last night. Probably some from holding her shoulders so stiffly after the guy tried to stab her, and she tried to keep from breaking down.

She hadn't been able to relax until she got home and Ted took her in his arms. And danced with her. And kissed her. Maybe it was the memory of those kisses. Maybe it was the wine, but when she crawled in bed, she had a smile on her face, and she completely blocked out the terror of last night's attempted stabbing. Now, cold dawn brought the reality of last night's incident back in chilling force. *That man had tried to stab her in the back! She could have been dead this morning or hospitalized with terrible injuries!* She remembered the look of the knife lying on the floor of the Hotel Compagne. The blade looked almost a foot long and serrated. She shivered and checked the time. Only five o'clock.

She stumbled to the Keurig in the kitchen and picked out her strongest brew, Dark Silk, trying to be quiet so she wouldn't wake Ted. In seconds her coffee was ready, and the smell alone revived her. She leaned against the counter as she drank. Thank God she didn't have a very taxing schedule today. Her brain knew that a workout on the treadmill would probably make her feel better. Her body rebelled.

She remembered that today Ted needed to go to Plainfield to take care of paper work and other preliminaries for his new job as Chief of Police, and John Tremayne would be her bodyguard for part of the day. Ted had only seven more days to be her protector. It scared her to think that Kendrick might still be out there. Still hounding her. Still wanting her dead. She hated the idea of hiring someone else for a bodyguard. She wanted Ted. Only Ted.

When he joined her in the kitchen, she clasped her arms around his neck. "Last night dancing with you and kissing you was a wonderful reprieve. Thank you so much."

He tugged her closer. "It wasn't a reprieve. It was a beginning." He embraced her and held her in the circle of his arms.

She nestled closer. "It was like a refreshing oasis in a desert. I could enjoy it, but I still have to get across the desert. And today I'm really scared. Kendrick just won't quit and leave the country, will he?"

"We can't count on that. But every move he makes brings law enforcement officers closer to him. We can assume he's in the Chicagoland area now.

Tremayne texted me early this morning. Yesterday's stabber has an address in Chicago. The airplane with the sign that was rented is from Palatine. The drive-by hoods were from Chicago. The guy that tried to strangle you that first night is also from Chicago.

"Kendrick has to have an accomplice to arrange for his hits. Thanks to the reward money, that person gets more vulnerable every time he makes a move. I don't know what Kendrick is paying for his help, but someone, somewhere may decide it would be simpler to just turn the accomplice in and collect the reward. That could happen. Once Kendrick's accomplice is out of the picture, Kendrick'll be in deep shit. He'll have to crawl out of his hole, which is probably some big hotel with room service. The Chicago and suburban police have been systematically checking hotels and will continue to do so."

"Isn't that like looking for a needle in a haystack with daily movement in and out of those places?"

"Sometimes that's what police work is all about, those needles in the haystacks." Ted replied regretfully as he released her from his embrace. "Right now, we need to get going on our workouts."

His phone rang, and when he hung up, he said, "That was Tremayne. We talked about coverage for the Civil War Reenactment tomorrow. The police chief is assigning extra policemen to the activity since the crowds will be so large. We'll assign each one an area of responsibility."

"What does that mean?"

"It's a simple thing, really. Each officer is assigned a specific area to cover. It's a procedure to have in place so that we can eliminate any crossfire issues."

Later, as Fiona fast-walked on the treadmill, her mind raced right along with her feet. Thoughts flew through her mind like a tag team at a relay race. As soon as she put one down, another took its place. What am I doing? Day after day I wonder if I'll die before I go to bed. I have a stiff neck from looking over my shoulder. Every time someone bumps into me, I over-react. I hate to go out in a crowd today.

I sure can't go back to bed and hide there. Kendrick's goon already saw to it that I couldn't be safe in my own bed, either. When is this going to end? When will Kendrick run out of money to pay killers? Will I ever be able to go for a run outside again? I'm mostly afraid that time is running out for Ted to protect me. His new job starts in seven days. What will I do without him? I could go hide somewhere like Kailee, but who can guarantee I'd be safe when I came back. I don't want to quit my job.

She realized that she was finished with her run. But even when she walked slowly to cool down, her mind still kept darting from one scary thought to another. She couldn't seem to turn them off.

When Fiona got off the treadmill, Ted could see that she was upset by the set of her shoulders and the straight line of her mouth. "Something the matter?" he asked.

"The matter?" she shrilled. "The matter? Of course, something's the matter! Once again, someone is probably out there waiting to kill me today. That's what's the matter! I'm so damned vulnerable it makes me furious."

Ted placed both hands on her heaving shoulders.

Fiona jumped sideways like a spooked cat. "I feel as if a giant target is attached to my back. I have a stiff neck from swiveling my head to see if it's safe behind me. I can't even go hide under the covers and be safe. A killer has already defiled my bedroom, my sanctuary. I feel like I'm brittle, and that I'm going lose it and start screaming over nothing. If I survive this . . ."

Ted interrupted her. "You will survive this You'll overcome your fear. Put your trust in God first. Then trust in my skills. Trust yourself. You're in good shape, and you can defend yourself better than most women I know. People are rallying around you."

"My nerves are jangling like keys on a key ring, and I want to smash everything in sight. I wish I had a punching bag."

"Everyone's allowed to have a meltdown, and you do have a punching bag." Ted grabbed a pillow off the couch in the corner. "Pretend I'm Kendrick. Give me your best shot," he said, holding the pillow over his middle.

"I'll feel stupid."

"Stupid is okay."

"Are you afraid I'll hurt you?" she asked, pointing to the pillow.

"No, I don't want you to hurt your hands."

"Hmph!" She drew her right arm back and punched at his chest, once, twice, three times.

"Forget the right moves. Just keep punching."

Using both left and right fists, she pummeled Ted till sweat was running down her face. When she finally stopped, she collapsed against his chest. "What's the matter with me? I was in a decent mood earlier today. Then I let a few thoughts about Kendrick get into my mind. The next thing I'm a blithering idiot! Am I losing it? Every morning I wake up, I hope that we'll catch Kendrick before you have to take over your new job. Oh God, I'm sorry I'm such a mess!"

"You want to be safe, and that's a very real human need. I'm watching the calendar, too. We'll work out something. When I go to Plainfield today, I plan to ask if the present chief of police can delay his retirement for another week before I start there. That will give me two weeks."

CHAPTER 45

When John Tremayne and Fiona left her second appointment of the day, John made a couple swift moves and neatly evaded the press. Fiona was relieved she didn't have to fend off questions as they headed for Hugo's Frog Bar to eat. Hugo's was a white tablecloth kind of restaurant with dark floors and woodwork, but the atmosphere was casual and prices were reasonable. Both ordered the grilled tilapia, served with Balsamic rice and green beans.

John entertained Fiona with anecdotes about the Naperville PD, as well as a commentary on the personalities and foibles of Naperville's leaders. He kept her laughing, and for a short while she forgot about Kendrick and his machinations.

At one point, Fiona asked, "How did you decide to become a policeman, John?"

"Or, why didn't I go into the family business?" John's family owned a national bakery chain with headquarters located in Naperville.

"Well, I did wonder about that, too."

"I had an uncle, on my mother's side who was a cop. I'd listen to him for hours, talking about catching the bad guys. I finished college with a business degree to please my family. Then I pleased myself by going to the Police Academy. I thought I was rebelling, but I found I genuinely liked police work. I even did undercover work for awhile. Had long hair and a gold ear ring. Got tired of that after awhile, and eventually made detective."

"Have you ever married?"

"You've met my mother."

"Be serious," she laughed.

"I came close only once. She dumped me."

"I'm sorry."

"Don't be. I like my life. The truth is, I haven't met anyone I wanted to settle down with. I kinda like being the playboy cop."

"Ted has respect for you as a detective. Says you are painstaking about detail, and that you also have good instincts."

"Wish I could come up with some good hunches about Kendrick. I have several contacts in Chicago from my undercover days. But no one has anything for me. Although it seems logical that he's in this area, if not out of the country."

"Ted says he's a risk-taker. And we'll catch him because of that."

"The cops in Chicago are checking every lead. We assume that he may be in Chicago."

When Tremayne and Fiona left the restaurant, the media were conspicuous by their absence. Again, Fiona felt relief, although she figured they'd be waiting for her at home. As they approached her subdivision, John had to pull over twice to allow a fire truck and two squad cars to pass. When they turned onto the street of her subdivision, Fiona saw the fountains splashing away on the right. On the left, she saw a tangle of emergency vehicles press vans, and bystanders in front of her house.

"What's going on?" she asked. Her stomach lurched and her heart jack-hammered in her chest.

"Something at your house," Tremayne said grimly, pulling as close as he could to the scene. They moved out of the car on the run.

"Here comes Fiona," someone shouted. The group of bystanders and press made way for her.

"What happened?" she cried.

"An explosion at your house. A person was killed," a cameraman yelled.

"Who?" Fiona worried about Ted. Or maybe her mom had stopped by with food.

"A paparazzi named Sonya Cerny," Bonnie Day said. Fiona recognized the matronly reporter from her old Chicago station.

Fiona gasped, but felt immediate relief that Ted and her mother were okay. John moved them closer to the house. He tried to shield Fiona when he saw the front entry, but he was too late. Fiona saw the blood, the blown out entry door, and the charred remains on her front stoop. She squeezed her eyes shut, hoping to squeeze out the pitiful sight. When she realized that the smell was burnt flesh, she covered her mouth with her hand, opened her eyes, and ran to the lawn to retch violently.

As she wiped her face, she asked, "Why was she on my front porch?"

"A box of flowers was sitting outside your front door," Bonnie said. "Sonya was curious and wanted to know who they were from. She went up on your stoop. We tried to tell her she was way out of line. We told her not to touch the box. She gave us the finger and pulled the card from the envelope. The thing exploded."

"What? The box of flowers exploded?" Fiona stopped short. "Oh, John, that was supposed to be me," she whispered, grabbing Tremayne's hand, her eyes moving back to her entry.

"Don't look," John said as he ushered her over to the side.

Fiona's neighbor, Nancy Hiller, ran over to her. "Come next door, to my house . . . away from the questions and the stares." Fiona followed her numbly. She needed mouthwash or something to get rid of the taste of vomit in her mouth.

Tremayne signaled to a couple police officers to follow them as well. Fiona heard one of them say to Tremayne. "This just happened. I was just calling you when I saw your car pull in."

"Tell me what you know,"

"According to Mrs. Hiller, a black panel truck stopped about ten o'clock, and a person delivered a long box to Fiona's house. He rang the doorbell, then set the box on the porch. The truck had white letters that said Florist. Mrs. Hiller didn't pay enough attention to the delivery person, just remembered that it was a man dressed in black, wearing a Cubs cap. Someone in the press said they lost you around eleven o'clock and came here. Ms. Cerny tampered with the package at twelve-ten."

"Did you know Ms. Cerny?" Tremayne asked Fiona.

"Not really, though I've seen her around." Fiona reached for her cell phone to call her mother immediately and assure her she was safe.

Barbara said immediately, "If you need a place to stay, I want you to come here."

"I don't know what the situation is, but I'll let you know. I don't want to put you in danger."

"With my friend, Steve, and Ted here, I'll feel plenty safe. Just plan to come here."

CHAPTER 46

Ted loosened his collar and rolled the windows down as he headed back to Naperville. He'd rather sit at a stakeout all day rather than fill out the mountain of forms necessary for his new job. He realized how much he'd missed being with Fiona that day. In a very short time, she had become the most important person in his life. He'd also hated turning her over to Tremayne today. The guy oozed charm, and he was only too happy to take over Fiona's protection detail. Ted decided he'd better let John know that Fiona was off limits. Then he wondered who he thought he was.

After last night, he knew Fiona felt the strength of their connection as well as he did. The faster he could help get Kendrick back behind bars, the better. Then he could concentrate on a relationship with Fiona.

When he saw the commotion in front of Fiona's townhouse and the damage to her front entry, and worst of all, the sheeted remains, his heart clenched. He could feel the muscles of his face twisting in anguish. He parked and ran like a man possessed.

"Oh my God, Fiona, oh no!" he shouted aloud. "No!" He knew what a bomb explosion looked like. He also knew what the smell of charred flesh meant. And he saw a sheet covering something on the front entry. He pushed his way through the crowd of people, oblivious to any words spoken to him. Overcome with emotion, he looked only for Fiona.

When he spotted Tremayne coming out of the neighbor's house, he shot in that direction. "Fiona?" he shouted.

"She's here. She's okay," Tremayne waved at him. "She's been watching for you."

Relief washed through Ted. Just then, Fiona burst past Tremayne and sprinted out of the neighbor's house toward him. Ted raced toward her. When they met, they wrapped their arms around each other. Fiona burrowed her face into his chest. They just held each other and rocked, too filled with emotion to talk and oblivious to the cameras and commotion around them.

As they separated, Ted tenderly pushed a tendril of hair behind her ear and gave her a melting kiss. When they became aware of the crowd cheering and clapping around them, they broke apart, but Ted kept his arm around Fiona's shoulder as he ushered her back into her neighbor's house.

They sat on the living room couch. Ted listened carefully as Tremayne and Fiona's neighbor, Nancy, filled him in.

"First of all, Fiona," Ted patted her hand, "neither John nor I would have ever let you touch that box of flowers, so you never would have died in the explosion. I'm sorry Ms. Cerny was killed, but she chose to over-step the ethical line of propriety even for a paparazzi. And anyone with half a brain should have warned her."

"Apparently they tried," Tremayne said.

"I know who Sonya is," Fiona said. "Or was." Her voice broke. "She was based here in Chicago. She seemed like a reckless, driven woman. What she lacked in brains, she made up for in sheer pushiness." She paused, and tears trickled down her face. "But, oh God, she never deserved such a gruesome death."

"Of course not," Ted said.

"Now that you're here, I'll head back to the crime scene," Tremayne, said, as he went back to Fiona's house.

Nancy offered to make iced tea and went to her kitchen. Ted sat next to Fiona on the couch and circled his arm around her waist. "When I saw the sheet covering Ms. Cerny on your front stoop I felt as if someone pulled my heart right out of my chest," he said. "Inside I was roaring with pain." He squeezed her. "And then I saw you come out the door. A rush of happiness swept over me like I've never experienced. I thanked God you were okay."

Ted ran his hands up and down Fiona's arms and sides. He smoothed her hair and ran his knuckles along the side of her face. "I have this need to touch you, to feel your vitality, and to hang on to you for dear life."

"I would feel the same way if something happened to you." Fiona reached up to cradle his face in her hands.

"One thing I know for sure. We have something special between us. And, I definitely need you in my life."

"Oh, Ted, I need you in my life, too, and it scares me. But, when the chips were down here, you were the one I wanted to see and hold."

"I'm sorry about Ms. Cerny, but I think that Kendrick has narrowed the field of possible assassins. Not many will want to take the job now that so much public awareness and media attention are focused on you."

Fiona turned to Ted. "I need to get back into my house, so I can change for my newscast."

"I'll call Tremayne to see if you can get in yet." Ted reported back to Fiona that John would unlock the sliding glass door in back for her so she could pick up clothes and necessities. But the front area could not be repaired in time for her to sleep there tonight.

"I'd like to go over there," Fiona said. Accompanied by Ted, she scooted out Nancy's back door and reached her sliding glass door in back without reporters seeing them. On the way to her bedroom, she could see that in addition to replacing the front door, there was a hole in the wall, and brick work would have to be replaced. Her foyer was trashed.

Debris was strewn around the living room, including pieces of her white wicker chair from the front entry. But, thankfully, most of her furnishings appeared intact. Both she and Ted quickly gathered clothes and toiletries and took them to Nancy's house where she called her mother back and said Ted and she would arrive after her five o'clock show.

Later as she stepped onto the small platform and seated herself for her broadcast at five, Fiona realized her hands were shaking. She'd been trembling on and off since she saw her front step with Sonya's covered body resting on it. And she could still smell charred flesh. Why was that? Maybe because the sense of smell triggers more memories than any of the other senses. She quickly grabbed a small cologne from her purse and sprayed it lightly at her neck and arms. Ah-h-h, much better. She wondered if today's explosion triggered any of Ted's memories of car crashes during his career as a policeman.

She saw him standing in the small studio, ever alert, but his eyes always came back to her. He steadied her when the going got tough, and just looking at his warrior face helped stabilize her now. She checked out her papers and the teleprompter. When her program started, she was back in control and smiled at her hidden audience.

When she reported on the incident on her front steps, her voice was clear and direct, and she had no hesitations. She breathed a sigh of relief when it was over, though. She and Ted left the studio for her mother's house as quickly as they could.

CHAPTER 47

Barbara Morgan wrapped her arms around her beleaguered daughter and just held her close.

"Mom, when will it end?" Fiona asked.

"Soon, I hope. Please God, it can't be soon enough."

Fiona greeted her mom's friend, Steve Wylie. She was glad her mother had him to rely on, and he had been staying at her mom's house since the news of Kendrick's escape.

"It smells so good in here." Fiona sniffed the odors of lasagna and toasting garlic bread.

"You know me. I always cook and bake when I'm worried." Barbara led them into the kitchen to sit at the table.

"Your mom was really worried about you," Steve said. "We're so glad you're safe."

"Thanks, Steve."

"Can I fix you something to drink?"

"A glass of white wine for me."

Ted opted for a beer.

While they visited, Fiona's phone rang in its Regan tone. She grabbed it and moved out of the kitchen. "Is everything all right, Regan?"

"We're fine. It's you I'm worried about. I just heard someone else got killed in an explosion on your front step. Was that explosion meant for you?"

"Afraid so."

"Are you okay?"

"As in not dead or injured, yes. Oh, Regan," her voice thickened, "when I saw the body on my front stoop, I was so afraid it was Ted or Mom. You know how she stops by to drop off a casserole or a cake. I was frantic!"

"I'm so sorry you had to go through such a traumatic time. You sure you don't want to come here to Spain?"

"How could I be sure Kendrick's thugs wouldn't just follow me? At least here, I can rely on Ted and the Naperville police to keep me safe. And I have a job here. What do I say to Mackay? I'll see you in a week or a year when it's safe?"

"I understand. But you're welcome here any time."

"Thanks. How are the kids?" Fiona changed the subject.

"They're turning into bilingual imps, picking up Spanish faster than I am."

"Give them each a big, smacking kiss for me."

"Stay safe, Fiona. Each time you call, I hope to hear that Kendrick is back in jail."

"Ted thinks we're getting closer to catching him."

"Any normal thug would forget the vendetta and get out of the country."

"He's not normal. He's obsessed with killing all of us. It's more important than his own safety." Fiona sighed.

"On that cheery note, I have to ring off," Regan said. "I have a luncheon appointment."

Fiona hung up the phone and returned to the kitchen.

"I just got a call from Brady. We have more information," Ted said. "Tory Girard's killer has been apprehended in New York City."

"Really? Any chance he can lead us to Kendrick?" she asked, hope shining in her eyes.

"Afraid not. He was a paid assassin who used throw-away phones and went through anonymous channels."

Disappointment sent Fiona's shoulders drooping. She picked up the daisy centerpiece on the kitchen table and set it down again precisely in the middle. "So we're no further ahead than before. How did the police find him?"

"He tried to pawn Tory's antique gold necklace. Evidently, Tory's mother and co-workers figured it was stolen because it wasn't found on or near her body. Pawn brokers across the country had been alerted."

"Did he kill Sandy, too?"

"Wish I could say yes, but he has a water-tight alibi."

"So Kendrick hired two different people. Was Tory's killer hired to kill me and my sisters?"

"He says no, that he was hired for one kill only."

"That sounds so matter of fact, that it's obscene, like one loaf of bread only. This is bad news, isn't it?" Fiona rolled her shoulders to get her muscles to relax.

"Not for Tory Girard's parents. Their daughter's killer will be brought to justice," Ted replied. "But you and your sisters are definitely still in danger. He probably hired two pros with different MO's to kill Tory and Sandy. The hitmen targeting Kailee and you sound more like street thugs. Maybe he used a different contact for the Naperville hits."

"Anything more on Sandy's killer?"

"No," Ted said, "but the police find it suspicious that her new boy friend hasn't come forward to help with the investigation. They're still trying to locate him, but she never mentioned his name to her coworkers."

"Dinner's ready." Mrs. Morgan set the lasagna pan on a trivet in the center of the table. After they finished eating, Ted and Fiona sat around the kitchen table with her mom and Steve drinking coffee.

Out of the blue, Fiona said, "Mom, I need to talk to you about Dad's death. Ted seems to think I'm wrong to blame myself for his suicide."

"Ted would be absolutely right." Barbara raised her eyebrows. "Why would you even think that?"

"I thought he couldn't stand the commotion of me testifying."

"Fiona, depression ran in your father's family. Both Martin's father and his brother committed suicide when they were in their forties."

"Didn't he take medication?"

"Yes, and he often changed medications, trying to get relief."

"I always felt my testifying put him over the edge." Fiona twisted her hair.

"Absolutely not. A project he'd been working on for four years had been canceled shortly before his death. He felt as if the company cut off his arm. He became very despondent. It was not your testimony. He was hardly aware of what was going on about the trial."

"Oh." Fiona moved her coffee cup in a left to right movement. "Weren't you afraid that one of us Trips would inherit the weakness for depression?"

"That would be impossible since Martin was not your biological father." Barbara Morgan sucked in a breath as she caught herself. Her usually cool eyes suddenly flared wide. Flustered, she covered her mouth with her hand.

CHAPTER 48

F iona banged her coffee cup down with a thump. She braced both hands on the table. "What did you just say? He wasn't our father. How can that be?"

Barbara's face twisted, her shoulders slumped, and she whispered, "I can't believe that I blurted that out. The tension over the last few days must be getting to me. I'm so sorry." Fingers trembling, she picked up her coffee cup, but set it down without drinking. "No, he wasn't your biological father, but I never wanted you girls to know that."

"Did our father . . . er . . . I mean Martin. Did Martin know that?" Fiona was relentless.

"Of course he knew it," Barbara shoved her hair away from her face.

Fiona shot to her feet. "Were we adopted?"

"No. I am your biological mother." Barbara heaved a big sigh. "Sit back down and I'll explain this."

Ted interrupted the conversation. "I think Steve and I should give you ladies some privacy." The two men left the room.

"I think I've said too much already," Barbara said. She took Fiona's hands in hers. "Thirty one years ago, I went to my high school reunion in Milwaukee alone. As you know, Martin didn't enjoy that type of thing. I met an old boy friend. We enjoyed talking and reminiscing. We danced, and I'm afraid we drank too much. He escorted me to my hotel room." Barbara squeezed her daughter's hands. "I should have sent him away, but I didn't. I chastised myself the next morning, and we didn't see each other again."

"I can't believe I'm hearing this." Fiona stood back up and paced the kitchen.

"I know. I know. I came home thinking that was the end of it. Several weeks later, when I knew that I was pregnant, I had to tell Martin what happened. He agreed to give my baby his name and to pay all expenses of rearing the child. But he warned me that he didn't know how to act around a child. I told him he wouldn't have to worry. I'd take care of the baby."

"So he just accepted this?" Fiona's jaw dropped.

"Yes, he did. As long as I took care of things. But the day we discovered that I was having triplets, he turned white as a new tube sock, and said, 'What about the noise? You know I have to concentrate on my work, even when I'm at home.'

"I reassured him again. He agreed that as long as his routine wasn't disturbed he could handle it. He also mentioned again that there was plenty of money, and that I should buy whatever I needed, including nannies and household help. Whatever it took so that he was not disturbed."

Barbara took a deep breath and looked at Fiona, who was still walking back and forth in the kitchen. "I hope you don't hate me too much. I made a bad decision, but I was never, ever sorry I got pregnant. Up until then, I had never conceived with Martin, and I wanted children . . . badly."

"I certainly don't hate you, but who is our father?"

"His name was Nathan Scott. He lived in Philadelphia at that time, and I heard through an alumni newsletter that he died in a car accident when you were six years old. He never knew he had daughters."

"All those years when I wished I had a different father, I really did." Fiona sat back down at the table.

"Martin couldn't help being the way he was. He was always off in his head solving some intricate computer problem. He just wasn't plugged into the real world like other people. But he always wanted to provide well for you girls, and you should appreciate that."

"We Trips always felt there was something wrong with us. He never hurt us physically, but being ignored like an insignificant bug is hurtful, too."

"I'm so sorry you felt that way. I see now I should have told all of you sooner. I guess I just hoped it would never come up."

"I wish you had, but at least today, you've taken a huge weight off my shoulders. I really thought Martin's suicide was my fault, because of all the commotion over the trial. And, from the time I was little I hated that he ignored me. I used to act up just to get his attention. But he'd just say 'Take care of this, Barbara.' I remember one time I fell off my bike. He saw me and left me there in a tangle. Said he's send you out to help me. Then he forgot to tell you."

Fiona's mom shook her head. "When I met him, Martin was a handsome, moody, but socially needy man. I was a romantic and an idealist. I thought I'd gently bring him out of his shell after we married. Of course, that didn't happen. How many women have thought they'd change a man after marriage?" She smoothed her placemat. "And, about the time I realized that he was never going to change, I got pregnant with you girls. At that point, my heart was so full of gratitude to him for agreeing to take care of us, nothing else mattered.

"I had no brothers or sisters. I don't know what I would have done if he had wanted a divorce. I would have been a single mom with three babies to raise. I couldn't even work to support you because daycare would have been too expensive. It was much easier to accept Martin's generosity and overlook his quirks and peculiarities. I tried to do what I could to make him comfortable. I orchestrated things so your paths didn't cross with his very much."

"I remember we had nannies."

"Yes, I hired two of them to be with me after you were born, so that none of you would ever lack attention. I also had a cleaning woman and laundress. If one of you got sick, I was always available. I had an ideal situation. I had time to cuddle and care for each of you without the burden of all the laundry, the feeding, etc. You each had your own bedroom . . . your own personal space. Frankly, I was in my glory. I fixed the basement like a little pre-school and sound-proofed it, so you could have friends over even up through your teens, and I wouldn't have to worry about disturbing Martin."

"Do I have other brothers and sisters?" Fiona's lips trembled.

"No, Nathan had no other children."

"Mom, you need to tell Regan and Kailee, too. They felt like I did about his ignoring us. They need to understand him the way I do now."

"I planned to do that, when you all graduated from college. I invited all of you for dinner, and I even had my yearbook and a reunion picture to show you. Then you all came in laughing and bubbling with good spirits, and I just couldn't do it. I put everything away. And, frankly, after that, I just thought I'd let things be. But now that you know, I'll certainly have to tell your sisters. Will your sisters accept it the way you do?"

"I think so. We all felt guilty that we didn't care for him more when he was alive, and, even more so, when he died. Kailee has the biggest heart and always tries to make excuses for other people. She'll be okay. Regan might take a little longer. She'll probably go right to the Internet and look up everything she can on Nathan Scott. Like I will. Can you describe him?"

"He was tall, over six feet. He was blond, athletic, and handsome. He had blue eyes, and he was smart. He would have wanted to know you, but I couldn't break up his marriage and mine."

"Do you still have those pictures of him?"

"I do, but they're packed away in the attic. I'll get them out tomorrow."

"I'd appreciate that." Fiona twisted her hair and took a deep breath. "I've got a splitting headache, and I can't seem to process this right now. If you don't mind, I think I'll go to bed."

"You've already had one terrible shock today. And now I accidentally gave you another one. I'm so sorry." Barbara put her arms around Fiona.

"Actually, it gives me something to think about instead of that terrible scene on my doorstep. That was so awful." She hugged her mom back. "The bottom line for me is that I love you and I'm glad you're my mom."

Chapter 49

As Ted followed her upstairs to the bedrooms, Fiona grabbed her I-Pad and said, "My mother was the paragon of truthfulness, but she lived a lie. I'm trying to get my mind around that."

"I assume she did what she had to do. She protected her babies and kept you all with her. And she gave you a good life full of her love."

"I remember always wanting a daddy who'd grab me in his arms and twirl me around and make me laugh. Maybe I did after all. We just never met each other." She brushed her hair back from her face. "Thanks for encouraging me to talk to my mom.

"Maybe I can let go of Martin's indifference now and concentrate on compassion for him. I can even respect him for taking on another man's babies. And we never did lack for physical comfort. Or toys, or clothes, or education. On the surface nothing is changed. But inside I feel a big upheaval. I need to process all this. I need to take another look at my mother. She was basically a single parent raising us. I never thought of her as a sexual being. Now I wonder if she and Steve have a thing going."

"If they are, it's none of your business."

"You're right. I know you're right."

She paused at an open bedroom door. "Mom said you can use Kailee's bedroom. Sorry about the ruffles. Mom kept our bedrooms exactly as we decorated them when we were in our late teens. And the bathroom is the next door down. I'll be across the hall in my old bedroom."

Fiona set down her I-Pad and clasped her hands behind Ted's neck. "My emotions are all over the place. Thank you for being you, and for being here for me today."

He tightened his arms around her. "I can feel you vibrating," he said. "I bet I know what you're itching to do when you get in that bedroom. You'll be Googling your father's name before you sleep."

"Yeah, I can hardly wait to see what I can find. I just realized that even my nationality is probably different. I wonder what I am. I forgot to ask Mom that."

"You'll have time tomorrow." His kiss was everything to her. It grounded her on a day that had been truly shocking. It was a tender reminder that he cared about her. A promise of more to come. And, of course, the usual fireworks display that occurred whenever their lips touched.

When he released her, he said, "Remember, the door stays open after you hit the sack."

"No argument from me," she smiled at him.

Karen J. Gallahue

When she stepped inside the bedroom, she grabbed her I-Pad and immediately Googled her natural father's name. Her headache soon forgotten, she read everything she could about him as her fingers tapped the keys. She discovered that he had been a sportscaster! She felt a tenuous tie with the smiling young man in the yearbook picture. She'd often been told she had the gift of gab. Sounds like he might have had it, too. She found other pictures of him, as well, and she studied them carefully. Her father also had a brother who was a Republican state senator. The brother had a wife and two children. They would be her cousins. Her fingers danced over the keys as she sought more and more information.

CHAPTER 50

Chicago, 11:00 p.m.

The multi-story hotel in downtown Chicago on Michigan Avenue was overwhelming for Kendrick after spending his last twenty years in prison. Ponzo had reserved a room facing the lake, and for the first few hours after they checked in, Kendrick spent most of his time at the window. It was dark now, and he liked seeing the lights out on the water.

"I remember one time when I was a kid," he said to Ponzo, "my dad chartered a fishing boat on Lake Michigan. We caught some big salmon and lake trout. That was one of the best days of my life. I even liked cleaning the fish, slashing them open and gutting them, cutting off their heads. It was great."

Ponzo grunted.

Kendrick continued, "I want you to get me binoculars and a gun."

"I can get the binoculars. I don't know about the gun,"

"You afraid I'll shoot you? Don't worry. I know I need you. If I wanted to get rid of you, I'd just grab that piece you're carrying and shoot you while you're snoring away at two in the morning." He picked his nose and wiped his hand on his pants. "What if you're gone, and some cop shows up? I need to be able to defend myself."

"Okay, okay."

"I need different disguises, too. I'll make a list of stuff."

"You realize that every time I leave this room, I put my life on the line?"

"I know. You're getting well paid for doing that. Remember?"

"Yeah, yeah, yeah."

After watching the late news and hearing about the explosion killing a paparazza instead of Fiona Morgan, Ralph Kendrick turned off the TV. "What the fuck is going on here?" He yelled at Ponzo as he kicked a footstool across the room.

"In Naperville alone, I've put out good money four times. Four fucking times! And for what? For nothing. The Morgan women are still all alive and well. And my killers are either dead or in jail. And the bomber dude didn't even kill the right broad!"

"It's not his fault the paparazza babe exploded the bomb."

Ralph snorted. "Then I find out that Tory Girard's killer has been arrested! What kind of half ass killers are you hiring, anyway? The only successful hitman

167

was the one in New York. And she was a broad. The one that killed Sandy Johnson. Hire her to kill Fiona."

Ponzo said, "I doubt she would take a second job. Too much media attention. Too much danger of sticking her neck out and getting caught."

"I say I want that woman. She did a fast, clean job."

"I tell you she'll be out of the country if she's smart."

"Get her. This Fiona chick has cost me plenty, and she's still alive. I want her dead."

Ponzo threw up his hands and stalked over to a box of throwaway phones. "I'll make the call. No sweat."

It took more than one phone call, but when Ponzo hung up his cell, he said, "My contact reached the woman who killed Sandy Johnson. She'll do the job, but I had to give her ten thousand more. And my contact said that's it. No more. You'll have to forget Regan and Kailee. None of his contacts will touch them. And we need to get out of the country while we can."

"All right. All right. As long as Fiona is killed. She was probably telling the truth. Why would she claim to the witness if she wasn't?"

"Whatever." Ponzo gave a big sigh of relief. "It's dangerous enough for me to get Fiona killed. Then we're outa here."

CHAPTER 51

Naperville, 1:00 a.m.

When she realized she was so tired she had to squint to read the monitor, Fiona turned off her I-pad and crawled into bed. She thought she'd fall asleep immediately. But she didn't. She tossed, turned, and replayed today's events. Seeing Sonya's body on her doorstep. Finding out Martin Morgan was not her father. One thought chased another.

She could feel that her hands were fisted, and she deliberately opened her fingers out flat. Her toes were tensed as well. She straightened them. Her jaw was clenched, and her lips were pursed. She relaxed them. She lay still, thinking sleep would come now.

It didn't. In fact, she was now wide awake again. She snapped on the light in her old bedroom. Still decorated with the same colors she had chosen in her late teens. Turquoise rug and duvet with hot pink pillows and accessories. She remembered that she and her sisters had each decorated her own room. They were amused, but not surprised that each chose turquoise as the main color, but Regan had turquoise and white, and Kailee had turquoise and gold. Fiona's room was loaded with pictures and memorabilia. She couldn't believe her mom was still dusting off her teddy bear collection. Small ceramic figures. Stuffed bears of all sizes and shapes. Other stuff, too.

She spied her karate picture back when she was eleven. Next to it sat a small red toy microphone. A Walmart special whose batteries died years ago. When she was six, Fiona went through a few of those. Drove her sisters wild trying to interview them over and over. And entertain them with Knock-Knock jokes. After a while Regan said no more and refused to let her come close with the mike. Kailee, more patient, said three times a day, and that's it. Already, Kailee was gifted with the art of negotiation.

An hour later, she heard a soft knock on the open door and saw Ted glaring at her."What's going on here? It's after two in the morning. What the hell are you doing?"

"Taking pictures."

"Why are you doing that?"

"I couldn't fall asleep. I looked around the room and realized mom and I should get rid of all this memorabilia. I read somewhere one should take pictures of treasures like this once you no longer collect. Then you call still see it all, but it doesn't take nearly the space."

"You're taking pictures with a cell phone in the middle of the night?" He rubbed his hair which had small tufts sticking up here and there. "You never cease to amaze me. You're like a handy rubber band. Some of the time, I think you're stretched as far as you can go. And the next minute, you snap back together and do weird things like this. Go to sleep!" He turned and stalked back to his bedroom.

Fiona figured she had enough pictures. She turned out the light and fell fast asleep in minutes.

When Fiona jerked awake the next morning, she felt disoriented for a moment. A quick glance answered her question. She was at her mom's house.

Suddenly, she remembered last night's conversation with her mother and the shocking news that blew her perception of herself right out of the box. She wasn't who she thought she was! She was thirty years old and was just finding out that Martin Morgan was not her biological father!

Yesterday, her thoughts had been in turmoil, rattling around in her brain like seeds in a tin cup. This morning she felt more relaxed in her mind. In one respect, she was glad Martin wasn't her father because at some level, she'd worried about the suicide thing, wondering if such behavior was hereditary. She thought of several more questions to ask her mom, too.

Fiona wished she could share her thoughts and feelings with her sisters. But she knew her mom had to be the one to tell them her well-kept secret. Who knew when that would be? It's not the type of thing one tells a daughter on a long-distance call.

Usually an early riser, Fiona couldn't believe it was already after eight o'clock. She had a lot more questions for her mother about her biological father. Was he called Nate or Nathan? What nationality was he? Was he honorable? Did he have a sense of humor? She had Googled pictures taken of him with players on both the Phillies and the Seventy-Sixers teams. She'd like to travel to Philadelphia sometime in the near future. Not to contact anyone, just to see what surroundings he had spent his life in.

She tumbled out of bed. Time to get moving. She left her gym shorts on, but put a bra on under her sleeveless top in deference to Steve and Ted. She apologized to her mom for missing breakfast.

Barbara Morgan replied, "I kept a plate of French toast warming for you. Ted and Steve are out on the back porch reading the paper." She touched Fiona's arm. "Are you all right? I tossed and turned all night worrying about you. And hoping you didn't think too badly of me."

Fiona threw her arms around her mother. "How could I ever think badly about you?"

Barbara said drily, "Anyone who discovered what you did last night would be bound to have a real jumble of feelings."

"Last night I was dealing with the shock of it. That and the shock of the explosion that killed Sonya. Today I'm thinking how lucky I am. My main feeling toward you is love. I asked myself what I would do if faced with your decisions. I would have done the same as you did. The only thing I'd do differently would be tell me sooner. At least after I turned twenty-one.

"I already feel relief that Martin Morgan was not my father, but I have warm feelings for him now for giving us his name. Kailee and Regan and I always thought we lacked something. That we weren't important to him. I'm dealing with the fact that I'm really not lacking. And I owe him a debt of gratitude. He provided for us really well."

"Thank you for accepting this so well. I hope your sisters react as well as you did."

"I Googled Nathan Scott last night and got a bunch of info. Do you want to see it?"

"Sure. But why don't you eat first." Barbara Morgan's beaming face showed her relief that Fiona appeared to be okay today.

171

CHAPTER 52

The next couple days were routine for Fiona. So far she and her sisters were still safe. Thank God! She plunged into her work and sought out more information on her biological father. When she and Ted attended mass at St. Raphael's Church on Saturday afternoon, she prayed fervently for Kendrick's capture.

On Sunday morning, Fiona woke to the sound of something screeching off and on. She flapped her arm out from under the covers to jam the off button on her alarm. The racket didn't stop. At the same time she realized it was her phone, she also recognized Regan's calling song. A wave of fear rushed through Fiona as she answered the phone with trembling fingers. It wasn't even five in the morning!

"What's wrong?" she stammered out the words, fearing the worst.

Her sister's voice chirped over the line.

"Nothing's wrong. I just wanted to talk.

"Do you realize what time it is here? I was sound asleep."

"Woops! I'm sorry, Fiona. I didn't remember the time change. I'm glad I'm in Spain, though, where you can't strangle me. I just saw a picture of you and Ted Collier kissing on CNN. They were airing the explosion event that killed the paparazza. And there you were. Wrapped in each other's arms. What's going on with you two?"

"It was a thank-God-you're-alive kiss. He's not seducing me. By the way, he listened to you."

"What?"

"I understand you told him what a needy person I am."

"Not really. I just didn't want him to hurt you, especially under the circumstances."

"You can lay off, Regan. I'm not a kid anymore."

"You're right, of course. I'm sorry."

The sisters continued the conversation. Regan kept Fiona laughing with stories of the boys' antics, her adjustment to a new country, and her husband's perks and aggravations as he learned the ropes of the new job. When they said goodbye, Fiona headed for the coffee pot and her morning workout.

"Banana bread coming up," Ted said, as he finished slicing the loaf Fiona had taken out of the freezer last night. Freshly showered, Fiona rinsed off some fresh, plump blueberries and spooned them on top of vanilla yogurt.

"M-m-m, this should sustain us since we're going to a battle today," she replied.

As they sat at the table, Ted pointed to a small map. "John Tremayne e-mailed this to us for this afternoon's event. He studied it as he spread margarine on his banana bread.

Fiona took a spoonful of fruit and yogurt. "I see you're checking the layout of the Naper Settlement. Have you ever visited it?"

"No, but I know it's a bunch of restored buildings from the 1800's moved to the area near Washington and Aurora Avenue."

"It's actually pretty cool. They call it a living museum. You can see a blacksmith working at a real forge. Or get a demonstration of how they used a printer in the mid nineteenth century. That kind of stuff."

She continued as she chose cream cheese to spread on her banana bread. "Anyway, the Naper Settlement hosts the Civil War Reenactment every year in May. The participants set up army tents on the settlement grounds and live there for the two days of the reenactment. During that time, they cook over campfires, wear authentic clothing, and participate in events."

"I spoke with Tremayne while you were in the shower, and he said about three hundred Civil War people come, and that the event could attract five thousand attendees over the two days. He also said that the chief of police has authorized extra police officers for the event. Apparently, he's feeling the heat, with all the national media attention. He really wants to get Kendrick and his assorted cohorts behind bars."

"Kendrick 's screwing up Naperville's record as a safe place to live with four attempted murders in the last few days," Fiona said.

"True, but Naperville's finest have brought down all the attempted murderers, except for the bomb fellow. That's better than New York City and Minneapolis can say."

"What's involved in planning for an event like this?" Fiona asked.

"At the Civil War event, my responsibility is to keep you safe. If I leave your side, another officer will take my place."

"Sounds as if I'll be well covered."

"Yes, you will. And for an event like this with a few thousand people, we always have to prepare for any eventuality. As you probably know, police procedures have really changed since Columbine and other incidents across America. The term *active shooter* is used frequently now, and it refers to any armed person who has used deadly force on others and continues to do so. If someone should target you, we need to know ahead of time how to respond quickly. Studies have shown that the faster action is taken, the fewer casualties are involved."

He stood up to remove his dishes from the table. "I never got to a Civil War Reenactment when I was on the force here. Tell me more about it."

"Some of the Civil War people represent the soldiers of the Union and the Confederacy. Others play other parts from that era, like politicians, snake-oil salesmen, surgeons, etc. They have all kinds of activities, including a mock wedding and the battle we'll see today. They also have hands-on activities, like I can try sawing a bone in the surgeon's tent after the battle. People come from all over the country to participate. The big attraction is the daily battle scene between the Blues and the Grays."

"With cannons and muskets?"

"Yup."

"And what will you be doing?"

"I'll circulate throughout the area. I plan to interview the bride and groom at the mock wedding. And I also want to talk with Abe Lincoln, Ulysses S. Grant, and Robert E. Lee. Plus I want to interview a couple soldiers from each side."

"So you'll be wandering around in crowds of people."

"Right."

"Where will you stand when the battle takes place?"

She wiped her fingers on her napkin and touched a spot on the map. "I'll stand right about here near the corner of the PawPaw Post Office building."

"PawPaw?"

"It's a tree. There's one standing near the building. It has big fat leaves."

As she talked, Fiona was aware that her hands were curled into fists, and she sounded much braver than she felt.

"So, what time do you want to arrive at the settlement?"

"Probably twelve thirty. I'll have some time then before the battle at two thirty. This morning I'll do some research for my show."

CHAPTER 53

Since the weather report predicted a hot and muggy afternoon, they dressed accordingly. Ted noticed that Fiona wore a silky green one-piece shorts outfit which ended above her knees. It would have looked better without the Kevlar vest, but, for once, she didn't gripe about wearing it. Ted wore tan shorts with a black loose-fitting shirt that covered the Glock holstered at his waist. He also wore his Kevlar vest.

Fiona seemed a little quiet as they walked through the kitchen to the garage. He patted her shoulder as he opened the car door for her.

"We'll be looking out for you, Tiger," he said.

"Thanks." She squeezed his hand with hers.

As Ted backed the car out, he swore under his breath when a skinny photographer actually laid on the hood of his car and tried to snap a picture of Fiona. Ted pushed the button for the alarm system. It blared, and the guy rolled off trying to both hold his ears and hang on to his camera. Ted smiled. The guy's ears would be ringing for the next hour. As always, several media people yelled questions; then they scurried to their cars to follow them.

"Where should we park?" Ted asked as they neared the Naper Settlement.

"In the City Hall parking lot. It's just north of the settlement across Aurora Avenue."

His lips twitched. "I do remember where City Hall is."

He pulled into the lot which was already almost full. Continuous waterfall geysers flanked City Hall and added a little class to the marble-faced building with its unique oblong rectangular windows. Ted and Fiona couldn't cut straight across from the parking lot because there was a barrier and a ditch, so they walked to the stoplight on Aurora and Eagle.

Across the street a six foot black wrought iron fence enclosed the Naper Settlement. Ted could see the white canvas army tents pitched inside the fence as far as they could see to the right. He could also smell the woodburning campfires.

"We'll see more tents pitched here and there throughout the settlement," Fiona said.

Charlie waved to them when they reached the Pre-Emption House/Tavern, a large rambling multi-use structure which held artifacts from the eighteen hundreds. Tremayne, dressed casually in shorts, introduced them to the other officers who would be on duty for today's events. Tremayne gave Ted ear buds and a lapel microphone, similar to what the other officers were using. Tremayne also assigned one officer, John Kraft, a bald, black man, to immediately cover

Fiona's protection if Ted was injured or left her side. The police officers dispersed as soon as they had their assignments.

Ted and Tremayne conferred briefly before the group stepped outside the Pre-Emption house, and Ted saw the Village Common, a large, grassy plot of land surrounded by several small buildings. Red brick pathways led off into various directions. He grunted when he saw there were a number of mature oaks, elms, and maples around the common. Thank God spring was late this year, and the tree leaves just hazed the branches. No sniper could conceal himself. Still, he and Tremayne would want the trees checked periodically.

The area seemed festive to Ted. Women wore hoop skirts. Children in period costumes played games. One young boy chased a hoop with a stick, and he invited children who were spectators to join him. People carried bottles of root beer and munched on popcorn being sold by a vendor.

Ted figured the plantings were probably authentic to the time. He saw wild roses, peonies and purple irises, as well as other plants he couldn't identify.

Wherever they went, members of the press followed them, edging in close whenever they saw an opportunity. Ted followed Fiona when she spotted a man dressed as Abe Lincoln and hurried over to interview him, first as Abe, then as himself, a tall, retired farmer from Indiana, who indulged his love of history and his interest in other people by traveling along with the Civil War group.

While she talked, Ted scanned the surroundings. Canvas tents were set up in several areas all over the grounds and participants wore authentic Union and Confederate costumes. Men and women of all ages participated. Earnest history buffs, immersed in their roles walked around and seemed willing to share their expertise with others.

When Fiona finished the interview, she led Ted to the first building on the left, the Blacksmith Shop. He peered inside and saw the smithy working at his forge. Ted didn't envy him on a day as hot as this one. The next building was a Print Shop, followed by a Stonecarver's Shop. Several people watched the artisans at work. All three buildings were only one story high. The last one on the left was the Firehouse.

The Paw Paw Post Office stood to the right of the Firehouse and looked more like a house than a place of business. It was two stories high with a welcoming porch on two sides. He alerted Tremayne that someone needed to be stationed upstairs, especially when Fiona was standing outside near there during the battle which would start at two-thirty.

Fiona pointed to a structure directly south of them and identified it as Fort Payne an authentic replica of a nineteenth century fort. "When the battle starts," she said, "most of the action will take place between the Pre-Emption House and the fort."

Ted, ever watchful, scanned the crowd, checking for body language or facial expression that might flag danger. He hated when so many people wore sunglasses which covered their eyes.

The day was heating up drastically. Not one cloud floated in the sky. The pitiless sun sailed high and just a little nasty, scorching and blistering the earth, as well as the people who walked on it. Ted saw a lot of pink cheeks and sunburned noses. Although it was only May, the weather felt like August.

He was so hot he swore he could feel sweat at the back of his knees. He also guessed if he tossed a raw egg on the red brick pathway, it would fry up just fine. They'd had unusually wacky weather in Illinois lately, with sudden shifts from hot to cold and back again.

As he wiped the perspiration off his forehead, he felt sorry for the men in the authentic wool Civil War uniforms. One had to be a dedicated history buff to participate so enthusiastically in spite of the discomfort.

In her pale green sleeveless dress with matching strappy heels, Fiona looked like a refreshing crème de menthe. She interviewed both participants and spectators and moved smoothly from person to person, her honey-rich voice drawing people out, asking the perfect question, making each feel important because she valued each opinion.

"I'd like to go inside the post office," Ted said.

When they entered the building. Ted noticed a small reception room to the right. A young woman in period costume explained that the postmaster operated out of his home back in the eighteen hundreds. The reception room was used by travelers who waited for the stagecoach. The next room included all the paraphernalia for the postman. The rest of the house included the rooms for the family.

Ted saw that the stairs to the second floor were roped off. He showed his credentials to the young woman, and she let him go up and confer with the police officer stationed there already. Ted quickly checked the view from each bedroom, and he pointed out to the young man where Fiona would be standing during the battle.

When he came back down he joined Fiona as she continued her walking tour of the settlement. They visited a doctor's residence, and they stopped at the schoolhouse. At each place along their route, Fiona interviewed more people. Many people recognized her and called her name. Several asked for autographs. They reached the chapel in time for the mock wedding.

As the time grew closer for the big battle, Fiona and Ted moved back to the Paw Paw Post Office where the brick sidewalks were being roped off for the spectators. Ted checked again at the post office to make sure an officer was in place upstairs.

At two thirty, a few muskets fired from the south from the Confederate army. The people milling around in period costumes all hustled to safety. And the battle

177

began. Answering shots were fired from the area of the fort. Gradually more soldiers appeared on each side, pulling cannons. Ted could see five cannons lined up on each side. The narrator of the action mentioned that, in an actual battle there were often one hundred fifty cannons on each side.

Soldiers from both sides formed lines, shoulder to shoulder and elbow to elbow, marching toward each other. They fired when they got close enough to see the whites of their eyes, about thirty-five feet.

As Ted watched the blue and gray-garbed men fall during the battle scene, he thought how differently war was fought in those days compared to the recent battles in the Middle East. But dead was dead, no matter what the weapon or the technology.

When the first cannon belched its orangey-gray smoke, a toddler shrieked in terror. Ted could imagine the sounds and the amount of smoke generated by three hundred of them. Ted constantly scanned with a lawman's keen eyes. At least people in summer clothes had a harder time hiding a weapon.

For the next thirty minutes, Ted scanned and watched the battle progress. As a soldier close by primed a cannon for its next belch of smoke, suddenly Ted's attention focused on sunlight glinting on something silver from a second story window of the post office. A gun. Pointing toward Fiona!

He yelled "Gun!" In one quick motion, he shoved his hand onto Fiona's shoulder.

CHAPTER 54

Fiona dropped to the ground, and Ted covered her with his body. He grunted as a bullet hit him in the back, but he had his Kevlar vest on. A second shot hit him in the left upper arm. That one hurt. But he didn't waste a second.

"Stay here. Officer Kraft will cover you," he yelled to Fiona. He snapped to his feet in one quick motion, his eyes on the post office. When he saw a shadow move in its back yard, he took off like an Olympic racer. He glimpsed a person with a backpack running behind the Stone Carver's Shop. Although his left arm was bleeding and hurting like hell, Ted used his lapel microphone to call for help, and he drew his gun with his right, never breaking his stride.

The crowd of people about ten deep parted for him, and he heard a kid yell that someone was really shot who wasn't a soldier. He could see the suspected shooter heading behind the Printer's Shop. The person had a backpack, wore sneakers, and ran like . . . a woman! Shit! The runner was a woman. He yelled, "Police. Stop or I'll shoot!"

In one smooth action, she turned and fired at him. The bullet barely missed him, and almost hit a large pot-bellied man to Ted's right. Ted couldn't chance a shot at her with all the people milling around, but he ran even faster, like a panther pursuing his prey. And now he knew she definitely was the shooter.

The woman was fast, but Ted had been a track star in high school, and he was gaining on her. She suddenly darted from behind the Blacksmith's Shop toward the red brick path, muscling through the individuals in her way. He still didn't dare risk a shot at her.

Ted spoke to Tremayne on his lapel microphone as he ran, "skinny white female wearing khaki cargo shorts, a dark green shirt, and a black baseball cap, traveling north, probably toward the City Hall parking lot."

He thought, "If she tries to go over the black wrought iron fence on Aurora Avenue, I'll have a shot at her." Instead, she flew into the Pre-Emption House, literally knocking people out of her way.

Without breaking stride, she flew out the other door leading to Aurora Avenue. No black fence in her way there. She tore across two lanes of heavy traffic. Cars swerved. Brakes screeched. People yelled, but she made it through. Ted plowed after her, causing more pandemonium.

She veered to the right to avoid a ditch and barricade and ran up the small ramp leading into the City Hall parking lot on the southeast side.

Several people were in the lot near their cars. Ted yelled, "Police! Take cover!"

People screamed and tried to hide themselves.

Tremayne radioed Ted that he'd be entering the southwest side of the parking lot in five seconds.

Ted yelled at the shooter. "Lady, you're stuck now! More police are on the way. You've already shot one cop. Your next stop is jail. How many years you spend there depends upon what you do now."

Ms. Cargo Shorts responded with a wild shot in Ted's general direction, and she ducked behind a white SUV in the middle lane of the parking lot. Ted stayed crouched. He saw her shadow underneath the car.

"Good," he thought. "I can keep track of her. If she stays there, Tremayne and I can set up an "L" formation ambush. I'll proceed toward her shooting from the southeast, and Tremayne can do the same from the southwest. We can avoid any unwanted fields of fire and neutralize her."

He could see her shadow move, as she tried to get into the car. "I hope that's her car," he thought as he shot out the tires on the side facing him as well as an additional shot he angled toward the dashboard. "If not, I'll probably have to pay for the damages."

He paused. Nothing happened. She didn't move. Ted saw three blue uniforms moving rapidly, one from the east, two from the west. A squad car blocked the only car exit from the parking lot. He saw another squad park in front of City Hall, and the officer jumped out to secure the building.

Ted's left arm still hurt, but it wasn't spurting blood, so the bullet hadn't hit a major artery. He tried to keep it elevated as he waited.

Then, like a panther, Ted moved from one parked car to another. He tossed a rock that hit the ground a few feet to the shooter's left. A shot rang out, but her shadow stayed put.

"I want a helicopter," Ms. Cargo Pants shouted.

"You have no hostage to bargain with. Come out with your hands up. No shots need to be fired."

CHAPTER 55

Back at the Civil War site, the minute Ted took off, Officer Kraft ran to Fiona's side. Fiona picked herself up off the ground, yanked off her strappy heels, and tossed her purse and I-pad to Charlie. She'd heard Ted grunt twice and talk into his lapel microphone. When she spied blood on her arm, she figured he must have been shot. She just didn't know where. She knew he was chasing the shooter. No way was she going to stay here while he ran off into danger on her behalf!

As she prepared to sprint after Ted, Officer Kraft grabbed her arm and said, "Stay here."

She shook her arm free. "You'll have to shoot me to keep me here. Ted's been shot. Come on."

Fueled by fear, Fiona tore after Ted behind the Stone Carver's Shop. Officer Kraft ran beside her with Charlie puffing behind them. She sprinted like a late airline passenger trying to make her gate in time. As her adrenalin kicked in, some senses seemed heightened. She was aware of the vivid blueness of the sky and the kaleidoscopic blur of people clad in bright summer hues, but she was oblivious to their faces. The smell of cannon smoke seemed to scorch her throat, but she barely felt the rocks and tree roots on her shoeless feet. When the cannons boomed again and belched dark smoke, she tried not to cough. At one point, she tripped over a tree root. Officer Kraft grabbed her elbow and kept her upright.

Like a posse in pursuit, she could hear press people behind her. And she could hear people shouting at them. At one point, she shoved a man out of her way. She could see Ted ahead of her.

Her heart stuttered when she saw the person that Ted was chasing turn and fire at him. Ted didn't break his stride, so she guessed he wasn't hit. Thank God! She wanted to yell at him to let the person go and stay safe. She didn't want him to get killed. But she knew he'd just shout at her to stay back.

When Ted veered left, alongside the Blacksmith's Shop toward the Pre-Emption House, she lost sight of him for a minute, but people were shouting and pointing at the Pre-Emption House. She headed there with Officer Kraft still by her side. When she hit the red bricks of the pathway she ran even faster so her bare feet wouldn't feel how hot they were.

She flew through the Pre-Emption House and heard the sound of brakes screeching and horns blaring out on Aurora Avenue. Heart hammering, she saw Ted dodge across the street safely and roll across the hood of someone's car. He seemed to be gaining on the shooter.

By the time Fiona and her entourage got to the street, cars stopped and stayed stopped. Fiona headed for the small pedestrian ramp leading to the parking lot. As she entered the area, she heard Ted's booming voice shouting, "Come out with your hands up. No shots need to be fired." The next thing she saw was another police officer join Ted behind a parked car on the southeast side of the parking lot.

Fiona clutched the stitch in her side and gasped for breath. Officer Kraft manually put her behind him and said, "Don't move." The damned Kevlar vest made a hot day hotter, and now her feet felt raw. Her lips tasted salty from the perspiration running down her face.

Office Kraft whispered to her, "The shooter is on the driver's side of that white SUV in the middle lane." Fiona peered from behind him and saw movement on the driver's side. Ted must have seen it, too, because he and the officer next to him fired their guns.

In the next moment, Fiona watched in horror as she saw Ted and the officer step out and move in a two-man formation toward the white SUV, guns blazing. My God, she thought. Either one of them could be killed! At the same time, she saw Tremayne coming from the southwest side of the parking lot. Also with his gun blazing. After an initial volley of shots, the shooter evidently decided the odds were against her.

She shouted, "I give up." The policemen's guns were still.

Tremayne shouted, "Toss your guns ahead of you on the ground, and lay flat on the ground behind the SUV with your hands behind your head."

Fiona saw a gun and a backpack tossed onto the pavement behind the SUV. The officers proceeded closer, guns still drawn. In the next nanosecond, Fiona saw the shooter swing herself back up and fire at Tremayne with yet another gun in her hand. Three officers returned fire, and she slumped to the ground, face down. The officers ran quickly to the shooter's side. Ted bent down and checked her pulse

"She's dead," he said. Fiona sank to her knees thinking, *suicide by cop.* A human being was dead, and for what? At least no other policemen was hurt, except for Tremayne who took a shot to his chest. Fortunately, he was wearing his Kevlar vest. Like Ted, he'd be badly bruised, but okay.

An ambulance peeled into the parking lot, as quickly as the squad car could be moved out of its way.

Members of the media who had chased Fiona snapped pictures, one after the other.

Fiona saw Ted's bloody arm and rushed to his side as soon as she could.

After a quick, but fervent, one-armed embrace, Ted said, "What the hell are you doing here? So much for me telling you to stay put. I'm trying to keep you safe from harm. And you run right toward it."

"I knew you were hit. I had your blood on my arm. I had to make sure you were okay."

"I'm fine," he said, but Fiona didn't like the gray tinge to his face, and she could see that the wound in his arm was still bleeding. When she saw three paramedics rush to the scene, she called one over. He was tall, freckled, and had Kelly green eyes.

The man checked Ted's arm. "The bullet didn't exit your arm," he told Ted.

"I'm aware of that," he grunted. "At least I'm carrying the evidence that it was from the shooter's gun."

"Lucky you. Should be easy to remove. Let's get you on a gurney."

"I can walk," Ted protested.

"Sorry, big guy, not while there's a chance of you going into shock. We need to get you stabilized. How long has this wound been bleeding?"

"At least fifteen minutes," Fiona said "And as soon as he was hit, he chased after the shooter from inside the Naper Settlement over to here."

By that time another paramedic joined them, and they moved Ted to the ambulance.

Tremayne moved to Ted's side and complained, "You repeatedly get to be the daring rescuer, and I still get all the damned paper work."

Ted said, "Thanks for the good teamwork. What the hell happened to the police officer that was stationed upstairs at the post office?"

"I've tried contacting him, but there's no answer. I sent a guy over to check."

Ted grunted. "Make sure they handle the shooter's guns carefully. It's important that we have her fingerprints on them. Should be a rifle, probably in that backpack."

"Right." Tremayne and Ted both got the message at the same time. "Officer Horak at the post office got hit with a stun gun and a vicious blow to the back of his neck. He's starting to come around. Paramedics are on the way to him."

"Thank God he's alive," said Ted, and he passed out.

Fiona gasped, and the paramedic said, "He's lost a lot of blood. As soon as we can replace it, he should be okay."

CHAPTER 56

While they loaded Ted into the ambulance, Fiona asked Tremayne to arrange for a police officer to bring Ted's car and Fiona to the hospital. Naperville's Edward Hospital had grown from a one-building facility to a large complex with buildings devoted to Cancer Treatment, Cardiac Treatment, and several other specialties. The Emergency Room was fairly busy with people being treated for heat exhaustion. After the necessary paper work, Ted was taken immediately to a cubicle.

The young doctor with the curly Afro that checked Ted's wound said, "I'm sure you want me to get rid of that bullet for you."

"The sooner, the better. It's a little crowded in there right now." Ted grimaced.

"It's a good thing you're in such good shape. We should have you stabilized within the next hour so that we can remove it."

"That's good to know."

Fiona's mother and Ted's mother reached the hospital shortly after he went into surgery.

"I can't bear it that Ted's hurt because of me," Fiona said.

"That's part of who he is," his mother replied.

The two moms waited with Fiona until they could see Ted after his surgery.

"Do you want me to take Ted home with me?" Ted's mother asked Fiona.

"If it's all right with you, I'd like to take care of him. He took a bullet that was meant for me. I owe him big time. Plus, even injured, his presence steadies me."

"I kinda figured that." Mrs. Collier turned to Fiona's mom. "I think we can leave after they bring Ted back to the room.

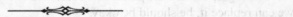

After Ted's surgery, the doctor came to talk to them. "He's going to have some pain, but the surgery went well, and we saved the bullet for him. A police officer took it away already. After all the blood Ted lost, I thought I'd have to keep him overnight for observation, but he's stable already and can be released in an hour or two when the anesthetic wears off."

All three women breathed a sigh of relief. A short time later, Ted was wheeled into the recovery room. When he woke up, he reached for Fiona's hand.

"How're you holding up" he croaked.

"Much better now that the bullet is out, and you're awake," she replied. "Can I get you anything?"

"Just a little water. My mouth tastes like dried paste."

Fiona handed him the water and asked, "Are you hurting?"

"Can't feel anything in the arm, but I sure can feel that bruise on my back where the first bullet hit my vest."

"I'm just so glad you were wearing that vest."

The two mothers fussed over Ted and then left.

By the time Tremayne and another police officer stopped by, Ted was fully awake.

"How's our hero?" the detective asked.

"Can it, Tremayne," Ted muttered. "You're the one who took the last bullet. I had a thought before I went under. And I can't retrieve it. It's driving me crazy. Something about the woman who shot me. I thought it might be important."

Fiona held his hand. "Your mind is like a steel trap. It'll come to you."

"What's the status on the shooter?" Ted asked Tremayne.

"Her fingerprints show she has a long history of aggravated assault. A Chicago girl, she's been in and out of prison since she was fifteen. Apparently, she has several aliases. A real tough broad."

"She sure could run." Ted turned to Fiona. "Now I remember that thought I had. The shooter today had the same body build as that footage we saw of Sandy Johnson's killer, leaving her apartment building. Also the same dark hair. It's a long shot, but it could be worth checking out."

"We'll check it," Tremayne said. "In the meantime, you get some rest. This is Officer Dick Waskiewicz. He'll be the bodyguard for both of you until Ted gets better."

They all shook hands. Tremayne took statements from Fiona and Ted and left.

The nurse sent Fiona from the room while she checked Ted's vitals. Fiona took her cell phone out in the hall, rang her boss, and said, "Mr. Mackay, I have a request for you. After what happened today, I need to take a break from public appearances. I can do my five o'clock show and interviews at the office for the next couple days, but I'd like to have time off from any public functions. I need to pull myself together. And I don't want to put anyone else in jeopardy. Also, Ted needs time to recuperate from his wound."

"No problem, Fiona," Mackay said, in his usual abrupt manner. "I'll contact Maureen Hansen. She can call you and find out what events you want her to cover. Tell Ted I hope his recovery is swift."

"I will, she said and rang off.

The next call was the hardest. She called her friend, Annie.

"Are you all right?" Annie asked. "I can't believe what you went through. The shooting at the settlement has been all over the news. A reporter said Ted was shot, but is in stable condition. Is that true?"

"I'm okay, and Ted is recuperating from the surgery on his arm. I can take him home in a couple hours." She took a deep breath.

"Annie, I'm afraid to put the wedding party in jeopardy after today's event. I don't think I should attend the rehearsal dinner or the wedding ceremony on Friday night and Saturday.

Annie burst into tears. "You can't be serious. I need you to be there. After all, you introduced Tom to me. Please say you'll come. Hold on while I tell Tom."

When Annie returned to the phone, she said, "Tom said to remind you that there'll be several police officers as guests, including the groomsman assigned to you. He'll alert them all to be aware of the situation. He agrees with me. He wants you to come. This won't be as large a crowd as the Civil War event. Only a hundred people for the ceremony. He said, hopefully by then, Kendrick will be captured."

Fiona knew Annie wouldn't let up. She said, "We'll talk more later. The nurse is leaving Ted's room. Maybe they'll let him go now. I have to hang up."

Nurse Broward gave Fiona directions for Ted's treatment at home. She wheeled in the mandatory wheelchair, which Ted tried to refuse. "I didn't get shot in the leg," he complained.

"Hospital policy," the nurse huffed, expanding her enormous bosom. "Deal with it! And don't forget to wear that sling."

Officer Waskiewicz stepped over to wheel Ted's chair out to the car. He asked them to just call him Dick. The police officer that had been maintaining order with the press outside the hospital had pulled Ted's car to the front entrance. The media crowd was bigger than ever, probably a couple hundred. They clapped as Ted and Fiona emerged from the hospital.

"Hey, Ted, way to go," one reporter shouted. "You saved her again!"

Ted rolled his eyes and got into the back seat. Fiona moved to get in beside him.

"Is Ted doing okay?" Kathy Turner asked. She was a good friend of Fiona's from Chicago's WGN.

Fiona turned. "Yes, the doctor removed the bullet which lodged against his humerus in the upper left arm. As soon as the wound heals he'll be fine."

"Did more than one bullet hit him?"

"Yes, the first one hit him in his back as he was shielding me. Fortunately, he had his Kevlar vest on. He has a bad bruise, but nothing more."

More questions peppered Fiona, but she shook her head and got into the car.

As they drove away, Fiona reached over and patted Ted's hand. Two minutes later, she realized she was still patting his hand.

"Are you nervous?" Ted asked.

"I guess so," she admitted. "I can hardly wait to get you home. I've never been comfortable in hospitals." She looked at her watch. "I can't believe it's only eight o'clock. So much has happened since the first shot of the battle."

When they reached Fiona's town house, Dick pulled into the garage and closed its door before they could get ambushed by more media people. As they entered the kitchen, Fiona said to Ted, "You'll be sleeping in my bed tonight."

"You're not going to sleep on the couch," Ted replied.

"No, Dick can sleep there. I'm going to use the blow-up mattress in the office."

Ted opened his mouth to argue.

Fiona heaved up her bosom like Nurse Broward and said, "Deal with it!" They both laughed.

Fiona found a pan of lasagna from her mom waiting for them in the refrigerator. She popped it into the oven to heat it up.

CHAPTER 57

Something was wrong with Fiona. Ted noticed that her hands shook as she set the table. She fussed over napkins. When Fiona, Ted, and Dick sat down to eat, she kept jumping up to get stuff like Parmesan cheese, or filling glasses of water. While Ted and Dick ate hungrily, she picked at her food, mostly moving it around the plate. She acted distracted, and she jerked when Ted had to ask a question a second time.

When they finished, she rose quickly from the table and refused any offer of help with the dishes. When the kitchen was clean, she pursed her lips and busied herself plumping pillows and straightening magazines. Finally, Ted asked Dick to go to the office for a few minutes while he and Fiona had a private conversation. He patted the couch next to him and asked her to sit.

Okay." Ted opened the conversation. "Tell me what's bothering you. You're unusually jittery."

Fiona twisted a strand of her hair. "Isn't the fact that a woman shot at me and hurt you enough to make me jumpy?"

"Of course. But you've been attacked before, and I don't recall seeing you this nervous."

"Oh, Ted," Fiona's face crumpled, and she threw her arms around his neck. "I was so worried about you. I think I need to hire a new bodyguard," she blurted.

"What? I take a bullet for you, and you want to fire me?" he asked, as he took her hand.

Fiona burst into tears. "That's exactly why I have to hire someone else," she sobbed. "You've already saved me from a strangler, a stabber, and a shooter. I can't bear the thought of you getting hurt . . . or killed because of me. I just won't have it. When I chased after you today, I was so afraid for you."

Her shoulders heaved and she couldn't continue. Her sobs seemed to be coming all the way from her toes. She grabbed a tissue and wiped her nose. "You could be killed. You almost were killed today."

Ted put his good arm around her and shifted her into his lap. "You won't get rid of me that easily. I refuse to be fired. I make my own decisions, my little guilt-catcher, and I also shoulder my own consequences. I decide to stay." He smiled a slow, easy smile. "You said you care about me? How much?"

"Too much to see you hurt or dead," she said, lips quivering and turquoise eyes glittering with tears. Ted kissed her thoroughly. When they separated, he gently framed Fiona's face with both hands. "I don't intend to step away and let someone else protect you. You're the most important person in my life. I *need* to protect you. When they said the bigger they come, the harder they fall, they were talking about me."

"You mean everything to me, Ted." Fiona's voice wavered. "I keep thinking this will be over. Yet it keeps going on and on."

"We'll get through this. I promise." He tilted her chin and angled his lips over hers. He gave her another long, soul searching kiss.

"We need to celebrate this moment," he said. "Kendrick has to be nearing the end of his rope."

He kissed her on the forehead. "Maybe we'd better let Dick out of the office," he smiled at her.

She slid off his lap and called to Dick. She came right back and snuggled close to Ted. As Fiona turned the TV on to CNN, they heard a news announcer say, "According to Naperville's Chief of Police, George Jansen, Naperville has been under siege by out-of-town killers."

The screen changed to a shot of the chief. "We don't take kindly to out of town assassins shooting our residents," he said. "And we especially do not take kindly to these same people shooting at our police officers."

He continued, "Fiona Morgan did the right thing twenty years ago when she testified against Ralph Kendrick. And we aim to continue to protect her. So far, the Naperville Police Department has a home invasion strangler behind bars, as well as a stabber, and a drive-by shooter. That shooter's sidekick is dead. And now we have another shooter dead."

He continued, "That woman, Lola Fields, fired two shots into a crowd of families today, some with small children. She then attempted to escape and shot again at the police officer chasing her. Prior to her death in a public parking lot, she pretended to surrender, then shot Detective John Tremayne in the chest. Fortunately, he was wearing a vest and was only bruised.

"At that time, she was shot and killed by police officers. Each policeman who fired at her was doing his sworn duty to protect the citizens of Naperville and their visitors. Each one of them placed himself in harm's way to do so. Several members of the media have offered their videos of the incident. We thank them. The videos have given us visible proof of what happened. Thank you for your attention. I will not be taking any questions at this time."

CHAPTER 58

Fiona soaked her tender feet the next morning. Running over uneven surfaces yesterday had taken its toll. She also skipped her workout. Instead of running to the scene of accidents, etc., she appreciated a quieter day doing research for future segments. Her only commitment was her five o'clock newscast.

Fiona also checked out every avenue on the Internet to get information on her biological father. She found out that her grandfather had been a state senator. He and her grandmother were deceased. She discovered that her father's wife was still alive. Although she had no interest in contacting her, Fiona decided someday she'd like to visit Philadelphia and kneel beside her father's grave. Apart from that, she could let the whole business go, at least until her mom told her sisters. She knew they'd have plenty to say to each other after that.

Ted had a follow-up visit for the gunshot wound and was told he was healing nicely. The day of the bomb incident on her front steps was a turning point for them. They both admitted how close their relationship had become. Fiona realized that Ted had become the main person in her life, the person she could turn to, confide in, and love. The events at the Naper Settlement made her bond even closer to him.

Ted proved to be very handy around the house. He oiled doors, fixed a drawer that was off its rollers, changed a light fixture in the garage, and did the maintenance on her air conditioner. As usual, he did all the tasks with competence and no fuss.

He spoke again to the outgoing chief of police in Plainfield and received another week's extension to his start date there. Ted's mother invited Fiona and Ted to dinner on Thursday where Fiona would meet Ted's brothers and their families.

As always, Fiona found relaxation when she organized something. One day she organized her ear rings. Up to now, she'd kept them in plastic ice cube trays. Recently, she bought a new ear ring organizer that hung in a closet and had thirty-five clear plastic pockets on both its front and back. Each pocket could easily hold a few ear rings. She organized them by color. If she needed silver ear rings, she could see at a glance what she had. She put the ones she never wore in a donation container.

As she sorted the ear rings, Fiona found the gold hoops Jeb had given her on the first Valentine's Day after their wedding. She looked at them for a moment, before tossing them in the donation box. She could afford to buy newer, nicer ones. She didn't need any reminders of Jeb. Especially now. No matter how things turned out with Ted, she discovered that she could actually risk caring about a man again.

Ted walked by and said, "You have that satisfied smirk on your face that tells me you organized something."

She pointed to her handiwork and said, "You're really getting to know me."

"Not as much as I'd like to," he replied and gave her a cheeky grin.

Ted felt they were getting closer to catching Kendrick. Someone at the PD with contacts in Chicago's underbelly reported to Ted that he heard of two hitmen who said they would refuse to take a contract on any of the Morgan triplets. Hopefully others would be scared off by all the publicity and the reward money.

At her five o'clock show, Fiona shared what info she could. The members of the press hammered her with questions every time she set foot outside her house.

"Do you think Kendrick'll ever come after you himself?" a lanky *Enquirer* reporter asked.

"I have to be prepared. At least, he'll be easier to recognize than some unknown hitman. He may or may not get me, but it'll be certain death for him if he tries. Hopefully, he'll be apprehended before he even gets anywhere close to me."

When they reached her town house, Fiona changed into casual clothes. She and Ted talked companionably on the couch in the living room. She sipped a glass of wine while he drank a beer. They could smell the pot roast in the crock pot that she had fixed this morning.

Fiona grabbed a turquoise toss pillow and plucked a thread on it as she said, "What was your wife like?"

"She was shy and sweet, a homebody. Very unassuming."

"She sounds very nice." Fiona pressed the thread back along its seam.

"She was."

"Do you have a picture of her?"

"I do." He reached into his billfold and handed Fiona a picture.

She saw a lovely woman with long, dark hair and chocolate-colored eyes. "She's beautiful."

"Yes, she was. I'll always care about her. But I'm finally over the intense grief and ready to explore the rest of my life. She'd want me to find happiness again. I'd feel the same way about her if our situations were reversed."

Fiona yanked the thread again. "I'm not anything like her."

Ted reached over and put his arm around her. "I wasn't planning to marry her clone. And, at this point in my life, I'm kinda attracted to the vibrant, cheeky, stubborn type."

"Oh?"

"Yeah, but both you and Lois are alike in that you have a solid core of goodness that's very special." He took the pillow away from her and said, "The way you were yanking that thread, I thought you'd unravel the whole pillow." He reached over and kissed her. Not once, but a few times. They almost forgot about the pot roast.

CHAPTER 59

Chicago, Illinois

Jimmy Ponzo hung up his cell phone and said to Kendrick, "I made the damn reservations at the Holiday Inn in Aurora for tomorrow night, against my better judgment. We're good for five days. But like I said before, what we should be doing is getting out of the country."

"Not yet, not yet," Kendrick said. "I want Fiona Morgan dead first."

"Yeah well, you don't have to put your ass on the line every time you go out the door."

Kendrick ignored the last remark. "At least, Aurora's closer to Naperville. I want to be there when the kill takes place. And don't forget; you're being paid to arrange that, well paid."

"Just remember our agreement. This payment I make tonight is the last one. We don't bother about the other two Morgan broads."

"Yeah, yeah." After Ponzo left, Kendrick worked on his laptop, checking maps of Naperville and locations of different landmarks. Later he sprawled on the bed, checking the time, as he flipped TV channels. At midnight Kendrick figured Ponzo should have been back from paying the last hitman by eleven.

Where the hell was he? Ralph found a motorcycle program and settled back down to watch. At a commercial break, he checked the time again. Twelve-fifteen. Crap! Ponzo wasn't back yet! Probably getting screwed somewhere. He kept checking every few minutes. By one o'clock, sweat beaded his forehead. He paced back and forth in the small hotel room.

At one-thirty, he flipped open a small suitcase, filled it with his few sets of pants and shirts, even a woman's pantsuit that Ponzo had bought for him. He also packed a woman's wig and makeup. He swore when he realized he didn't have the combination to the safe which held passports, fake driver's licenses, and more cash. He briefly thought about calling the management, but nixed that idea. Most important, at least his new gun and box of bullets weren't in the safe. He found about five hundred dollars in twenties laying around. Plus, the latest schedule of Fiona's movements.

He decided to go for the old man disguise. Placing putty inside his cheeks and securing a moustache and goatee to his face only took a few seconds. He put on a white wig and tore open a pillow and put padding on his upper back.

He used the back stairs to exit the building, and he went out the door to the rear parking lot where he walked briskly away from the hotel. When he was far enough away, he hailed a cab on Michigan Avenue and told the cabbie to take him to Union Station. He used a British accent.

After he reached the train station, he located the commuter trains heading for the western suburbs and found a departure for three a.m. He moved to a different area while he waited. When he boarded the train forty-five minutes later, he allowed himself a smile. Who needs Ponzo? If the guy was okay, he'd find Kendrick in Aurora. If not, it's all the fault of the bitch.

It took an hour for a thirty minute ride, but the train stopped at every podunk town between Chicago and Aurora, which was the end of the line and one stop after Naperville. Only one cab sat in the otherwise empty parking lot when he left the train. On the way to the hotel, the cabbie said, "You're out in the dead of night."

"I'm here for a funeral," Kendrick responded sadly.

The night clerk was involved in a conversation with her boy friend. She barely looked at him when he checked in. When he reached his room, he locked the door. He set his stuff on the floor and didn't even bother to pull the duvet off the bed. Instead he collapsed on it and fell asleep.

CHAPTER 60

Naperville, Illinois

Shortly after six the following morning Ted received a call from Tremayne. Ted put him on speaker phone as he and Fiona walked down the basement steps for their morning workout.

Tremayne said, "The Chicago police called me, and I think we finally caught a break."

Ted and Fiona both stopped on the steps and looked at each other, hope lighting their eyes.

"It's a good news, bad news thing," Tremayne continued. "Last night in Chicago an event occurred that definitely affects you. A man, Jimmy Ponzo, seeking to hire an assassin to kill Fiona Morgan, was killed by an undercover cop after Ponzo pulled a gun on him. Police are now checking out Ponzo's connections to Ralph Kendrick. I'm on my way into Chicago to confer with the Chicago cops."

"What about Kendrick?" Both Ted and Fiona shouted in unison.

"The cops are hoping some items in Ponzo''s pockets will lead them to Kendrick. No news on that yet."

"Hang on while I get my laptop," Ted said. "The name Ponzo rings a bell." He ran back up the steps, accessed his computer, and pulled up his list of names of possible connections to Joe Toro and the lawyer.

"Bingo!" he said into the phone. "Jimmy Ponzo is one of Joe Toro's many nephews. His sister's boy. Finally! A break!"

"I'll relay that info to the Chicago guys. Got an address on the guy?"

Ted quickly rattled off the personal information he had on Ponzo. When he hung up, Ted grabbed Fiona and swooped her off her feet and around in a circle. "Finally we're getting some place." They hugged and went downstairs to work out, hoping every minute that Tremayne would be calling back with more good news.

When the phone rang an hour later, Ted grabbed it quickly and again put Tremayne on speaker.

"A hotel room key and a bar receipt for the Russell Hotel on Michigan Avenue were found in Ponzo's pocket. Police immediately went to that hotel, but Kendrick wasn't there."

"Oh, no!" Disappointment swept through Fiona.

"However," Tremayne continued, "Fingerprints belonging to both Ponzo and Kendrick were found in the hotel room. Police assume Kendrick left the hotel in a hurry because the room safe contained phony passports, drivers licenses, and a large sum of money. They're wondering if Kendrick may not have known the combination to the safe."

"That would be a break for us," Ted said.

"In addition to his fingerprints, Kendrick left behind a wheel chair and, in the trash, an empty box of bullets. Security tapes at the hotel showed an older man leaving the hotel about one thirty in the morning with a small suitcase and a laptop computer. The man left through a rear door of the hotel into the parking lot. His body build matched Kendrick's.

"A picture of Ponzo is being shown to the assorted hitmen now in jail. Cab companies are being notified. All bus, train, and airport terminals are being checked. And hotels. He may have checked into a different hotel in Chicago."

Ted said, "If Kendrick's smart, he'd at least leave the state. If he doesn't do that, I have a gut feeling that he'll come to Naperville to kill Fiona himself. We know now that he probably has a gun. We don't know if he has another contact for a passport. Or, if he has much money. He probably took other disguises with him. Based on the wheelchair he left behind and the security video, he's disguised as an old man. My guess is he took a train to Naperville or one of the surrounding suburbs. He can't rent a car without a driver's license. He could steal one, but that's pretty risky."

When they ended the call, Fiona said, "Do you really think Kendrick will try to kill me himself?"

Ted grabbed her arms. "He may not have a viable choice now that Ponzo's gone. The good news is that the authorities should have enough evidence to arrest Ponzo's uncle, Joe Toro, for aiding and abetting Kendrick. I doubt that Kendrick'll get any further help from Ponzo's uncle. It's falling apart for Kendrick. And he no longer has Ponzo to run his errands and bring him food."

Fiona was glad she had no public events to attend that day. Instead, she and Ted stayed glued to the TV and to their cell phones.

She felt as if she was living in limbo, though. Sort of like the lull before the storm. Kendrick was still out there somewhere. Had he given up on his vendetta? Did he have a new helper to replace Ponzo? Had he left the country? Maybe he had, and she was scared and worried for nothing. That thought was really annoying. She'd hate to waste time worrying over nothing.

They knew he had a gun. Maybe he took someone hostage. Who knew? She talked long distance to Regan and really missed connecting with Kailee. She hoped her younger sister was having a good time in someplace warm while she was in exile, but it felt as if a part of herself was missing. In the past, the trio of sisters had all stayed in touch via phone through the college years and afterwards.

CHAPTER 61

Aurora, Illinois, Noon

When he woke up at noon the following day, Kendrick ordered room service lunch. Then he turned on the TV. His attention riveted to the screen when he heard on a Chicago channel that a man named Jimmy Ponzo was killed last night in Chicago when he resisted police after trying to pay a man to kill Fiona Morgan. The man was an undercover cop.

"Damn!" Kendrick shouted. He didn't have anything close by to throw, so he stomped his feet as he sat.

The newscaster continued, "Fiona is the young woman from Naperville who has been terrorized by killers hired by Ralph Kendrick, a convicted murderer who escaped from a Minnesota prison. When the undercover policeman tried to arrest Ponzo, he opened fire. The policeman suffered a shoulder wound. The officer shot and killed Ponzo.

"After a bar receipt and hotel room key were found in Ponzo's possession, a SWAT team was sent to the Russell Hotel on Michigan Avenue, hoping to apprehend Ralph Kendrick. He was gone, but fingerprints found on the scene indicated he had definitely been there."

"Glad I got out of there," Kendrick` muttered to himself. He picked up the toss-away cell phone and dialed the number he had used after the prison bus accident. No one answered. He looked at the phone, unbelieving. That number was his only tie to getting out of the country. What the hell was going on?

CHAPTER 62

Naperville

Fiona woke up slowly the next morning. She couldn't remember her dream, but it had been about something good, not some terrifying nightmare. Maybe that's a positive sign, she thought hopefully, swinging her legs to the floor beside the bed.

A few little tendrils of hope crept into her mind. She allowed herself to think for just a minute that if Kendrick was captured, she could go on her daily runs along the Riverwalk again. Running on the treadmill really sucked compared to running out of doors, especially at this time of the year when each day held its new spring surprises. Also, she wouldn't have her peers dogging her every step. And no more trash in the front yard for Ted to complain about.

This morning she refused to let herself shudder about Tory and Sandy. Ted had protected her from a strangler, a stabber, and a shooter. She had to believe that he would protect her again.

She fixed her coffee and looked out the sliding glass doors to the back yard. The new hot pink petunia plants she'd bought since the tornado looked perky. She missed the homely task of watering her own plants. Tonight she and Ted were going to his mom's house for dinner. She was looking forward to meeting his brothers and families.

At her five o'clock show, Fiona had plenty of news. Maureen and Charlie had taped scenes at a home fire caused by a barbecue too close to the house, a huge traffic accident, a bomb scare at a high school, and a groundbreaking ceremony for a new elementary school.

After the show, it seemed strange to Fiona to be pulling up at Ted's mother's house on Blackberry Court, rather than at her mom's house. Mrs. Collier welcomed them warmly. Fiona discovered that the three Collier men resembled each other enough to almost be triplets themselves. All were wide shouldered, dark haired, take charge men with smoky gray eyes. Mark was two years older than Ted, and he had more gray hair. He was the stock broker who had made such good investments for Ted.

Mark's wife, Eva, was a tiny brown haired dynamo with snapping brown eyes who seemed to have as much energy as her kids. The two boys, Chad and Owen, were ten and six. Their little sister, Cara, was three. All three children were obviously fond of their Uncle Ted. Chad asked where Ted got shot. Owen wanted to know if it was true that he was a hero, and Cara headed for Ted's lap every time he sat down.

Ted's younger brother, Jack, was the priest. His gray eyes sparkled with fun and a genuine interest in others. The Collier men had an easy camaraderie, and the evening was full of good-natured put downs and a lot of laughs.

Fiona's mother was included in the group. Ted's mother had said she wouldn't think of entertaining Fiona without asking her mom to join them. Fiona and Ted weren't surprised and shared a grin. The two moms seemed very chummy. The closer Ted and Fiona became, the wider the moms smiled.

Halfway through dinner, Cara asked Fiona in a loud voice, "Are you going to be my auntie?"

Fiona didn't miss a beat. She smiled at her. "If I knew you would be my niece, I might consider it."

Later, as they drove home, Fiona asked Ted how he felt about having children.

"Is that question based on the antics of my nieces and nephew?"

She laughed. "Not at all. I fell in love with all three of them. I just wondered in general."

"I'm all in favor of having children," Ted replied.

"What if the person you marry couldn't have any?"

"Then I'd probably want to adopt."

"I always wanted children, but I never got pregnant. I saw a gynecologist, and she found nothing wrong with me. She wanted Jeb to be tested, but he refused. He had some macho image of himself. So I really don't know if I can conceive or not."

"It sounds pretty likely you can. However, as I mentioned before, I'm open to adoption."

"I'm liking you more and more, Mr. Collier. I feel the same way."

"We probably wouldn't have any problem together then, since I've already fathered a child." He squeezed her hand and gave her a come-hither smile. "And I'd be happy to father a child with you."

Fiona leaned over and kissed his cheek.

Each day that passed brought them closer to Annie's wedding. Whether or not Fiona would attend was still up in the air. Fiona talked to Annie each day. The conversation was always the same. Annie wanted Fiona in the wedding. She was willing to have the ceremony inside the Visitor's Center if need be. But she kept saying that the wedding with only a hundred guests was nothing like the Civil War Reenactment, and she really preferred to have it outside. And she was sure it would be safe.

Ted and Fiona visited the Carillon site to see what security measures would be needed . . . The Carillon, or Bell Tower, was about sixty feet feet from the parking lot off Aurora Avenue, across the street from Naperville Central High School. Red-bricked pathways meandered from the Carillon to the Visitor's Center, to the covered bridge crossing the DuPage River off to the left, and to the Quarry for the paddleboats off to the right.

The concrete, round tower jutted out of the prairie like a sentinel. The Carillon had an interior circular staircase which wound around the massive bells housed in the center. It reminded Ted of the Statue of Liberty, and Fiona had mentioned it was almost ten feet taller than Lady Liberty.

"Annie said the ceremony will take place here at the front of the tower," Fiona said, pointing to the seven wide steps leading from a grassy area to the Carillon, which looked like a natural place for the bridal bower. "Folding chairs will be set up to form an aisle in front of this area. What are you thinking?"

He scanned the area. "We have to be ready for people strolling the grounds, but I'm thinking that this could be doable. Thank God for the late spring. If the leaves were fully mature, there would be plenty of places for a sniper to hide, but at least the area where the ceremony will take place is relatively open. We'll have to make sure the tower itself is checked and locked until the ceremony starts." He looked around. "Where will the bridal party get ready?"

"At the Visitor's Center." Fiona led the way to the left where a flat-topped stone building nestled in the woods. "We'll process from here to the site of the ceremony."

"With all the trees and bushes along the path, we'll need extra security here," Ted said, "And I'll need to walk alongside the path while you're processing to the Bridal Bower.

"That's fine with me. Does that mean I can be in an outside ceremony?"

"If it were up to me, I'd wrap you in bubble wrap and never let you out of your town house until things are settled. However, I spoke with the Chief of Police this morning. We agree that Kendrick or any paid assassin will not likely come after you in your home or at the TV station because you're well protected. They also will not be able to tamper with my car because of the protection package I have on it.

"They could try following us to the store or a restaurant, but I'm pretty good at spying a tail on my car. As long as we continue as we have been for the last few days, you and everyone around you will be reasonably safe."

She interrupted. "You're going to say *but*, aren't you?"

"Yeah, the problem with that is that Kendrick or an assassin could lie low or wait you out."

"And how long can I hide out if I want to continue in my job? And how long can I count on having you to protect me?"

"We agreed that at some point you'd probably have to appear in public again, and it might as well be the wedding. One hundred guests is a far cry from the thousands at the Civil War days."

Karen J. Gallahue

"The one good thing about the wedding is that it's a personal rather than a public appearance. The wedding is not a work-related public function. Kendrick may not know about it," Fiona said.

"That's a plus."

"And don't forget, there's always the possibility that Kendrick will run out of money . . . or be identified and captured. Trouble is, we can't count on that." She sighed.

"As the chief said, if President Obama, or a famous sports figure, or a movie star came to town, people would not be encouraged to stay home to be safe in case someone tries to kill them. He'll provide extra security for you if I give the go ahead." He put his arm around her waist. "Why don't you call Annie and tell her she can have the ceremony outside."

"I'll do that right away before you change your mind." She grinned and grabbed her cell phone.

CHAPTER 63

Aurora, Illinois, 5:00 p.m.

Kendrick unlocked his hotel room door and slumped against it after closing it. Today was nerve-wracking. He went to Naperville for a ground-breaking ceremony at a new school, an event that was on Fiona's schedule. He kept looking over his shoulder and wondering whether someone recognized him. He couldn't be sure of any of his disguises, thanks to the media for printing pictures of what he might look like. And all that worry for nothing.

When he reached the ground-breaking ceremony for the new school, Fiona wasn't there! Some other broad took her place. Kendrick didn't want to get too close. Only a handful of people attended the ceremony. He couldn't take any chances.

The day wasn't a complete bust, though. He knew how to get to Naperville's Carillon now, where Fiona would be in a wedding ceremony later on Saturday. He checked out the area, and found out he could take a bus from Aurora that would drop him off within walking distance of the Carillon.

He kicked off his shoes and flopped on the bed while he figured out what disguise to wear that day. After that, he called room service and ordered two sirloin steak dinners. Good thing the maid restocked the bar today because yesterday he drank up all everything that was there.

He realized he missed Ponzo. Not because he liked the guy, but he liked bossing him around after being bossed himself for so many years in prison. He wished he had a toss-away phone. He wanted to call Fiona and taunt her.

CHAPTER 64

On Friday evening, the wedding rehearsal turned out to be a snap for security. The skies opened and rain scourged the area just as the wedding party left their cars for the rehearsal. Ted didn't need to worry about bystanders strolling up close; they were all running for shelter.

Tremayne and three police officers who had secured the outside area met them at Ted's car. Under their umbrellas, the bridal party members followed the minister to the Visitor's Center so that he could explain the following day's procedure. Another police officer met them at the door of the building and assured Ted that all was secure inside.

Reverend Carlin's face was seamed like a bulldog's, and he had the engaging smile of a cherub. He walked with a slightly pigeon-toed gait as he led them to the room which the bride and her attendants would use as a staging area. He also showed the men of the bridal party the room they would use down the hall from that.

Following that, he led them to a large room where the actual ceremony would take place if held inside.

"Because of the rain, we'll do our rehearsal here," he said, "since the ceremony will be the same whether it's held in or out. Folding chairs will be set up to form an aisle, and the Bridal Bower will be here." He pointed to the front of the room. When the Carillon bells ring, it will be a signal for the mothers of the bride and groom to be escorted down the aisle by the groomsmen."

"After the mothers are seated, the bells will stop, and a bagpiper will play while the groom and his men enter the room over here." He pointed again.

"When the bagpiper changes to the Wedding March, the women will process from the staging area to the Bridal Bower. After the procession, the attendants and groomsmen will face the congregation. I will face the couple." He beamed at Annie and Tom. "You two will face each other in front of me,"

When the women practiced the procession to the Bower, Ted noted that Fiona would be standing between the maid of honor and the other bridesmaid, but not at the end. That was good.

As she moved through the steps they'd follow in the wedding tomorrow, Fiona thought back to her own wedding day and all her hopes and dreams. She had been so excited, so sure that Jeb was her perfect choice for a husband. She had been so wrong. His charm and charisma had blinded her to the fact that she couldn't trust him . . .

He was her first lover. After his death, she was sure he'd be the last. In spite of what she'd said to Ted. Fiona still worried a little that she might be lacking in the sex department. She had no wish to find herself with another man who found her lacking. Until recently. Until Ted. She found that he could stir her feelings by a touch to her hand, or by tucking her in close when he escorted her. He could run his finger along the side of her face and turn her to mush.

As the bride and groom practiced their vows, Fiona looked for Ted. The man moved like smoke. One minute he was in one location. A minute later he was somewhere else. Ted had told her that he was satisfied that the cop who was Fiona's groomsman could protect her up close. Ted felt the need to patrol the area. She finally spied him talking to the sweet-faced woman who had let them into the Visitor's Center.

After Revered Carlin finished rehearsing the ceremony, he said, "Grab your umbrellas, and I'll quickly show you how you'll do this outside."

By this time, the rain had let up a little. The minister showed them the winding path they'd take to the Bridal Bower at the Carillon. Ted fell in line alongside Fiona.

Since the wedding guests would total only one hundred people, Ted wouldn't have hordes of people to deal with tomorrow, except for the traveling press circus, of course. Even now, they prowled around the edges of the area. And their numbers increased every time he checked them out. Trouble was, Kendrick could pretend to be a member of the press. Ted walked over to the group to remind them again to contact a policeman if anyone was present with them that they didn't recognize, especially tomorrow.

When the rehearsal ended, Fiona came to stand near Ted who was meeting with the other policemen who would be wedding guests. The men discussed strategy for the actual ceremony, and they set up a grid that each would take responsibility for. Ted assured them that the Carillon would be checked and re-locked an hour before the ceremony.

CHAPTER 65

After the drippy rehearsal the night before, Fiona was glad to see the sun shining as brightly as a big lemon lollipop on Annie's wedding day. Unless the weather changed, the wedding would be held outside.

In the morning, she and Ted drove to the beauty shop to meet the other ladies of the wedding party. Ted had grunted with chagrin at the idea of bodyguarding in a beauty shop, but he sat stoically at the salon while the bride and her attendants had their hair and nails done. Fortunately, he had his computer with him, so he wasn't totally bored. He even put up with the good natured comments of the bridal party. And offers from the hair stylists to touch up his few gray hairs.

Fiona's long hair was drawn back at the sides and curled and tickled into a cascade of curls that hung down the back of her head. Baby's breath was woven into the intricate arrangement. A few tendrils of hair dangled at the side of her face. She hoped Ted liked her hairdo. She caught herself and smiled. It was a long time since she'd cared if any man liked her hair. Or her dress. Or anything else about her. It was a good feeling. No, a great feeling. She felt herself drawn more and more to him. And he touched her mind and heart in a way she'd never experienced before. He was definitely a keeper.

Ordinarily, Fiona's sisters would be wedding guests today, and she missed them. She was glad her mom and Steve would be in the congregation.

She wished she could talk to Kailee, to bounce off her thoughts. Kailee would listen intently while Fiona talked, until Fiona solved the problem herself. If she called Regan, she'd probably tell her to grow up and that it was about time to trust another man again. And she'd be right. It was time.

Fiona still felt a few stomach flutters and a vague uneasiness about being in the wedding. Kendrick was still out there somewhere. She tried to ignore the feelings, and she put on her biggest smile when she walked over to talk to Annie while the nail technician finished the bride's nails.

A few hours later, Fiona stood before her full length mirror and checked to see if her three inch matching heels were the proper height with her long royal blue taffeta gown with the pencil slim skirt. The color was chosen because it was one of the colors in Annie's Scottish family's tartan. A sash in the tartan colors of royal blue, dark red, green, and white hung diagonally from Fiona's left shoulder to the right side of her waist. The groomsmen would wear matching cumberbunds with their black tuxes. Annie would wear a traditional white gown, with her own diagonal tartan sash.

When she walked into the living room, Ted said, "I didn't think you could look any better than you did the night of the Silent Auction, but I was wrong.

That color is terrific on you, and today your eyes look almost royal blue to match."

"Thanks," she smiled. "I just hope everything goes smoothly for Annie's wedding."

When Fiona and Ted reached the Carillon, he escorted her to the room where the members of the wedding party would make the finishing touches to their finery and wait for the procession to begin. Fiona saw that Katie Archer, the policewoman, had arrived ahead of them . . .

"I checked out the adjoining bathroom and closets," Katie said.

"Thanks," Ted replied. "I'll check out the rest of the building. He gave Fiona a quick hug and left the room.

Annie rushed over to greet Fiona. The bride was a vision in her wedding gown, and the deep red in her tartan sash matched her titian hair exactly. Excitement filled the air. And happiness. And anticipation. The open windows gifted them with a soft breeze that smelled of honeysuckle, and it blended well with the smell of deep red roses, white lilies of the valley, and royal blue carnations from the bouquets, as well as from the pleasant perfumes of the bridal ladies.

As he prowled the area around the Carillon, Ted felt confident that things were under control. But he still felt a prickling at the back of his neck, and he stayed on high alert. As he scanned the area where the wedding guests were gathering, Ted noticed what a beautiful May day it was. A benevolent sun rode high in the sky, sending out perfect weather rays. Pudgy little white clouds nudged each other gently and seemed to have no obvious destination. The air smelled like fresh-cut grass and honeysuckles. Nice for the bridal couple. Too many walkers out and about, though. Although, so far, no one he saw resembled Kendrick in build. Most were families or couples out for a stroll. And they usually moved on after a quick peek to see what was going on.

He was dressed in a new gray suit, with a white shirt and maroon tie. As he checked out the suits on the other men, he decided his suit looked okay, but he'd better buy some new shirts and ties. The other guys' shirts were as colorful as the ladies' outfits, including pastel shades of pink and lavender. Well, maybe he wouldn't pick those colors.

Ted wished he was marrying Fiona today. It couldn't be soon enough to suit him, although he still wanted to court her properly when she wasn't afraid for her life.

As he had with the press, Ted made arrangements for people on both the bride's side and the groom's side to alert him if someone they didn't know tried to be seated. So far, so good there. As planned last night at the rehearsal, the area was divided into grids and each of the cop guests knew which one he was assigned to. Just in case something unexpected happened.

When the bells pealed out joyfully, Ted saw that the groomsmen were escorting the parents of the groom and the mother of the bride down the center aisle which had been set up with folding chairs on either side. He knew the wedding was ready to start, and he moved to the Visitor's Center.

Inside the Center, Annie's niece, Ginny, rushed in to tell the women of the bridal party that the parents were being seated. The women picked up their bouquets of flowers. At the sound of the bagpipes, they knew that the groomsmen were walking to their places for the ceremony, and the women lined up for their own procession until the bagpiper played the Wedding March. As Fiona walked along the winding, red brick path to the arbor, she saw Ted walking beside the path on her right side. He looked so good in his suit that matched his eyes, and he exuded competence. She felt her lingering worries fade away, and she gave him a big smile.

CHAPTER 66

As Ted fell in step alongside Fiona, a ray of afternoon sun hit Fiona's blond hair and gave her a temporary halo. His breath caught in his throat. In spite of the Kevlar vest, she looked so lovely.

His eyes moved from Fiona to check the area constantly. The sound of the bells and the bagpipes evidently attracted more attention because a few more people drifted over. But again, none had Kendrick's body build. The women took their places on the left side of the bridal bower, and the minister opened the ceremony with a welcome to the bridal party and the congregation. According to plan, Fiona stood in the middle of the bridal attendants, not on the end.

The time-honored words of the wedding ceremony rang out on the lovely afternoon, and Ted saw that both mothers of the bride and groom looked a little teary.

Just as the minister pronounced Annie and Tom man and wife, Ted saw a woman pushing a buggy head toward the congregation.

She was a chunky black woman with dark long hair, wearing a navy pantsuit. But she had the height and build of Kendrick, so he watched her more intently. His finger itched to shoot first and ask questions later, but he was a professional, and citizens didn't like cops killing other innocent citizens. He tensed as he waited to see if she was headed to Fiona's side of the congregation, just as the minister pronounced the bridal couple man and wife.

But the woman didn't move toward Fiona. She moved to the outside edge of the groom's side. He started to relax. He and the cop assigned to that grid nodded at each other.

As the minister introduced the new couple to their family and friends, the black woman suddenly darted like a snake making a strike and grabbed a blond child of four or five who was sitting at the end of one row on the groom's side of the congregation. The child screamed, struggled and shrieked, "Mommy! Daddy!"

A man's voice shouted, "Anyone move, and I shoot the kid. I'm going to toss her off the tower, unless Fiona Morgan steps forward to take her place."

Members of the congregation took a collective gasp and stared unbelievingly.

Ted thought, "What the hell? It had to be Kendrick. *I should have shot him when I had the chance.*"

Fiona's head whipped to the right when she heard the man's voice. Her eyes widened to see the "woman" holding the terrified child. She knew instinctively it was Kendrick. The little girl continued to struggle and scream for her parents.

Rage and fear coursed through Fiona to think Kendrick would snatch a small child. She knew he would kill the little girl without a qualm if she didn't take her place. Adrenalin surged as she thought of the way Ralph had blighted her life and made her sisters suffer. Then fear receded, and fury took over. She made an instant anguished decision.

"I'll take her place." Fiona stepped forward with grim determination.

"Oh my God," a voice moaned in the congregation.

"No, Fiona, no!" Fiona could hear her mother's voice from the congregation.

Fiona felt it was her only choice, but she planned to do everything she could to stay alive.

"Don't anyone else move," Ralph shouted, as the little girl's mother and father stirred.

Someone said, "That's a man's voice."

"I'm coming," Fiona said loudly. She walked as quickly as possible past the bridal couple toward Kendrick and the screaming, wriggling child. Kendrick transferred the gun from the child's head to the back of Fiona's neck instantly. He squeezed his left arm like a vise around Fiona's waist. The little girl scurried to her parents. Every police officer in the congregation prepared to fire. Not one of them could get a clear shot at Kendrick without risking a reflexive shot from the gun at Fiona's neck.

"We're going up to the top of the tower, Fiona, and all your friends can watch your body land splat on the ground." Kendrick's lips widened into a grotesque smile.

CHAPTER 67

Just then, a chunky, pony-tailed paparazzo charged down the grassy area outside the groom's side with his camera. Kendrick didn't blink an eye. He shot the man in the chest and immediately pressed the gun back against Fiona's neck. It took three seconds.

The paparazzo clutched his chest and fell to the grass. His camera bounced beside him. Screams erupted in the congregation. People crouched down. Parents shielded their children. Some people ran off and away, heedless that Kendrick might shoot them, too.

Fiona felt as stunned as if she had taken the shot herself.

"Move, Fiona," Kendrick snarled.

Momentarily, she couldn't move at all. Kendrick jerked her closer, and he pressed the gun harder against her neck. He also pulled her backward as a shield as he took the few steps to reach the door leading to the tower steps. His left arm was still tight around her waist. She felt the nozzle of the gun, cold and lethal against her neck.

Kendrick made Fiona open the door to the tower. Once they were inside, emotion thickened Fiona's voice. "You may kill me, but you'll die up there too, Kendrick."

"We'll see about that. Even if I die, my name will be known from one end of the country to the other. No one will forget Ralph Kendrick."

"I'm a newswoman. Trust me. They'll forget you in a week," she replied, her chin high. "You're not going to be a hero for killing me. I'm the person you hate, and you're going to make me a heroine. How will you like that? You'll be known as the swine that killed me!"

"Shut up, bitch, and move ahead of me up the steps."

As he shoved her past him, she saw the face of a crazy man. A furious, crazy man. His eyes bulged. His face contracted into a fierce scowl. He seemed beyond logic and common sense.

Thoughts flooded her mind as she awkwardly tried to step past him in three inch heels and a pencil-slim long skirt. Thank God it had a slit, she thought stupidly. She wished she could tell her family how much she loved them. She thought of Ted, too, and wondered where he was. She loved him. She knew that fact with complete certainty. She knew he would help her if he could kill Kendrick without killing her. She knew any of the cops in the congregation would do the same.

She deliberately sagged, hoping to slow down the climb.

"Keep doing that and I'll shoot you in the leg," Kendrick threatened.

"Then you'll have to carry me up."

"Stay ahead of me, and don't try anything. I don't really care how I kill you. Just so I get the job done."

He pulled her left arm back into a quick hold like a hammerlock, and Fiona grimaced. She realized how strong he was. *Strong, like a mule. With a gun. Desperate. Well, she was desperate, too!*

CHAPTER 68

Fiona tried to remember all the tricks and tips Ted had taught her. She knew she'd have to outsmart Kendrick. She repeated to herself the target areas: eyes, head, crotch. She was supposed to have the gift of gab. Well, now was the time to use it! What could she say to slow him down? To catch his attention? *Why was her mind blank? She needed to focus.*

Fiona knew from her research that there were two hundred fifty-three steps on the circular staircase leading to the top floor. One part of her brain clicked into numbering the steps as they moved upward.

She knew she was on *Step Ten*. She needed to make this the longest climb in history. Fear clogged her throat. She had a hard time swallowing. Her breathing was choppy. She reminded herself to inhale and exhale. Now it was *Step Nineteen*. She could hear the sounds of sirens in the distance. She debated kicking back at Kendrick suddenly, but even with the slit, her long, slender bridesmaid dress wouldn't allow it. Her stomach was still clenched like a fist, and she tried to relax it. Now she could feel the sweat slicking under her armpits.

She couldn't hear a sound from the wedding group outside. But the sirens sounded closer. People must have been herded away from the Carillon. Apart from the sirens off in the distance, it was as if she and Kendrick were alone in the world. He kept them close to the center of the building, well away from the viewing areas of the tower.

"If you kill me, you'll be committing suicide, Kendrick," she said. *Step Twenty-four*.

"Yeah, suicide by cop," he spat, as he gave her a shove forward that almost caused her to fall to her knees. "I'll never go back to prison. And I needed Jimmy Ponzo to help me leave the country. It's all your fault he's dead, bitch. You spoiled everything."

Fiona bit her tongue. There was nothing she could say about that idea. He'd felt that way for twenty years. She wasn't going to change his mind.

"*Step Thirty*," she counted in her head. Sweat moistened her upper lip. She licked her lips and found them salty. As she struggled to move up the steps, her right shoe fell off, the thin strap dangling. She said, "I lost my shoe. I need to take my other shoe off. I can't make it the rest of the way when I'm lopsided."

"Too bad."

"If I trip, I'll drag you right down with me."

He grunted and stood still, and she took her time removing her shoe. She had to. Her fingers were trembling like an elderly person with Parkinson's Disease. *Step Thirty-four*.

She thought she heard a slight rustling sound from below them. Kendrick must have heard it, too. He shot in that direction and immediately transferred the gun back to her.

I should have tried something, she thought, but there really hadn't been time. For a man built like a bull, Kendrick had moves that were astonishingly fast.

"Get behind me, again," Kendrick growled. "You can be my shield."

They awkwardly changed positions. Fiona stumbled on the circular stairs, and he cursed. He grabbed her right arm above the elbow, always keeping the gun pointed at her as he almost side-stepped upward. She hated having his hand on her.

Fiona hoped Ted hadn't been shot. She worried about him. He suffered such grief when his wife and child died. She couldn't bear it if knowing her cost him more suffering. She heard no more sounds from below. *Step Forty.*

Searching for something to distract him, she asked, "How did you know I'd be in this wedding today?"

"Ponzo had an informant in Naperville. He met a fellow in a bar who used to work with you. The guy fed him info on your schedule."

"That must have been Ben Hamilton." Fiona was appalled. "The bastard! I can't believe he would be so low." She paused. "If I could get ahead of you again, it wouldn't be so hard to move backward up each step." *Step Fifty.*

"Forget it!" Kendrick snarled. "You just want to put me in the line of fire from below. At least I know no one's above us. I checked this tower early this morning. It was locked until the puny bell ringer lady went up before the ceremony. And I'll shoot her if she shows her face."

Fiona felt Kendrick wouldn't kill her going up. She figured he wanted to make a drama out of her death. He wanted the notoriety. She hoped she was right. He'd have to shoot her if he wanted to dump her over. She would fight and kick up to the last minute. She thought again of places on his body she could target. *Step Sixty.*

Fiona thought she heard a whisper of movement from below again. Kendrick fired two quick shots and returned the gun quickly to Fiona. The movement below stopped. *Step Seventy-nine.*

CHAPTER 69

Fiona wondered how many bullets were left in Kendrick's gun. *Did he have more of them if he ran out?* She needed to make this trip as difficult as possible. She would not let him kill her without a fight. She tried to find her chance. With him going ahead of her, it was physically impossible to flip him over her head. She couldn't head butt him or gouge his eyes, not with that gun pointed right at her. She still heard no sounds from outside. The crowd was probably dispersed. Poor Annie! Her wedding was in shambles! *Step Eighty-four.*

She pretended to pant. "I can't go this fast," she gasped.

Kendrick turned to snarl at her and suddenly sneezed. She cringed as droplets from his nose shot through the air toward her. He wiped his nose on his sleeve. She couldn't cover her look of revulsion.

"I tell you I can't go this fast," she repeated.

Kendrick arched his eyebrow, pointed his gun. *And shot her!* The bullet nicked about an inch below her left elbow. Pain lanced her arm. It happened so fast. She couldn't believe it. *He shot her!* She wiped at it with her right hand and saw blood. She wanted to gag. *It was her blood!* She swallowed her scream, but inside she quaked. The man was a maniac. *Step Ninety-three.*

"That shut you up, didn't it?" Kendrick taunted.

She tried to think of a reply when more noise erupted from down below them. It sounded like several feet rushing up the stairs. Kendrick fired again in that direction. The movements stopped again. *Step One hundred two.*

"Everybody's afraid to come and save you. Maybe I'll have time to rape you before I toss you over. In fact, that's what I'll do," Kendrick jerked her after him.

"In your dreams," Fiona muttered to herself. Maybe she'd have a chance if he had to set the gun down to rape her.

"You run out of words? Look at me, bitch."

She looked at him. She didn't know how or why, but in the midst of terrible peril, she started to laugh nervously. She tried to keep a straight face and couldn't. Kendrick's long dark wig had slipped to one side. His blackened face had smeared in the struggle, and he had spittle oozing out of the sides of his mouth. He looked like a mad dog.

"I didn't run out of words. I was thinking you don't look so hot in drag."

"You've got a nerve laughing at me. You're a smart-mouthed bitch. You should be saying your prayers." He whacked her on the side of the head with the gun. "Her neck snapped, and her vision blurred momentarily.

She didn't give him the satisfaction of a reply. *Step One hundred fifteen.*

"I haven't seen hide nor hair of your brave bodyguard," Kendrick sneered. "He must have run like a coward after I shot that cameraman."

Fiona was silent. She knew Ted would be doing anything he could to save her. She twisted to look up at Kendrick.

"Do you think that puny old lady will save you? Or maybe someone else flew up ahead of us?" Kendrick laughed and moved away a little, gesturing upwards with his gun.

CHAPTER 70

Fiona thought she heard Ted's voice saying "Yup" *just as a bullet cracked out and hit Ralph in the head*! Horrified, Fiona flinched and saw an explosion of blood and brain material immediately above her. She gasped and then gagged. She felt Kendrick's hand loosen and drop from her arm.

"Move, Fiona" Ted's steady voice commanded from above.

She did.

Another shot hit Kendrick's chest, and Fiona instinctively moved even further out of the way. His body slid sideways down three steps and went still.

Ted appeared from above her and immediately checked Kendrick's pulse "He's dead," he assured Fiona. He quickly moved to Fiona's side and took her in his arms.

"Sorry it took so long, sweetheart. I was a few steps above you all the way, but I didn't have a good shot at him until he moved the damned gun away from you and pointed it upward."

Fiona couldn't move. She stood stock still on *Step One hundred thirty-four*. She couldn't speak either. Ted yelled out the viewing window, "All clear. Fiona is safe."

He turned back and saw the blood coming from her arm. "That bastard shot you in the arm, didn't he?"

She nodded her head and heard shouting and the pounding of feet ascending the stairs from below. Ted held her shoulders gently, and said, "It's over, sweetheart. It's over."

Fiona whimpered and burrowed herself closer in his arms. "I was really scared, Ted."

He smoothed her hair back where the tendrils hung loose. "You're the bravest woman I know. I'm so proud of you."

He looked her straight in the eyes, "But promise me you'll never offer yourself as a hostage again during my lifetime. I could feel my hair turning white for the last twenty minutes."

"I promise. No argument from me." Suddenly fatigue hit her, and her legs felt wobbly.

"Thank God it was a circular staircase. I knew if you fell it would only be a step or two. But I had to hit him just right, so he couldn't reflexively shoot you. I was a little braver because at least you had the bullet-proof vest on."

He angled his mouth over hers. "Thank God you're safe," he murmured as he kissed her with all the pent up emotion of the last hour. In between kisses, he kept repeating, "It's over now."

Fiona clung to him as if she would never let him go.

"Uh-oh," said the first police officer who arrived up the Carillon stairs. "I think we interrupted something."

"Damn right," Ted said, and he kissed Fiona again.

By then several people came up the circular staircase. Fiona could hear a voice outside over a bullhorn saying, "Fiona Morgan is safe. Please stay where you are until the police clear the crime scene."

Fiona could also hear shouting, and whistling, and clapping.

Ted pulled away from Fiona and checked her arm. "You need to see a paramedic." He swooped her in his arms to carry her down the steps.

"Wait," she said. "I want to look at Kendrick before I go down."

"I don't know, Tiger. It's a pretty gruesome sight."

"I know, but everything happened so fast. I need a final picture of him dead to carry in my mind. So I can remind myself that he can never hurt me, or you, or my sisters again."

Still holding her, Ted turned so she could see the body. In death, Ralph Kendrick was a horrific sight. His wig had been knocked off and lay like a rat by his head. Kendrick's smeared black face was covered with blood and brain matter. His body had twisted, and his head was below his feet.

Fiona shuddered and offered up a prayer of thanks that she'd never have to worry about him again. When she nodded to Ted, they started downward.

"You can't carry me down all those steps," she protested.

"Wanna bet?" With his usual economy of movement, Ted moved quickly down the staircase in no time.

CHAPTER 71

A s Fiona and Ted exited the tower, a huge shout went up from the crowd off to the far left. People yelled, "Fiona, we're so glad you're safe." Fiona could see the little blond girl Kendrick had grabbed, and she heard her reedy shout, "I love you, Fiona." Annie shouted the same thing. Soon the entire crowd including the members of the press yelled, "We love you, Fiona."

Tears streamed down Fiona's face, and she couldn't seem to stop them, as Ted and several policemen ushered her back to the room used for the women of the bridal party. Her mother and Steve were waiting for her there.

"Thank God you're safe," her mom hugged her. "I've been praying so hard for you. It was the worst moment of my life when Kendrick took you up those stairs."

"I know. Mine, too."

"I already called Kailee to tell her she can come home," Mrs. Morgan said, as she hugged her again. "And I contacted Regan as well."

"Thanks, Mom."

Ted yelled for a paramedic and a gurney.

"I don't need a gurney for a little scratch," Fiona protested.

"You do if you're starting to go into shock," Ted said. "Your eyes are dilated, and your face is a little gray."

"First, I need to wash my hands and arms. I don't know if it's Kendrick's blood or mine. I just know I have to get rid of it."

"The paramedic can help you clean up, sweetheart," Ted said. "Here he comes now."

"Well, look who's here," the paramedic said. He was the same freckled, green-eyed guy who worked on Ted's bullet wound after the Civil War battle. "Are you two trying to keep me in business?"

"Not really," Fiona sighed.

"She's starting to go into shock," Ted said.

"Let's get her on the gurney," the paramedic said, "and I'll check her out." Within seconds he pronounced, "You'll need a few stitches to close your wound properly, but the bullet just grazed you. In the meantime, lay quietly, and I'll cleanse your wound and get rid of the blood spatters."

Just then Tremayne appeared. "You doing okay, Fiona?" he asked.

She nodded her head.

Tremayne turned to Ted and said, "Once again, I get stuck with all the paperwork. This time it'll be a pleasure!"

Fiona called to Tremayne from the gurney, "It's really over, isn't it, John?"

"Yes, it is," he replied, getting down on his knees to give her a careful hug. In my worst nightmare I saw you take the little girl's place when Kendrick had a gun on her. There aren't too many people as brave as you."

"You're wrong," she murmured, "You or any of the other police officers here would have done the same thing."

Tremayne squeezed her hand and said, "For once, I'm glad that the members of the press were here. We have several videos of Kendrick grabbing the little girl and of Fiona taking her place. I'll take your car, Ted, and follow the ambulance. I'll need to take statements from both of you about what went on inside the Carillon."

When Ted and Fiona left the Visitor's Center for the ambulance, she shuddered once as she saw the body bag being carried out of the Carillon. Then she shook her head and shrugged her shoulders. It was time to put Kendrick out of her mind permanently.

Members of the press surged forward, asking one question after another. The police kept them from getting too close. She could hear them wishing her well as they drove away.

She turned to Ted. "How did you get to the tower ahead of us? I had no idea you were up there."

"As soon as I heard him mention throwing you off the tower, I knew I had to get ahead of him and try to get a shot. Everyone was watching you and the child."

"I always thought you moved like smoke. Did you hear the part where he spoke of the Naperville contact and a fired employee? Do you think he meant Ben Hamilton?"

"We'll certainly check that out."

"Now Kailee can come home! I've missed her so much. And Regan can relax and enjoy Spain."

"I'll need to call Detective Brady in Minneapolis and have him notify Warden Elmore. So he can contact Kendrick's mother."

While the doctor stitched her up at the hospital, Fiona suddenly realized that Ted didn't need to protect her any more. He didn't need to be at the town house, either. She might be all alone tonight. From the high of her elation, she felt a sudden horrible emptiness. If he went back to his mom's house, at least he'd have a bed to sleep on. She hated that idea.

She parked the thought when Tremayne arrived in the Emergency Room and took their statements.

Later, when Ted and Fiona went to the parking lot, he asked, "Where to?"

"My town house," she replied. "I need to get out of this bedraggled dress and the Kevlar vest. And I need to take about five showers to feel really clean again." Her hand moved to twist the hair on the side of her face, but she stopped herself. She chose not to do that anymore. The stress was finally over. "I'll have to find something else to wear to the wedding reception."

"How about that little black number you wore to the auction?"

"That'll do. Um . . . will you be going to your mom's tonight?" she asked.

"Not tonight. I want to be sure you're okay after all this trauma." He turned to her. "But you know what this means."

"What?" she answered.

"It's a new game now, with new rules. Finally, I can take you on dates, and bring you roses, and pursue you with every damned maneuver I can think of. I want to marry you, Fiona. But I promised myself I wouldn't rush you."

"You know what they say. If you save a person's life, you're responsible for them. You saved my life four times. I'm afraid you're stuck with me forever."

"Then we'll definitely have a short courtship." He sealed that statement with a kiss.

EPILOGUE

Five months later

A s Fiona stepped outside to water the flowers on her new patio, she thought back to the events leading up to today. Ted had been true to his word. He intended to court Fiona before he asked her to marry him. And he did. He wanted to give her time to adjust back to a normal life. He told her he didn't want any decision based on adrenalin rushes of fear. He didn't want to be the dolt who rushed her into marriage when she was vulnerable.

Fiona hated that he moved out of her town house, and she told him so. He said that was a positive sign, that she would miss him. But he said that since everything about her turned him on . . . her scent, her voice, her soft skin . . . he could no longer sleep in the same house with her and keep his hands off her.

Ted started his job as Chief of Police in Plainfield. He worked long hours the first few weeks, but he spent every waking hour that he could with Fiona. When he left her at night, he told her how much he missed her company, her laugh, her wit, her earthiness.

Fiona's eyebrows had lifted at the term earthiness. "Earthy as in mudball, or earthy as in hot?" She'd wanted to know.

"Hot. Very hot."

It only took two weeks for Fiona and Ted to decide that they were both more than ready to marry. Both had had large weddings for their first marriages. Neither wanted that again. They both wanted to stand before Ted's brother, the priest, with only immediate family members and a small circle of friends present. Their wedding took place three months after Annie's. Regan and her family flew home for the wedding.

Fiona smiled when she thought of her wedding night. When she and Ted finally came together as man and wife, they were completely awed by each other. Ted quickly dispelled any doubts she had about her desirability. He was a lover both passionate and tender. He touched her heart and wrenched her soul. She loved being married to him.

Ted was glad he hadn't bought a condo or a town house before he met Fiona. Instead, they sold her town house and found a one family home. The patio she was standing on was that of her new home.

Tom and Annie's wedding received national coverage following the ceremony. A well known travel agency gave them a two week package to Hawaii. Free airfare and all expenses paid.

Kailee and her husband returned home the day after Annie's wedding. Her latest ultrasound indicated she was expecting a boy.

Mrs. Kendrick's first words when she heard the news of her son's death were: "I can sleep now. And he can, too." She set up a substantial fund for rewards to aid in the capture of other killers. She named the fund the Fiona Morgan Fund, with Fiona to head the committee which would choose recipients. Already it had been used once in the capture of a man who kidnapped a young girl in Alabama.

Fiona was interviewed by Brian Williams on Rock Center where she described the Fiona Morgan Fund and the good work it was already doing. "If you have an opportunity to testify against a person who commits an evil act, do it," she urged. "I feel as if I protected other women from Ralph Kendrick during the years he was in jail. Mine was a very extreme case. If I could survive his retaliation with all his paid assassins, anyone can."

Fiona had numerous job offers following Ralph's death. She preferred to stay at NKTV, but she did accept a contract from NBC for six in-depth interviews with prominent national figures.

Ben Hamilton was arrested for aiding and abetting a criminal by supplying the details of Fiona's schedule to the unknown contact in Naperville. Ben got the information from Daphne by telling her he wanted to talk to Fiona about a new job. Daphne couldn't be arrested for stupidity, but she resigned from her job at NKTV because of the disapproval of her co-workers.

Ralph's offshore account had not yet been found. He took the numbers of his account to his grave.

As Fiona finished dead-heading her petunias, she looked down at her flat stomach. According to the ultrasound she had yesterday, her stomach wouldn't stay flat for long. Both Ted and she were elated.